MURDER BY THE BOOK

This brand-new historical mystery series represents an exciting new direction for award-winning science fiction writer Eric Brown.

London, 1955. When crime writer Donald Langham's literary agent asks for his help in sorting out 'a delicate matter', little does Langham realize what he's getting himself into. For a nasty case of blackmail leads inexorably to murder as London's literary establishment is rocked by a series of increasingly bizarre deaths. With three members of the London Crime Club coming to sudden and violent ends, what at first appeared to be a series of suicides looks suspiciously like murder – and there seems to be something horribly familiar about the various methods of despatch. With the help of his literary agent's assistant, the delectable Maria Dupré, Langham finds himself drawing on the skills of his fictional detective hero as he hunts a ruthless and fiendishly clever killer – a killer with old scores to settle.

A Selection of Further Titles by Eric Brown

THE DEVIL'S NEBULA
HELIX WARS
THE KINGS OF ETERNITY
NECROPATH
STARSHIP SUMMER
THRESHOLD SHIFT

MURDER BY THE BOOK

A Langham and Dupré mystery

Eric Brown

Severn House Large Print
London & New York

This first large print edition published 2014
in Great Britain and the USA by
SEVERN HOUSE PUBLISHERS LTD of
19 Cedar Road, Sutton, Surrey, England, SM2 5DA.
First world regular print edition published 2013 by
Severn House Publishers Ltd., London and New York.

British Library Cataloguing in Publication Data

Brown, Eric, 1960- author.
  Murder by the book. -- (A Langham and Dupré mystery)
  1. Murder--Investigation--England--London--Fiction.
  2. Detective and mystery stories. 3. Large type books.
  I. Title II. Series
  823.9'2-dc23

  ISBN-13: 9780727897008

Severn House Publishers support the Forest Stewardship Council™
[FSC™], the leading international forest certification organisation. All
our titles that are printed on FSC certified paper carry the FSC logo.

Printed and bound in Great Britain by
T J International, Padstow, Cornwall.

*To Beth Dunnett and to Phillip
and Liz Vine, with thanks*

ONE

Langham sat at his desk and pecked with two fingers at the keys of his battered Underwood. He was halfway through the last chapter of his latest novel and the end was in sight. Sam Brooke, his private investigator, was trailing a villain down Regent Street, little realizing that he was being lured into a trap from which it would take all his ingenuity and resourcefulness to escape.

The shrill summons of the phone sounded beside him on the desk. He cursed it initially, then decided to take a break. There were times, especially towards the end of a book, when his enthusiasm to get it finished needed curbing. He'd answer the call, then have a spot of lunch and think about the dénouement.

He laid aside his pipe, long extinguished but still gripped between his teeth, and picked up the receiver – the 'bakelite bone' he'd called it in one of his early, more flowery novels. 'Donald Langham here.'

'Donald, Donald, my dear boy. Forgive my importunate call. You must curse me, curse me! Be honest now, have I interrupted the muse?'

Langham smiled to himself. 'Not at all, Charles. I was just about to knock off for lunch.'

7

'You assuage my guilt, my dear boy. Did you say lunch? Similar thoughts crossed my mind not two minutes ago. If you hie yourself towards Pimlico in thirty minutes I'll stand you a repast at the Beeches – though their standards have fallen somewhat of late. I recall the feasts we enjoyed in those far off, pre-war days...'

Lunches with Charles Elder were always protracted, boozy affairs, with one postprandial drink turning into three or four, and often finishing not a minute before four o'clock. That would rule out an afternoon shift at the Underwood ... but the novel was almost finished anyway. He'd complete it in the morning.

He interrupted his agent's purple musings. 'Lunch would be excellent. I'm on my way.'

'I have,' Charles said, 'a delicate matter to put before you. Very delicate indeed.'

'I'm intrigued.'

'Not over the phone, dear boy. Drop by the office and we'll pop around the corner. No doubt you'll want to pay your silvery-tongued respects to Maria.'

'She's working today?'

'On the phone to some spotty sub-editor at Gollancz as we speak. I've had to increase her hours of late – the agency has never been so busy. I'm working like a demon for my seven-and-a-half per cent, and the thanks I get?'

'You know I never begrudge you your pound of flesh, Charles.'

'I'm not talking about you, Donald. I refer to the baying hounds of Grub Street, the semi-literate hacks who think they're Hemingway and demand advances commensurate with their delusions. As if the importuning of talentless scribblers were not enough, now *this*.'

'"*This*"?' Langham echoed.

'Over lunch, Donald. All will be revealed. Now, my ample stomach rumbles its discontent. Come hither, Donald, *post haste*!'

Langham replaced the receiver, fetched his overcoat and descended the staircase to the quiet side street. His battered Austin Healey sat in the bright April sunlight, as reliable as an old dog that had seen better days. He eased himself in behind the wheel and winced at a sudden twinge in his lower back. He was forty and, despite his usual sanguine take on life, had begun to feel old of late. Aches and pains, along with the fact that his father had died of a heart attack in 'thirty-five at the age of fifty, ushered in unwelcome thoughts of mortality.

He checked in the wing mirror and pulled out into the street.

Over the course of the past two decades – with a break during the war – he'd published over twenty mystery novels, several of which he was reasonably proud. He had a small group of friends, mainly men of his own age and in the same line of work, and a two-bedroom flat at the respectable end of Notting Hill.

He told himself that if his life lacked excitement these days, then that was fine by him. His wartime experiences had provided more than enough excitement to last a couple of lifetimes, and anyway he'd always daydreamed, during intolerably hot nights in Madagascar and India,

9

of living the quiet life in London, writing mystery novels and seeing friends over pints of bitter in snug hostelries.

Now he was living that life and sublimating any subconscious desire for action by putting his hapless private detective through all manner of life-threatening perils. It was true what a friend had said in the pub last week: he lived vicariously via the exploits of Sam Brooke.

The tree-lined streets of Pimlico hove into view and Langham turned the corner into Cambridge Street. The Charles Elder Literary Agency was situated down the leafy side street, surrounded by expensive mansions and the occasional high-end solicitor's office. Elegant women in their fifties, draped with fox stoles, walked bouffant poodles and yappy Pekinese. This was a million miles from Sam Brooke's usual stamping ground, and Langham's, if truth be told, and he never visited his agent without being aware that he and Charles inhabited two entirely different worlds.

He parked outside the agency office, bought a bouquet of mixed blooms from a roadside vendor, then hurried up the steps and pressed the bell. He slipped inside, assailed by the scent of beeswax, and took the short flight of stairs to the first floor. Everything about the premises exuded a luxury at odds with the general post-war penury that prevailed in the capital: the brilliant white gloss paint that covered, in multiple coats, the banister and handrail; a carpet so new and thick that he was in danger of turning an ankle as he climbed.

He tapped on the door to the outer office and entered when Maria carolled, 'Come in!' with a slight Parisian accent.

She was seated behind her desk, leaning forward with her hands clasped and her chin resting on the ridge of her knuckles, and a smile irradiated her features when she saw the bouquet.

'Donald! You are always smiling and bearing flowers.'

He handed them over. 'To brighten the place, not that the place needs brightening, what with—'

She stopped him. 'Always the same old line, Donald! And you call yourself a writer?'

He pointed to the communicating door. 'Charles...?'

'He is waiting for you, but he is not well. I will tell you that now.'

'Not well?'

'Something is troubling him, I know.' She held her head to one side and regarded Langham.

'No doubt he'll pour out his woes over lunch,' he said.

'Lunch,' she said almost wistfully, 'and while you are enjoying steak tartare and *crème anglaise*, I will be eating my Bovril sandwiches.'

He almost suggested, then, that she might like to share a more substantial meal with him that evening ... but his damned innate reserve stopped the words on his lips. Maria Dupré was ten years his junior, breathtakingly gorgeous, and the daughter of the French cultural attaché to London. She worked in the agency three days a week, but of her life outside the office Langham

11

knew nothing.

What he did know was that, despite the superficial banter and the ease with which they swapped jokes when their paths crossed fleetingly, he was constitutionally unable to do anything to escalate the terms of their relationship. Charles Elder found his reserve amusing, and mercilessly baited Langham about it whenever he had the chance.

'Right-ho, I'll go and see what's troubling his nibs.'

Maria arranged the flowers in a vase and Langham tapped on the communicating door.

A stentorian baritone boomed, 'Enter!'

He stepped into Charles's hallowed, book-lined sanctum where the ever-present scent of Havana cigars vied with overtones of whisky. A monstrous aspidistra, which Charles playfully referred to as his child, loomed in one corner.

Charles himself was standing at the far end of the room, his corpulent figure silhouetted against the sunlit window. He resembled, Langham thought, a tweed-clad brandy glass.

'Donald, my dear boy! Delighted, absolutely delighted. Had you turned down my suggestion of lunch, I would have been bereft. Bereft.'

He approached Langham with his hand outstretched like some beseeching dowager, as if desiring it to be kissed. He took Langham's hand in limp fingers and squeezed. '*So* glad you could make it. Let's eat!'

Charles's face was almost as vast as his stomach, pink and porcine and topped with a snowy peak of white hair. He was such a caricature of himself that passers-by were apt to turn and stare as he sallied forth, swinging his gold-topped walking stick and harrumphing snatches of Bach.

As they left the office – followed by an ironic *'Bon appétit!'* from Maria – Charles was muttering about the quality of the menu at the Beeches, which Langham knew from experience would be excellent.

He had known Charles Elder for almost twenty years, ever since his first novel was taken on by the agency, and Charles had changed little in that time. He seemed always to have been in his mid-fifties, gargantuan and patrician, a refugee from an earlier, grander era that had vanished with the war.

At their first meeting, Charles had intimidated Langham with a casual remark. 'Very interested in the book. We don't usually touch *mysteries*, dear boy, but this one shows distinct promise. Now tell me, where did you school?'

'Ah...' Langham had flushed, swallowed, and told the truth: 'I ... I didn't. That is, I left school at sixteen and worked in my father's office.'

'Good God, sir, for someone with no education you write like an angel. You read, of course? I mean Shakespeare, Milton, Marvell. If I'm not mistaken, I detected their influences.'

Langham had used this as a ladder to climb from the hole he'd dug for himself. 'All those, yes,' he'd lied.

'Had you down as a fellow Oxford man, my dear boy. But no matter...'

Over the years he had come to know and like

13

the man – despite, or even because of, the fact that he was unlike Langham in every respect.

They strolled down Gloucester Street, Charles swinging his stick and humming to himself. Usually Charles would have been enquiring about Langham's latest book, muttering encouragingly about the next advance he'd screw from the shysters at Harrington, but today he was decidedly quiet. Preoccupied, Langham thought. Maria was right: something was troubling him.

They entered the Beeches and Charles made straight for his usual table by the window, the head waiter in flapping attendance. Langham watched the waiter slide the chair beneath Charles's buttocks, and mused that two chairs might soon be needed to bear the load. Charles busied himself with the wine menu, his piggy eyes scouring the vintages, and in due course ordered a claret.

'Chateau Pontet, nineteen thirty, Donald. One of the finest.'

Langham smiled, wishing he could order a pint of bitter. He glanced around the room at the well-dressed clientele. He forever felt out of place when dining with Charles, conscious of his elbow-patched tweed jacket and threadbare corduroy trousers.

They ordered: Charles a steak *au poivre*, and Langham a pork chop. The wine waiter poured Charles a taster, and he duly swilled the mouthful with a series of theatrical grimaces and pronounced it satisfactory.

Langham watched the waiter depart. 'The delicate matter?' he asked.

14

Charles pulled a pained face, took a swallow of claret, then said, 'I will come to that in due course, my dear boy. Such things cannot be rushed.'

Langham ventured, 'Harrington getting cold feet about the Sam Brooke series?'

'What?' Charles waved his napkin. 'They love the books, dear boy. Don't fret on that score.' He paused, the acreage of his pink face rearranging itself into a frown, as if he were attempting to recall something. 'Remind me, Donald, immediately after the war ... what did you do?'

Thrown by the question, Langham sat back, nursing his glass. 'A friend I met in field security in India, Ralph Ryland, set up an investigative agency. He wanted someone to do the legwork.' He shrugged. 'I decided to write part time and work three days a week for Ralph. I saw it as an opportunity to get some experience that might feed into the books.'

'And I think it did, dear boy. Your books positively *reek* of your time spent chasing cut-throats through Whitechapel.'

Langham smiled. 'I'd hardly say that...'

'Too modest! Too modest by half. That is why maiden aunts up and down the country positively lap up your thrillers, Donald. Authenticity. You scare the pants off them with your villains because you're so *convincing*. The doyen of the lending libraries!' Charles finished.

'Thank you. I'll have that carved on my gravestone.'

Their orders arrived and Charles, goggle-eyed at the prospect of tucking into his inch-thick

15

steak, inserted a napkin between the collar of his shirt and his bullfrog's throat. He looked for all the world, Langham thought, like a pensionable Billy Bunter.

'Why the interest in what I did back then?'

Charles slipped a wedge of steak into his mouth, chewed, then said, 'Let me ask a question of my own, dear boy. Is the investigative agency still running?'

'Well, it was when I bumped into Ralph just before Christmas.'

He started on his chop, watching Charles as he did so. His agent was nodding slowly, mulling something over behind his bright blue eyes. 'That is interesting...'

Langham leaned forward. 'Would you mind telling me what all this is about, Charles? Do you need a private investigator?'

Charles masticated another mouthful of steak with porcine industry, laid down his knife and fork, and stared across the table at Langham. 'My dear boy, how long have you known me?'

Langham blinked. 'Twenty years, give or take a few months.'

'And you know very well what I am?'

Langham found himself smiling. 'An agent of impeccable taste, a gourmand, a *bon viveur*, a collector of *objets d'art nonpareils*...'

'Your flattery brings a blush to my already sanguine countenance. I mean,' Charles persisted, 'you are well aware of my predilections? My – how shall I say? – my *preferences*?'

'How could I not be?'

'And yet, for a man of your age and upbring-

16

ing, you show a remarkable tolerance.'

Langham smiled. 'I had my eyes opened during my time in the army, Charles.'

'Ah, the armed forces, my boy! I attempted to enlist in 1916; did I ever tell you? Myself and a sweet little thing I first met at Eton. We drilled together in the OTC. Needless to say, I was deemed surplus to requirements. And tragic Crispin stopped a bullet at Ypres.'

While Charles's dewy eyes focused on the past, Langham smiled as he considered his shock, back in 'thirty-seven, when he first realized that Charles Elder was homosexual. He'd kept his agent at a mental arm's length at the time, and it was not until Madagascar, when he met and fought alongside other men of the same persuasion – one of whom became a good friend – that his prejudices were dispelled.

'Very well, Charles. Out with it. What's happened?'

'That's what I like about you. You're down to earth, you speak your mind, and if you have any prejudices you keep them well hidden.'

'You haven't heard my drunken rants about the local Tory council.'

Charles smiled. He wiped his mouth with his napkin, stared at Langham, and then sighed. 'I've been a damned fool, Donald.'

Langham nodded. 'Tell.'

'The same old story, Donald. The cravings of the flesh are tied ineluctably to the desires of the heart; in my case, my boy, the sexual and the personal are, shall we say, conflicted ... In here,' and Charles lodged a fist against his breastbone,

17

'I want nothing more than the bliss of domesticity, the faithful love of a good man, while another part of me loves, I mean *loves*, the thrill of the chase ... Do you appreciate my meaning?'

'Ah...' Langham nodded. 'I think so.'

'I waffle, Donald; I waffle. I could never write with the clipped precision of yourself. My screeds would run to Jamesean prolixity. But I digress. Where was I?'

'Conflicted desires.'

'Quite. You see, in a word, I made a silly mistake and now I am reaping the dire consequences. I met a young gentleman ... Gentleman? What am I saying? He was a scallywag, albeit a charming scallywag. He works in Hackney swimming baths, where I am wont weekly to disport myself. One day, perhaps six months ago, we found ourselves in conversation and he tipped me the old "How do you do" and suggested I come back at six, when he'd be closing the place, for a few extra-curricular lessons. Do you see what I mean, Donald, about the weakness of the flesh?'

'You succumbed?'

'That is one way of describing it, my dear boy. I will spare you the details, suffice to say that we had the place to ourselves and the rapscallion exhibited a desire to please matched only by his gymnastic prowess. I'm sorry, I'm making you blush.'

'The wine,' Langham said.

'That was the first occasion. I returned monthly, and again last week, which is when the wretched photographs were taken. To cut a long

18

story short, the photographs – lurid beyond your imaginings – arrived yesterday, along with a typed demand for a hundred pounds.' Charles shook his head. 'The sad thing is that my recollection of our intimacy is so beautiful, and yet the photographic evidence of the act suggests a grim carnality.' He pushed his plate away, having demolished the steak. 'I must admit to a terrible rage when I think that our time together meant nothing more to Kenneth than the opportunity to fleece me.'

Tears filmed his eyes like silver cataracts. Langham looked away while Charles dabbed at them with his napkin.

'And you would like me to approach my contact at the investigative agency and have him look into the matter?'

Charles smiled. 'Would that be possible, dear boy? I mean, how might this continue? A hundred pounds now – and what next week? I know I'm not short of a penny or two, but a hundred pounds! If I don't pay...'

'There was a specific threat in the letter?'

Charles waved. 'Something along the lines of "what might some of my more respectable clients think if the truth got out?" To be honest, I fear more the opprobrium of the judiciary. I fear, I admit, a spell of her Majesty's pleasure in the Scrubs.'

Langham thought about it. 'Can I give you a word of advice?'

'I'm all ears, dear boy.'

'I suggest you don't take it to an investigative agency. I'd keep mum about it. Inform no one.'

Charles looked incredulous. 'What, and cough up a hundred pounds to the little villain?'

'Charles, leave it with me. I'll look into it. I'd like to see the note, and I want to know a little more about this young man, Kenneth.'

'Are you sure you want to get mixed up in all this, my boy?'

Langham reached across the table and patted Charles's hand. 'I'm doing this for a good friend. I'm sure I can put the frighteners on our Kenneth.'

Charles winced. 'The frighteners? Now you're sounding like Sam Brooke.'

'I learned a thing or two at the agency. I just never thought they'd be of much use outside my fiction.'

'You don't know how grateful I am, dear boy. What say we adjourn to the office? I have the most wonderful twenty-year-old single malt we might sample...'

Maria was on the phone when they arrived back at the agency.

'The contract stipulates six per cent, Mr Kenyon. And my client wants it understood that the delivery date, as agreed, will not be before the thirty-first of July.'

Maria listened to the response with her head tipped to one side, her lips pursed in an amused moue. Her long dark hair fell around an aquiline face, which with hooded eyelids and down-turned mouth gave her a look at once exotically foreign and droll. Langham found it hard to tear his gaze away from her.

20

'That's all very well, but my client insists that the agreement – the *gentleman*'s agreement – was for a delivery date of the first of August, and I, too, must insist that we keep to this.'

Charles stood beside Maria's desk, a fingertip pressed to his pursed lips as he listened. He winked at Langham, a gesture eloquent of his pride in Maria's negotiating skills.

He waved Langham into his office, eased the door shut and poured two stiff whiskies.

'She really is the most accomplished *aide-de-camp* I could hope for, Donald. You don't know what a relief it is to be able to leave the running of the agency in Maria's capable hands.'

Charles dropped into his chair behind a vast mahogany desk piled high with books and manuscripts. He raised his glass – reduced to the size of a thimble in his padded paw – to his lips, sipped and closed his eyes in bliss.

'Ah ... Drink has charms to soothe the savage breast, to misquote Congreve.'

Langham sat opposite and took a sip of whisky; it filled his mouth like honey, with a smooth afterburn on the swallow.

Charles said, 'I suppose you need to see the letter, my boy?'

'And the envelope.'

His agent opened the top right drawer of his desk and withdrew the envelope.

'When did you say it arrived?' Langham asked-ed.

'Two days ago. By some fortuitous stroke of providence Maria was half an hour late, or she would have opened the mail...' Charles closed his eyes in a theatrical display of horror. 'I don't know what I would have said had she found this ... this terrible testimony to my weakness.'

'She knows about...?'

'She's no fool, Donald. Of course she knows. But there's a difference between knowing and having one's face rubbed in the sordid facts.'

'I don't want to see the photos,' Langham hastened to add, 'just the envelope and the note.'

Pulling a distasteful face, Charles withdrew the photographs, slipped them quickly back into the drawer and passed the envelope to Langham.

The agency's address was typed on the manila envelope, and the postmark at the top right corner was smudged beyond legibility. Langham opened the flap and took out a single sheet of paper.

The short, typed message was brutally, gloatingly, to the point.

Dear Charles,
Enclosed, six of the very best showing you in flagrante delicto, *shall we say? I'm sure you would not want your clients* au fait *with your peccadilloes ... The price for my silence is a bargain at a mere hundred pounds.*

Langham looked up. Charles was wincing. 'What do you make of it, my boy?'

'Interesting.'

'Interesting? Is that all?'

Langham asked, 'Whoever did this didn't stipulate a time or place for the delivery of the hundred pounds.'

22

Charles placed a hand on his brow. 'I have that missive to anticipate. I await the postman's arrival with the eagerness of a lovesick beau. I've told Maria I'm expecting an important communiqué and I want her to send *all* the post in to me.'

Langham read the note again. 'I might be wrong, but this doesn't sound like the type of language a young swimming instructor might use. Or am I being unfair? What do you think?'

'It is a trifle flowery, and the use of the French...' Charles frowned. 'I agree. Kenneth is a cockney tyke, and I assume his reading tastes run to the *Wizard*, not Proust.'

'Maybe it's the work of his accomplice, the photographer?'

'In all likelihood they're running a very lucrative business, preying upon the lovelorn and the lonely. If only they could see the heartache they cause.'

Langham slipped the letter into the envelope and passed it back to Charles. 'I'll pay Kenneth a visit and see what he has to say for himself. Try not to worry. I know that's easier said than done, but I'm pretty sure I'll have the matter sorted out in no time.'

'My boy, you don't know how grateful I am.'

Langham looked at his watch. It was almost four. 'And as they say, there's no time like the present.'

Charles forestalled him. 'The baths are closed half a day today, my boy. The queers of London are spared Kenneth's poisoned charms.'

Langham finished his whisky. 'In that case I'll

23

pay him a visit tomorrow. I'll be in touch, and notify me as soon as you get another letter.'

Charles reached across the desk and grasped Langham's hand. 'My dear boy, my gratitude knows no bounds.'

Maria was busy typing a letter when Langham passed through the outer office. He waved as he went and said goodbye.

She tipped her head to one side, prettily, and trilled, *'Au revoir*, Donald!' Her contralto buoyed his steps as he left the agency and emerged into the late afternoon sunlight.

He considered his promise to Charles, and wondered if he'd made a mistake in appearing so overtly confident. Blackmail, he knew from his limited experience, was a messy business which rarely, if ever, redounded to the advantage of the victim.

TWO

Maria stood before the bay window of her father's Hampstead townhouse and gazed, without really seeing anything, across the darkening heath. She nursed a glass of champagne and wondered how many times she had stood in this very place while a party surged behind her.

Her earliest recollection was as a twelve-year-old, way back in 'thirty-seven when her father had first been posted to London. It had been

24

winter then, and she had been delighted by the blanket of snow which had covered the capital. Before the outbreak of war her father had been recalled to France, only to flee a year later to work in the cabinet in exile in London. Maria recalled standing here in the summer of 'forty at the age of fifteen, before being sent away to boarding school in Gloucestershire. While her father's political colleagues had schemed away, she had worried about how she, a foreigner, might be received at her new school. In the event she need not have worried. Half the girls there had been from overseas and she had made friends quickly; in many ways it had been the happiest time of her life.

Now her father held these soirées every month and invited everyone who was anyone in French émigré society: artists rubbed shoulders with writers, politicians with philosophers and professors. Her father always invited her along, he said, in order to add youth and beauty to the ageing mix of largely male guests, and for her father's sake she always attended. She disliked the formality of the gatherings, the stilted manners of everyone present, and most of all she disliked her father's expectations that she should circulate and be sparkling.

She had worked at the Charles Elder Literary Agency for almost five years now, and though she liked the work and loved Charles, she had found herself wondering lately where her life was taking her. Originally she'd decided to go into publishing with the hopes that one day she might become an editor, but after six years with two major London firms she'd come to the realization that it was not only her nationality that was holding her back: the fact was that publishing, like every other walk of professional life, was so dominated by the male of the species as to be practically closed to any woman with aspirations.

At least Charles treated her as an equal, and had even told her that one day she would be made a partner. So, she asked herself for perhaps the fiftieth time that day, why the sudden, indefinable dissatisfaction?

'Maria, my darling, forgive me – I've neglected you. Old Henri was bending my ear about some convoluted trade agreement and I couldn't get away. But here, I saw your glass was almost empty.' Her father passed her a full, fizzing glass and she smiled up at him.

The French cultural attaché to London was tall, slim and impeccably attired in a sharp evening suit. His face was proportionally thin and aquiline, his silver hairline receding gracefully. He combined the contradictory attributes of artistic acuity and business acumen never found in British politicians, but *de rigueur* in the politicos of her own country.

At the gatherings her father insisted on introducing her to the latest French literary lion – and to men who were neither French nor literary. She found it hard to forgive him for introducing her last year to Gideon Martin, an overbearing narcissist who'd had a few literary novels published in London in the late forties. They had sold abominably – for good reason,

Maria thought – and ever since Martin had trudged the gutters of Grub Street, picking up trifling commissions here and there and churning out hack novels.

She had made the mistake of dining with him several times last year – before she realized quite what a self-piteous, self-centred creature he was – and he had followed her like a lovelorn ghost ever since, swaggering with his trademark swordstick.

To her horror she had glimpsed him tonight, and had spent the evening so far attempting to avoid him.

'You seem withdrawn, *ma chérie.*'

She smiled. 'I'm tired, Papa.'

'Then drink. I have always found champagne to be a great enlivener.'

She laughed. 'To be honest, it sends me to sleep!'

He made to take it from her. 'In that case, would you prefer a cup of English tea?'

He was forever, in his own gentle way, making gentle digs at all things English. She wondered if he secretly resented the way she had taken to her adopted country. Well, she thought, if so then he had no one to blame but himself.

'Come, Maria. Look who arrived from Paris just this morning! None other than Monsieur Savagne. He is eager to see you again.'

She allowed herself to be steered across the busy drawing room to a knot of guests by the hearth. She wondered what the dear little man was doing in London this time. On their last meeting – and that must have been over two

27

years ago – he had regaled her with the details of a monograph he was working on: a history of Satanism in Paris and London.

Her father announced her to the small crowd as if introducing royalty. 'Ladies and gentlemen, my daughter, Maria. M Savagne, Maria has never stopped talking about your book.'

Which was an exaggeration, but she smiled anyway and said to the diminutive man, 'And what brings you to London this time, Monsieur? Research?'

He waved away the suggestion of another monograph. *'Non!* Certainly not research. I am afraid my scholarly days are behind me. The thought of writing another book...' His blue eyes twinkled at her. 'Do you know how old I am, my dear?'

She sipped her champagne and said, 'I'd guess at not a day over sixty.'

'You flatter an old man! I am eighty next week, eighty!' He went on with something like sadness in his tone, 'It is too old to be doing what I am doing, my dear.'

'Which is?'

He smiled, and launched himself into an account which seemed to have little bearing on his current business. 'During the last war, when the Nazis invaded Paris, they ransacked various apartments, though I think they used the word "commandeered" – but that is by the by. They also "appropriated" various works of art. One of these was my late uncle's pride and joy, an eighteenth-century Italian statuette of the virgin and child. For many years it was thought lost in

28

Germany, but it has recently come to light.'

'In London?'

'Actually, my dear, in Rome. But a little bird told me that it was coming up for open sale at Sotheby's this week.'

'And you hope to purchase it?'

M Savagne pulled an expressive face. 'If only I had the financial wherewithal to do so, my dear. No, my only hope is to approach the purchaser and appeal to his better nature. I hope to propose something along the lines that the buyer might, in his altruism, donate the statuette to a Paris museum. At least then it would be back where it belongs.'

Maria laid a hand on the little man's arm. 'A noble sentiment, but do you think the buyer might agree?'

'That remains to be seen. But that is why I am in London, and later this week I shall attend the auction at Sotheby's when the statuette will come under the hammer.'

Maria raised her glass. 'To your success,' she said.

A waiter arrived and recharged their glasses, Maria declining by placing a hand over hers. M Savagne said, 'But I will bore you no longer with my trivial concerns, my dear. I must say you are looking enchanting tonight – and how goes life in the Smoke, as I think they call this metropolis, and for good reason?'

For the next ten minutes they chattered amiably about literary life in London and her job at the agency; she managed to make her rather humdrum daily routine sound interesting, with exaggerated anecdotes of bidding wars between publishers and gossip about Big Name authors.

Canapés were served and her father, perhaps fearing M Savagne was overstaying his daughter's welcome, pounced and said, 'If you will excuse me while I steal my daughter for just one moment. My dear, I must introduce you to an eminent young man of letters...'

She smiled at M Savagne and wished him good luck at the auction. As her father escorted her across the room, he said, 'I feel sorry for the poor fellow. He told you about his crazy idea? The trouble is, which collector in his right mind would consent, after paying for the statuette, to have it sitting in some Paris museum when it could be gracing his private collection?'

'Perhaps an arrangement might be made for a part-time loan?' she suggested.

Her father smiled. 'The optimism of youth...' he murmured. 'Ah, here we are.'

The eminent young novelist turned out to be a bore in his forties who wrote sub-Proustian, stream-of-consciousness tracts and who was looking for a London publisher.

Maria tried to come up with a tactful way of telling the man that his book was unlikely to find a market in this country. 'The English,' she temporized, 'are more interested in whodunits than literary experimentalism.'

He rallied; she listened politely, her attention wandering. She looked up, and wished she hadn't. Her gaze was snared by that of Gideon Martin, who took the establishment of eye contact as permission to hurry across the room and drag her away.

'Do excuse us,' he said to the bemused writer as he gripped Maria by the elbow and steered her towards the window. He tapped her on her upper arm with the brass top of his swordstick and said, 'Now, why on earth were you talking to that ghastly little man?'

Her blood boiling, she snapped, 'Because my father introduced me, and actually I found him rather interesting. I was advising him how to go about getting a decent publisher.'

'If only you would do the same for me!' he said peevishly.

Gideon Martin – he insisted that his surname was pronounced in the French manner, as his mother had been from Paris – was a small, portly man in his late forties, with a huge, barrel-like chest and short legs, whose undeniably handsome face belied his age. On being introduced to Martin last year, she had assumed him to be no older than forty – and initially he had been the epitome of charm.

She had agreed to a dinner date with him, enjoyed the evening and Martin's witty company, and found herself swept off her feet by his urbane manners and wide knowledge. In retrospect she told herself that at the time she had been lonely, and therefore desperate. She had gone out for drinks with him on a few other occasions, until she saw the writer in his true colours. He was a desperately jealous man who resented more talented authors their success and blamed everyone but himself for his current situation as a jobbing hack.

She had screwed up her courage and told Martin that she no longer wished to see him, citing differences of personality and taste as the reason. He had been distraught, threatening to throw himself beneath a tube train if she did not agree to see him again – always the last refuge of the morally bankrupt, she thought – and had dogged her steps ever since.

He had even submitted some of his more literary efforts to her agency, under a pen name, but she had seen through his ruse and his over-wrought prose, and returned his manuscripts only partially read.

Now he said, 'His experimentalism is passé. Merely stylistic, lacking any intellectual content.' He had the annoying habit of not looking at the person to whom he was speaking; his gaze was forever fixed, broodingly, on something distant. Maria thought it was an indication of his egotistical self-absorption.

Maria almost said, 'Very much like your own "serious" work, then?' but stopped herself just in time. Instead she found herself snapping, 'And I suppose yours is brimming with intellectual content?'

His gaze came to rest on her face, swiftly, before flitting away. 'Maria, why must you treat me like this?'

He really did have the ability to annoy her. 'Like what?'

'As if...' His gaze flicked to her, then away. 'As if I were less than nothing.'

She was tempted to say, 'Because, Gideon, to me you *are* less than nothing.' Instead she said,

'My treatment of you is nothing of the kind.'

'Then why do you ignore me?' he asked intently, his moody gaze fixed on a point far beyond the confines of the room. 'Why do you refuse to answer my letters? I wrote to you just last week.'

'I'm extremely busy. Your letter must have gone astray among all the others—'

'As if my letters matter less to you than those of the hacks you represent.'

She gritted her teeth. She should turn and walk away, or tell the conceited little man just what she really thought about him.

He went on: 'Maria, can't you see how much you mean to me? Our time together last year ... Our meetings meant the world to me. They live in my memory as times of fulfilment and joy.'

She stared at him. 'Please. I told you, some things are just not meant to happen.'

'How can you say that if you do not give me another chance? What did I do wrong?'

He stared at her, and the sudden intensity of his attention was intimidating. 'You did nothing *wrong*...' she floundered.

'Then why do you treat me so cruelly?' he implored. 'What is wrong with me? I have looks, erudition and, I think I am correct in saying, not a little literary talent.'

She almost laughed at his inability to see himself as the insufferable, arrogant prig – and failed writer – that he was. She said, 'There is nothing wrong with you. It's just that ... there needs to be a certain ... chemistry between people, no? A spark?'

'And you are saying that I fail to ignite that

33

spark?'

She deplored the weakness in herself that would not allow her to tell him the truth: that he was an insufferable egotist whom she hated a little more every time they met.

'I don't know...' she said, and took refuge in a long drink of champagne.

His livid gaze fixed on the far door, he said, 'You are seeing someone else, aren't you?'

She spluttered on the bubbly. 'No, I am *not*! Why should you think...?'

'Then if you are seeing no one, why cannot you at least consent to accompany me occasionally?'

The arrogance of the man! 'My God...' she muttered under her breath.

A silence simmered between them. She was about to walk away when he said, 'I recall the last time we met. We had drinks at that West End bar, and then I took you to Bertrand's Gallery. You admired a rather nice watercolour by Myles Birkett Foster.'

She shrugged as if to say, *what of it*?

He went on: 'You made me appreciate the qualities of the painting, Maria. I went back and bought it last week. It looks rather good in my hall...'

She stared at him, simmering with rage. Fortunately his gaze was elsewhere and he did not see the fury in her eyes. She had told him – she was sure she had told him – that she intended to buy the watercolour as a present for her father's sixtieth birthday.

She was determined not to show her anger.

34

'Well, I'm delighted for you.'

He glanced at her. 'And on Thursday I hope to make another small purchase. At Sotheby's,' he finished.

She looked at him, suspicious. 'Sotheby's?'

'There is a very nice Italian silver statuette coming up for sale. I've heard on the grapevine that M Savagne is interested in the piece, and I've also heard that he is down on his uppers. I intend to purchase the piece before he can accumulate the requisite funds.'

She stared at him, open-mouthed, and he went on: 'I have, with considerable effort, raised three thousand, and I have always admired the statuette.'

Poor Monsieur Savagne, she thought; he would never persuade Gideon Martin to part with it.

He said, 'But enough of that. Did I tell you, Maria, that I think you the most beautiful girl in London?' He reached out and grasped her hand.

Salvation, in the looming form of Dame Amelia Hampstead, hove into view. 'Martin, unhand the girl this minute, or I shall report your febrile molestations to Monsieur Dupré forthwith!'

Martin started and looked up at the glowering dowager. *'You!'* he almost spat.

Maria pulled her hand from his grip and Martin, muttering to himself, turned on his heel and hurried from the room.

Maria touched Dame Amelia's plump hand. 'You don't know how grateful I am!' she laughed.

'Is that awful little man still chasing you, my dear?' Amelia asked.

Maria sighed. 'He never leaves me in peace! Had I known he would be here tonight, I would not have accepted my father's invitation. He really is *intolerable*.'

Amelia patted her hand. 'Well, your fairy godmother has saved your day. Waiter!' she called. 'I think we shall have another two glasses of this rather excellent champagne.'

Dame Amelia was one of her favourite people on the London literary scene, which had nothing to do with the fact that she was also one of Charles Elder's leading authors. Amelia penned light-hearted but technically accomplished whodunits in the Christie and Sayers mould, did not take herself at all seriously, and treated Maria like a favourite niece.

'Did I ever tell you that I penned a rather trenchant review of Gideon's first novel, back in 'forty-seven? He's never forgiven me for it.' She leaned closer to Maria and whispered. 'But it deserved every word I wrote, and I must admit I was savage. It *was* terrible!'

'I can imagine,' Maria said. 'I made the mistake of reading one of his efforts after our first meeting. It was almost as conceited as the man himself.'

Dame Amelia laughed. 'We really should have lunch very soon and catch up,' she said. 'I will call you at the agency and arrange something at Martinelli's next week.' She peered across the room. 'My word, am I mistaken or is that *really* Maurice? You haven't met? Then I shall introduce you!' And, taking Maria firmly by the hand, she escorted her across the room.

The evening wore on and, in comparison to Gideon Martin, the other guests were the acme of sophistication and courteousness. Maria had a third glass of champagne and at one - point scanned the crowd for any sign of the obnoxious man, but he had taken the hint and left the party.

It was only later, on her fourth glass of champagne while she was thinking of Monsieur Savagne being outmanoeuvred by Martin, that an exquisite notion occurred to her. She cornered her father and regaled him with her idea, and to her delight he said that he would think it over.

She enjoyed the rest of the evening and it was after one o'clock by the time she arrived back at her Kensington apartment.

THREE

Langham sat in his Austin Healey and glanced at his wristwatch.

It was five twenty-six and he told himself he'd enter the swimming baths on the dot of five thirty. Now that it was almost time to confront the youth, he was having second thoughts. It was all very well to promise Charles an expedient outcome in the comfort of his office after a stiff drink, but the reality of the situation was another thing entirely. It was nine years since he'd

37

worked at the investigative agency, and since then had cosseted himself in a safe fictional world that existed entirely within the bounds of his imagination. He was about to confront someone who was obviously not averse to criminal acts, and he was more than a little apprehensive.

He was parked in a quiet side street off Lower Clapton Road. The public swimming baths, a solid Victorian pile in grey Portland stone, dominated the street like a duchess down on her luck. Parents with children exited through the peeling blue doors, along with individual men and women carrying rolled towels. The baths closed at six and were emptying fast.

He watched a couple pass along the pavement. Hand in hand, they gazed at each other as they walked, welded together by the force of obvious mutual attraction. He felt a sudden pang when he mistook the woman for Maria – they shared the same slight stature and gamine good looks – but then the woman laughed and he realized he was mistaken. Maria was far lovelier.

He looked at his watch and smiled. So much for punctuality. It was five thirty-three. He left the car and hurried across the road and up the steps.

The overwhelming chemical stench of chlorine hit him as he pushed open the heavy double doors. He was confronted by low turnstiles, and memories of his schooldays came flooding back. Once a week his class had walked through the streets of Nottingham to the public bathhouse, similar in every respect to this one. He'd loathed these trips, hated the shock of immersion in what

38

seemed like ice-cold water, hated the dead cockroaches bobbing in the water along with the wadded sticking plasters. But most of all he'd hated the swimming instructor, a vindictive old man dressed all in white who mocked poor swimmers, like Langham, and was not averse to using a thick bamboo pole as a painful, prodding weapon.

'Are you going to stand there all day or do you want to go in?' A sour-faced woman stared at him through an arched grille beside the turnstile. 'It's thruppence, but you'd better be sharpish. Baths close at six.'

Langham paid the entrance fee and pushed through the stiff turnstile.

The pool itself was situated in a cavernous, eerily echoing chamber where the reek of chlorine was even stronger. The rectangle of blue water was a shimmering lens magnifying the dirty white tiles. Changing cubicles with swing doors, like the entrances of saloons in cowboy films, flanked the pool. During the war the pool itself had been boarded over and the chamber utilized as a recruitment station, and even now, ten years after VE Day, faded posters exhorted the wartime populace to Keep Calm and Carry On, Buy War Bonds, and Dig for Victory.

The last of the swimmers hauled themselves from the pool and hurried, dripping, across the tiles to the changing cubicles. Within seconds Langham was all alone in the chamber and he felt his gorge rise with nausea as the smell brought back unpleasant memories.

At the far end of the pool a figure in white, like

39

a younger version of his one-time persecutor, leaned against the tubular chrome frame of the diving boards and fixed him with a level gaze.

Langham walked around the pool, his footsteps ringing on the tiles. 'Kenneth?' he asked.

The boy nodded, suspicious. Langham was surprised at how young he appeared, and amazed that Charles had allowed his head to be turned by such an unprepossessing specimen. Kenneth was skinny, unhealthily pale, and his thin face was made even more unattractive by a sullen scowl.

'Don't like the stink?'

'Is it that obvious?' Langham replied.

'Either that or you don't like the company.' The youth continued to lean casually against the bars. He nodded to the cubicles. 'Young boys, they piss on the boiling hot water pipes. Charmin', they are.' Without a change of tone, he said, 'You a copper?'

'Do I look like one?'

The youth perked up. 'A guardsman, then? You look the military type.'

'I was sent by Charles Elder.'

No flicker of recognition passed across the youth's face. 'He a customer?'

'That's right.'

The boy nodded, pushed himself languorously from the diving frame and said over his shoulder, 'This way.'

Glancing around self-consciously to ensure he was not being observed, he followed the youth from the pool and along an ill-lit corridor. Kenneth's shoulder blades were prominent beneath

40

the white shirt, the material of his trousers tight across his buttocks.

He considered Charles's lack of inhibition, his readiness to assuage his libido. Langham had been celibate for over six years now, sublimating his desires in work and more work, and the occasional binge drink, and lacking ... what? The gall or bravery to confront his loneliness and do something about it.

Not that one-night stands with women would help him, he knew, just as Charles's assignation with the youth had done nothing to ease *his* loneliness; it merely provided a release of his needs.

Langham felt a quick surge of revulsion, soon quashed.

They came to a small room equipped with massage tables and leather-upholstered benches. He looked around, searching for the vantage point from which the youth's accomplice would have taken the photographs. There were a couple of doors leading to other rooms, and an interior window looking into a room equipped with gym apparatus and punch bags.

The youth locked the door behind him, then leaned against it and smiled at Langham.

'I don't come cheap,' he said. 'S'cuse the pun.'

'I know that,' Langham replied. 'A hundred pounds?'

Kenneth looked startled, then elated. 'A hundred knicker? Christ, what you want me to do for that?'

Langham smiled. 'You misunderstand me, Kenneth. A hundred pounds is what you're demanding from my friend, Charles.'

41

Kenneth's face was a picture of mystification. 'You're talking in riddles, mate.'

Langham studied the boy's expression, watching his eyes for tell-tale signs of duplicity. 'Last week you and Charles were photographed in here. Now someone wants a hundred pounds from Charles in order that your little assignation is kept quiet. Would you happen to know anything about that?'

The youth swallowed. He shook his head. 'Don't know nothing about any blackmail, honest.'

Langham kept his expression neutral. 'Who was your accomplice? Who took the photographs from...' he nodded towards the interior window, 'from in there, while you and Charles...?'

Kenneth turned a shade paler. This time, no words came.

Langham found himself relishing the sudden sensation of power. He stepped forward. The youth flinched, a sudden galvanic reaction to Langham's proximity. He lifted his hands quickly before his face and scuttled sideways along the wall until he collided with a massage table and had another start of shock.

Langham found himself pitying the boy. 'There's an easy way to go about this, Kenneth, and there's a hard way.'

Petrified, the boy nodded.

'The easy way,' Langham said, 'is to give me the name of your accomplice, then I'll walk away and you won't see me ever again. It's that simple.'

42

The boy nodded again.

Langham went on: 'And then there's the hard way. You don't tell me the name of who was in on this with you, and I go to the police and tell them about the little racket you've got going on here. And don't forget, I have photographs – one in particular that doesn't show my friend, but shows you very clearly indeed.'

If the boy suspected Langham's bluff, he didn't show it; if anything, the frozen look of fear on his face intensified.

'So ... what is it to be?' Langham leaned casually against the massage table, watching Kenneth.

'OK. OK, I'll tell you everything I know. But I swear – I swear I don't know the name of the bloke.'

'The "bloke" who took the pictures?'

Kenneth nodded. 'He made me do it, honest. I never ... I've never threatened punters. It's how I make ends meet, OK? I mean, it's what I do to earn a bit more than the lousy five bob they give me here. I never threaten the punters!'

'What happened, Kenneth?'

The boy took a breath. 'About a month ago, this bloke comes in – a short, gingerish chap in his fifties. Fattish. Didn't like the look of him. He said a punter had sent him, recommended me, like.'

'What happened?'

The boy shrugged. 'We came in here and he took me. He was rough. Hurt me. Wanted me to teabag 'im.'

'Teabag?'

43

Kenneth began to describe the act, but Langham held up a hand. 'OK, I get the picture. And then?'

The boy shrugged. 'And then nothing. He paid up and went.'

'But he came back?'

'Right. He came back, and I felt right sick at the sight of the bastard. Only this time he didn't want sex.'

'What did he want?'

'He said his brother was a copper, and that they were coming down hard on this kind of thing – cottaging and things. Said he'd turn me in if I didn't do what he wanted.'

'Which was?'

'He said he wanted to photograph me with someone, someone who came here pretty regular. He said he'd hide himself in the gym and take pictures of me and the punter.' He shrugged. 'That was it. What could I do? If I hadn't said yes, the bastard would've turned me in to the coppers, right? What could I do?'

Langham stared at the grime between the white tiles next to Kenneth's head. He looked around the room at the filthy, sweat-stained benches, the floor tiles stained with what might have been dried blood. The stench of chlorine seemed less prevalent here; instead, Langham could smell rank body odour and what might have been stale urine.

Oh, Charles, he thought, *Charles*...

He said, 'Tell me about him, the photographer. Did he give you his name?'

Kenneth shook his head. 'Punters don't, very

often. It's just in here, get the business done, then out like a shot.'

'He was short, fat, ginger-haired?'

Kenneth nodded. 'He was balding, but the bit of hair he did have was ginger.'

'You said he was in his fifties?'

'Around that.'

'Any distinguishing features?'

'Not that I noticed. He was just another creepy old punter.'

'And have you seen him since the day he took the pictures?'

Kenneth shook his head. 'Not a whiff of him.'

Langham nodded. 'I'll give you my phone number. If he comes back, if you find anything else about him, I want you to contact me immediately, understood?'

Kenneth nodded. 'Yeah, OK.'

Langham scribbled his number on a scrap of paper and handed it over. Kenneth took the paper with trembling fingers, then glanced from the number to Langham. 'And you won't tell anyone about...?'

'I won't say a thing.' He made to leave.

'Mr...'

He turned to face the boy, who was smiling timidly.

'You seem an OK kind of bloke, whoever you are.' He waited, then said, 'Seeing as we're here, you fancy a bit?'

He pulled a cord at the waist of his trousers and they dropped to reveal his penis, disproportionately meaty in comparison to his slight frame.

Langham shook his head. 'Save it for the customers, Kenneth,' he said, unbolted the door and walked from the room.

He made his way around the silent pool and crossed the foyer, where he found that the doors were bolted. He shot the bolts, stepped out and paused on the top step. All around him life went on as normal – couples strolling, kids playing football in the street, workers hurrying homewards. An old man shuffled along the pavement, clamped in a sandwich board which proclaimed: The End of the World is Nigh!

Langham returned to his Austin Healey and drove through the backstreets to Notting Hill.

It was after six by the time he reached his flat and poured himself a Scotch. It was a cheap blend, different entirely from the single malt he'd shared with Charles yesterday. He moved from room to room, from his bleakly spartan bedroom to the equally minimalist sitting room and then to his study, this room by contrast invested with personality. His collection of books lined the shelves, and next to the desk, in their own bookcase, were the titles bearing his name along with the magazines and anthologies he'd contributed to over the years. It was an eloquent testimony to the time he'd spent alone, losing himself in make-believe.

On the desk, piled beside the Underwood, was the manuscript he'd finished that afternoon. As ever, he felt satisfaction at the fact of its completion. Soon it would join the other titles on his shelf, and by then he would be well under way with the next one.

He moved to the sitting room and stood in the gathering twilight. A framed photograph stood on the grey-tiled mantelshelf. He picked it up and gazed at the man and woman staring out at him. The man, a younger version of himself with his arm around the woman, could have been a stranger.

He was hungry, but the thought of preparing a meal did not appeal. There was a Lyons' Corner House nearby, and after that he'd pop into the Bull for a couple of pints.

He was awoken the following morning at eight by the shrill summons of the phone.

He rolled from bed and groaned, smitten by a pounding headache. Last night he'd bumped into a writing friend who churned out romances for a new paperback company. The beer had gone down easily and talk had turned to the iniquities of the writing trade, the perfidy of publishers and the fickle nature of the reading public.

He trudged into the study and picked up the phone, the cessation of its din like a balm. 'Hello?'

'My dear boy,' Charles carolled. 'Did you by any chance manage to have words with young Kenneth yesterday?'

'Charles ... Yes, I saw him. I'll come over and tell you all about it. I have a manuscript to deliver, anyway.'

'And I have received another missive from you know who, this time with instructions.'

'Instructions? Right, I'm on my way.'

'How about breakfast? The finest meal of the

47

day, I believe. Mrs Bledsoe is preparing a veritable feast of devilled kidneys, bacon and eggs as
I speak.'

Langham smiled, despite himself. 'I think I'll
pass on that, but I could kill a cup of tea.'

'The finest Earl Grey it shall be! I await your
arrival with anticipation.'

Langham replaced the receiver, returned to the
bedroom and dressed.

FOUR

Maria was arranging books on the shelf behind
her desk when Langham entered the outer office.

He'd let himself in without knocking, not
expecting her to be here this early, and it was
obvious from her absorbed preoccupation that
she hadn't heard him come in. He paused by the
door and watched her. She was standing on
tiptoe to reach the top shelf with her back to him,
her legs braced and her back arched; she was
wearing silk stockings and a body-hugging jade
green two-piece. The effect was breathtaking.

Langham cleared his throat and Maria turned.
She swept a tress of dark hair from her face and
gave him a dazzling smile. 'Oh, Donald!'

'Sorry. Didn't mean to startle you.'

She gestured to the flight of stairs that led to
the top floor, where Charles had his London
pied-à-terre. 'He said he's expecting you for

48

breakfast.' She peered at him. 'But you look terrible!'

He smiled. The way she pronounced terrible – in the French manner, *terr-eeble* – made it sound even worse.

'That bad? I was out last night. Had one too many. Anyway,' he went on, hefting the manuscript, 'here's the latest.'

She took it, feigning collapse under its not inconsiderable weight. 'Charles will be delighted,' she said, with what he thought might have been a trace of sarcasm.

She dropped it on the desk with a thud. 'Donald, have you ever written anything else? I mean, not mystery stories?'

'Guilty.' He held up both hands. 'I might, if pressed, admit to a few westerns in the early days.'

She tipped her head and said, 'But never literature?'

He shrugged. 'I'm happy writing the Sam Brooke books. Why?'

'Oh, no reason. It's just that you write very well, do you know?'

'Why, thank you.'

'Perhaps,' she said, 'we should talk about this at some point in the future, no?'

He regarded her. Her head was still tipped prettily, and she was smiling. How to interpret the invitation? He made light of it, and laughed. 'Are you thinking of setting up your own agency, Maria?'

She shook her head, serious. 'And leave Charles? Perish the thought, as you English say.'

He indicated the stairs. 'I'd better...'

She inserted herself behind the desk. 'Ah, *oui*. Off you go.'

He climbed the thickly carpeted stairs to the luxurious suite of rooms on the top floor, knocked and entered. Charles was seated at a breakfast table in the bow window, and Mrs Bledsoe, who did for him, was serving a gargantuan plate piled with a full English.

She smiled at Langham as she hurried to the kitchen. 'And the same for you, Mr Langham?'

The very idea made him feel queasy. 'Tea and toast will be fine, thanks, Mrs Bledsoe.'

She cast him a critical eye. 'No wonder you look as thin as a rake, if I may say so. You need feeding up, you do.' She disappeared into the kitchen.

Langham took his place opposite Charles.

His agent speared half a kidney and held it before him. Langham winced at the noxious offal, slick with melted butter.

'Whatever slings and arrows the world throws at us,' Charles declaimed, 'whatever obstacles fate tosses in our path, there is always the consolation of the humble kidney!'

He popped it in his mouth and chewed vigorously, then perched his pince-nez upon the bridge of his porcine snout and peered. 'You look, if I might be so bold, dreadful. Have you shaved this morning, my boy?'

Langham rasped his stubbled jaw. 'Didn't have time.'

Charles harrumphed, as if neglecting one's toilette was a serious breach of etiquette. He

50

reached out for a silver teapot. 'May I?'

He poured, and Langham took a sip of Earl Grey. 'Ah ... that's good.'

'Now,' Charles said, 'you mentioned seeing young Kenneth yesterday.'

'That's right.'

Charles forestalled the conveyance of a plump mushroom towards his equally plump lips. 'And?'

'And he's innocent – well, innocent of the blackmail. Turns out he was threatened.' He gave Charles a synopsis of his conversation with the boy. 'None of which alters the situation.'

Mrs Bledsoe arrived with a rack of toast and a pot of marmalade. 'Now eat up. And there's more when you've finished that.'

Langham helped himself to a slice of toast, buttered it but forewent the marmalade.

Charles waited until Mrs Bledsoe had returned to the kitchen and closed the door behind her, then said, 'I knew it, my boy! I knew it.'

Langham eyed him over his toast. 'Knew what?'

'I knew beyond doubt that Kenneth was innocent, as much a victim in this foul matter as am I.'

Langham refrained from reminding Charles of his curses directed at the boy just two days ago.

His agent was in full spate. 'You see, it is always the downtrodden and impecunious who find themselves shat upon – I said positively *shat* upon – by the system.'

Langham eyed Charles warily. 'By that I take it you're referring to Kenneth?'

'Do you realize how much the boy earns at that sweatshop, my boy? Three shillings a week! Is it any wonder he is forced into supplementing such a meagre stipend?'

Before Langham could enlighten Charles as to the boy's actual wage – or at least the sum Kenneth had told him he earned – his agent went on: 'And now that it eventuates that the poor boy is innocent of all charges, I might have second thoughts about visiting again and bestowing upon him my largesse.'

Any largesse, Langham mused upon recollection of Kenneth's parting gesture yesterday, was unlikely to be bestowed by Charles. 'I would have thought that once bitten...'

Charles waved this away. 'But the poor boy needs support from someone, Donald. The poor and deprived have been neglected for too long!'

Langham sipped his tea. 'All this talk of injustice, Charles ... I never had you down as a socialist.'

Charles stopped chewing and pointed a fork at Langham. 'You and I might have many things in common – and I am thinking here of intelligence and wit – but we are *not* fellow travellers. Call me an old-fashioned liberal, if you will.'

'I will,' Langham said, 'but I'd be careful about going back there.'

'But the lure, the lure...!' He squinted at Langham. 'You obviously fail to see the attraction?'

Langham laughed. 'Charles, to be honest, and I don't mean this as any form of criticism ... but what I saw in Kenneth was nothing more than an ugly, underfed youth.'

52

'But underfed in such a *romantic* way!' Charles waved his napkin. 'But each to his own, is my motto. I, for my part, fail to see your attraction to Maria, for instance. And on that score, when do you intend to do something about it, my boy?'

'Do something about it? As if Maria would look twice at me.'

'Donald, Donald ... For an intelligent man, you can be remarkably dense. Maria practically drools when you enter the office.'

'Nonsense!'

'Ask the girl out to dinner, my boy!'

Langham felt himself redden. 'Anyway, I thought she was seeing—'

'They went out a few times last year,' Charles said. 'But no more. Gideon Martin is an egotistical cad, and between you and me he is making her life a misery.'

Langham looked up. 'How's that?'

'He trails her like a lovesick puppy and will not, will *not*, take no for an answer.'

'Gideon Martin...' Langham said. 'The name rings a bell.'

'He had a few faux literary novels published in the late forties, which went down well in Paris but failed miserably here. He's reduced to penning travel guides and anonymous encyclopaedia entries, and hates the world for it. We are not exactly on best terms, ever since I turned down one of his efforts a few years ago.' Charles beamed at him. 'But the fact remains: you really should make a move and ask the dear girl to dinner.'

53

'That,' Langham said as he finished his toast, 'is hardly what I came here to discuss. The actual point—'

'The point? What is the point of life but the essence, the very quiddity, of our relations with our fellow man?'

'I'm not denying that, Charles, but I'm here because you're being blackmailed and we need to do something about it.'

'Ah, *that*...' Charles adopted a pantomime glum expression. 'For a moment there I had almost walked out from under the shadow of *that* dark cloud.'

'The simple fact is that someone, a man in his fifties, short, fat, ginger—'

'You paint *such* an attractive portrait, my boy—'

'—is blackmailing you. There are a couple of reasons he might be doing this.'

'For the filthy lucre, presumably?'

'Obviously. But, is he attempting to extort the money from you because you're a rich punter? Or is it more personal?'

Charles squinted across the table. 'Come again?'

'What if you're being targeted because he bears you a grudge?'

'But my dear boy, I don't have an enemy in the world!'

Langham shrugged. 'I don't imagine you have. But that doesn't mean to say that someone might not hold something against you for whatever reason. The description of this fellow doesn't ring any bells?'

'Short, fat, ginger?'

'Ginger but balding.'

Charles shuddered. 'It brings no one of my acquaintance to mind, thank the Lord.'

'You're absolutely sure? No one at all? No one in publishing, perhaps?'

Charles shook his head.

Mrs Bledsoe bustled into the room and cleared away the dirty plates. 'Will that be all, sir?'

Charles glanced at his watch. 'My word, it's ten o'clock already. I think the hour calls for a pot of lapsang souchong, Mrs Bledsoe.'

'I'll be right back with it.'

When she had left the room, Langham said, 'Which brings us to the second letter...'

Charles made a pained face. 'Arrived this morning, Donald, first post.'

He passed a manila envelope identical to the first, and Langham withdrew a single typed sheet of notepaper.

Dear Charles,

Having given you ample opportunity to dwell upon the content of the first letter and withdraw the monies, the time has arrived for you to make the delivery – Thursday the 10th at two p.m.

Place a hundred pounds in used five-pound notes in an envelope and bring it to the following address: 22 Earle Street, Streatham. You will find it off Streatham High Road. Number 22 is a derelict cotton mill. Enter through the main delivery door and continue until you come to an interior wall. Place the envelope on the floor and walk back out into the street without turning around.

Needless to say, if the above instructions are not carried out to the letter, the police will be in receipt of the incriminating photographs.

Langham looked up. 'The tenth. That's today.'

He read the note again, then replaced it in the envelope. He examined the postmark, which this time was clear and unsmudged: the letter was posted in Streatham, not that this told him much.

He passed the note back to Charles.

'Well, my boy?'

'I don't see how we have any option other than to go through with the delivery.'

'But Streatham, my boy? I've never been south of the river since before the war!'

Langham shook his head, smiling. 'And most people would be more concerned about the hundred pounds.'

'Well, there is that, too. But I don't really see how I can go through with this.'

'You don't have to go through with it. I'll make the delivery.'

'You? But my dear boy ... think of the danger! What if this person is violent?'

'Charles, I can look after myself. I'll be delivering a hundred pounds, after all. There would be no reason to attack the messenger, as it were.'

'Only if you're absolutely sure...'

'I want to sort this mess out. If I make the delivery, I might even come across something that might help to catch the bastard.'

'You're a steadfast friend, Donald. Steadfast! Ah, I do believe this is the lapsang.'

Langham parked the Austin on Streatham High

Road, crossed the busy street and turned down Earle Street towards the bombed-out mill. It was one thirty, half an hour before he was due to make the delivery. He had plenty of time to look around, check the place out, and perhaps even witness the arrival of the blackmailer. Though he doubted this latter possibility. If the blackmailer were experienced – or even if he had an ounce of sense in his head – he would have chosen the site so that he could approach without being seen.

He had to admit to the first flutterings of apprehension, maybe even fear. He might have left Charles with a cavalier claim that there was nothing to worry about, but that had been more to reassure his anxious agent. The fact was that he had no idea who he was dealing with – other than someone who treated male prostitutes with brutality – and who was to say that, contrary to what he'd told Charles earlier, the blackmailer might not decide to attack the messenger?

As he made his way down Earle Street he passed a row of red-brick terraced houses, abbreviated courtesy of the Luftwaffe. Exposed interior walls bore poignant reminders that the empty spaces had once housed families, with peeling wallpaper still in place, the zigzag palimpsests of vanished stairs and the outlines of fireplaces.

Five minutes later he came to the bombed-out mill. Its façade still stood, with daylight showing surreally through the rows of upper windows. To the right, a towering chimney rose defiantly. A flimsy wooden fence fronted the building, a feeble sop to public safety, decorated with old posters advertising Crystal Palace speedway, long-gone circuses and the Festival of Britain.

He looked around for a place which might afford him a vantage point of the mill's interior. A low factory stood to the right of the mill, and to the left a bomb site, this one boasting a crater which had filled with water and sprouted attendant shrubbery like some unlikely urban oasis.

Across the road from the mill was a row of neglected back-to-backs, none of which appeared to be occupied. He approached the closest and tried the door; it swung open at his touch and he stepped inside. He was faced with fungus-infested walls, bare floorboards and a flight of broken stairs. He climbed them, stepped over a collapsed roof beam, and entered what had once been a bedroom.

From the broken window he had a good view of the mill opposite. Beyond the high, arched entrance he made out the concrete floor, pitted where cluster bombs had detonated during the Blitz. Fifty yards beyond the façade was the interior wall the blackmailer had mentioned, perhaps ten feet high and coated with scabbed whitewash.

He could not see what lay beyond the derelict mill. He looked at his watch: it was one fifty. There was no time to circumnavigate the building and check a possible rear approach. Anyway, he suspected that the blackmailer might already be in position, awaiting his arrival.

On the bomb site to the left of the mill, a gang of children played with makeshift wooden

Tommy guns and half-brick grenades. Their feverish cries, and the frenzied barking of a dog, drifted to him on the warm breeze, along with the scent of red roses which wound up the drainpipe beside the window. He closed his eyes and he was back in Madagascar: the warm wind, the scent of frangipani, even the heart-thumping fear.

He opened his eyes and asked himself what he was doing in a bombed-out terraced house in south London waiting to deliver a hundred pounds to some desperate blackmailer. Oddly enough, in the fragrant, balmy evenings outside Antananarivo he'd often asked himself what he was doing there, awaiting the first shells of the night from the Vichy French.

He scanned left and right. Other than the marauding kids, there was no sign of life.

He climbed down the broken stairs, emerged into the sunlit street, and crossed the road to the mill. The timber planks in the fence were fractured in places, or entirely missing in others. He found an accommodating gap and eased himself through. The façade rose before him, dark and satanic. He passed through the high archway and paused just inside the threshold. The floor before him was an obstacle course of deep pits, tangled pipework and fallen beams. He plotted a route through the debris and set off. As he walked, he was very aware of his thudding heartbeat. He knew that in all likelihood the blackmailer was watching him. He clutched the envelope in his coat pocket, wishing he'd had the time to seek out a weapon more deadly than the flick-knife that rested beside the envelope.

He picked his way through the mess of fallen bricks and tangled electrical wiring. The interior whitewashed wall was perhaps ten yards away now, with the dark, rectangular shape of a doorway at its centre. He approached the wall and, when he was three yards away, stopped. He slowed his breathing and listened. Only the distant sound of birdsong reached him, a child's protracted war cry, and the ever-present drone of city traffic in the background.

He reached into his pocket, placed the envelope on the ground, then stood and began walking back towards the façade.

He was beginning to breathe a little more easily when the blackmailer struck. He heard a footfall behind him and half turned, but not quickly enough to catch sight of his assailant – and not fast enough to evade the blow directed at the back of his head. The impact knocked him off his feet and he fell face down, groaning with pain. He tried to get up, force himself on to all fours, then stopped as he felt something cold being applied to the base of his skull. He heard a shout from far away ... or was he drifting into unconsciousness? Blackness and blessed oblivion engulfed him.

He had the impression that he was out for minutes only, though he had no way of knowing for sure. A pain in his ribs brought him to semi-consciousness. He forced himself on to his elbows in order to alleviate the pain in his chest caused by the sharp corner of a brick. He opened his eyes and stared down at a collage of broken

glass, weeds and powdered stone. He felt something poke his flank, and realized that it was this
prodding which had brought him around. The
blackmailer?

He heard a timid, 'He's still alive.'

'Hey, mister, you OK?'

'Watch it, he's getting up!'

He struggled to his knees, then managed to
twist around and sit down.

Perhaps a dozen dirty-kneed boys and girls
surrounded him, staring with big eyes in grubby
faces. They gripped wooden weapons and half-
brick bombs. The bomb site army.

'The bloke caught you a good one!' a blond lad
piped up.

Langham managed, 'Did you ... did you see
him? What did he look like?'

The lad looked at his mates, then said, 'He was
too far away, and he had one of those funny hat
things on.'

'A balaclava,' a mate provided.

A little girl said, 'He was going to shoot you,
he was, wasn't he, Dennis?'

Another lad nodded. 'He put a shooter to your
head, just here—' He indicated the back of his
skull. 'But I yelled, "Wot yer doin'!" and the
bloke saw us and scarpered.'

The girl nodded earnestly. 'Got away on a
motorbike.'

Langham felt the back of his head. His fingers
encountered a deep, painful gash and came away
glutinous with blood. He inhaled, then looked
around at the gallery of staring faces. 'Any of
you smoke?'

'Why?' the blond lad said. 'You got any ciggies?'

He inhaled again and made out the fading aroma of cigarette smoke.

He forced himself on to his knees, then paused like a sprinter on the blocks before making a concerted effort and standing. He screwed his eyes shut, then opened them. He felt dizzy.

He reached into his trouser pocket and found a ten-shilling note. He passed it to Dennis. 'For scaring him off,' he said.

The lad goggled at the note. 'Ten bob,' he whispered, and his mates crowded around him excitedly, jostling and exclaiming, before he ran off with the rest of the gang in hot pursuit.

Langham made his way back towards the façade, pain pounding through his skull in syncopation with his heartbeat. The short walk seemed to take an age, and he realized he was favouring his right knee, which throbbed painfully.

He pushed through the timber fence and limped along the street towards Streatham High Road, then stopped. The front of his overcoat was marked with whitewash; he would attract attention if he staggered on to the high street with a filthy coat and bloodstained hands. He wiped the blood on his handkerchief, then dusted most of the whitewash from his coat. When he set off, he made a conscious effort not to sway.

By some miracle he made it back to the Austin without either arousing public alarm or falling over. He sat behind the wheel for ten minutes, then started the engine and set off.

He drove north slowly, grateful for the light traffic. His vision was only slightly blurred, and he convinced himself that the pain was abating. When he saw the red light at the last second, and halted with a squeal of brakes, he knew he wasn't going to make it home.

He was in Chelsea, perhaps a mile from Charles's office in Pimlico. Very well, then ... he'd head there. He turned right, crawled along Royal Hospital Road, and willed himself to stay conscious long enough to reach the office.

He abandoned the car a couple of streets from the agency, his vision swimming. He pushed himself from the driving seat and staggered across the pavement. As he weaved his way west, he wondered why he was doing this ... and then came to some understanding. Maria. He wanted to see Maria.

Or did he want her to see him?

What seemed like an hour later the glossy black door of the agency came into view, and with a last, supreme effort he climbed the steps, barged through the door and staggered up the stairs to the outer office.

When he pushed through the door and collapsed on to the floor, Maria screamed and ran around the desk. The last thing he recalled before passing out was the sight of her stockinged calves and her small hand as she reached out to touch his cheek.

When he came to his senses he was lying in bed in Charles's apartment, with a bandage around his head. Charles and Maria sat beside the bed, watching him.

Charles was gripping his hand. 'My dear boy! I knew it, I knew! I should never have let you go. I curse myself for being such an abject, pusillanimous fool!'

Langham attempted a smile and squeezed Charles's hand.

Maria said, 'We called a doctor, Donald. He stitched your head and said you must rest. You will be fine, but you *must* rest!'

Langham looked from Maria to Charles, who said, 'I've told Maria everything, Donald. The whole sorry story.' He looked abject.

Langham whispered, 'The delivery ... it was worth it.'

'Worth it? But my boy, the beastly man almost killed you!'

Langham recalled the gun to his head and wondered if the blackmailer had really been about to pull the trigger.

'Worth it,' he managed, 'because I learned two ... two very important things. One, the black-mailer ... he rides a motorbike, and he smokes ... smokes Camel cigarettes.'

He drifted towards sleep, feeling more than wonderful, and the last thing he saw was Maria's pretty face staring down at him, her bottom lip nipped in concern between brilliant white teeth.

FIVE

The newsroom of the *Daily Herald* was a mael-strom of noise and activity. Fifty typewriters set up a deafening cacophony of clacking keys and harried journalists called back and forth through a fug of cigarette smoke.

Langham sat on a swivel chair across the desk from Dick Grenville, filled his pipe from his tin of Capstan's Navy Cut and listened to the review editor's predictable monthly tirade against the standard of publishing in general and the woefulness of crime writing in particular. It was the price Langham paid for being the *Herald*'s resident crime fiction reviewer.

'I mean, some of the stuff they put out these days. ... Listen to this.' Grenville snatched a hardback from a tottering pile on the desk, open-ed it and read the description on the front flap. 'Another adventure featuring Tommy and Suzie Rogers – not forgetting their canine accomplice Bonzo – sees the intrepid trio thwart the evil doings of international jewel thieves. The fun begins when Bonzo...' He snapped the book shut in disgust. 'Need I go on? How does this drivel see the light of day?'

Grenville sat back in his chair and glared at Langham as if he were solely responsible for the dire state of the genre. The editor resembled less a literary type than an officious town clerk, with his high, starched collar and impeccably snipped toothbrush moustache.

Langham gestured with his pipe. 'I'll give that one a miss.' He pulled the pile of hardbacks from the desk and sorted through them.

Grenville said, 'Why not cover it, Langham? Give it the pasting it deserves.' Grenville paused, then said, 'And if you don't mind my saying, I think you've been rather kind of late. I recall your pieces from years ago, when you had real teeth. If something was bad, you said so. These days you dismiss a shocker with a few bland platitudes.'

'Perhaps I'm becoming kinder in my old age.'

'Well, how about reinvigorating your pieces with some real venom? If a book's bad, then say so, and state why it's so bad.'

Langham ignored the editor and concentrated on selecting four titles. The fact was that he *had* become kinder of late; or at least less inclined to dish out cutting criticism. Nowadays he was loath to make enemies, not so much because he feared earning retribution in the competing review pages for his own novels, but because he thought that most writers – despite Grenville's assumptions otherwise – were actually trying their best. The only time he allowed his spleen full ventilation was when he came across a lazy novel obviously hacked out by a writer who should have known better.

Grenville leaned forward, squinting at him over his half-moon spectacles. 'If you don't

66

mind my asking, Langham, what on earth happened to your head?'

'Oh, this,' Langham said, touching the bandage that looped around his neck, partly concealed by the turned-up collar of his overcoat. 'I was coshed by a blackmailer while delivering a ransom demand on behalf of a friend.'

Grenville snorted. 'You've been writing too many Sam Brooke yarns, Langham. More likely you fell down the steps of a public house, hm?'

'Are you accusing me of inebriety, Grenville? Perish the thought!'

'Speaking of which...' the editor began.

'Inebriety?'

'No, Sam Brooke,' Grenville said. 'The early titles were put out before the war by Douglas and Dearing, weren't they? Did you know an editor there – Max Sidley?'

'He edited my first three,' Langham said. Sidley was an editor of the old school, a classical scholar with the sagacity and unruffled manner of a sleepy owl.

'Well, the poor blighter topped himself yesterday. Can't say I blame him, some of the titles Douglas and Dearing made him work on. It must have been more than his good taste could tolerate.' He pointed across the room to the editor's office. 'Nigel Lassiter's in there now, delivering the obituary.'

'He killed himself?' Langham said, shocked. He'd last met Sidley just after the war, but had always harboured a fondness for the man who'd bought his first novel and thus set the course of his subsequent career.

67

'He was seventy-five and still wielding the blue pencil. Poor sod should have got out years ago. A salutary lesson to us all.'

Langham squinted at Grenville, wondering if corrosive cynicism was a requisite for the post or the result of editing other people's tired copy.

'I'll take these four,' he said, slipping the books into his briefcase and standing. 'When do you need the piece?'

'First thing Friday. And remember, do inject a *soupçon* of venom, hm?'

'I'll see what I can do.'

He was threading his way through the tightly-packed desks when a stentorian summons sounded above the clatter of typewriters.

'Donald! Hold on, old man!'

He paused by the door while Nigel Lassiter exaggeratedly mimed jogging the last few yards and arrived panting before him. He was a tall man in his fifties, running to fat from the good life provided by two-dozen best-selling titles, the proceeds of which afforded him a big house in Islington, a yacht in the south of France and a table at the Ivy perpetually reserved in his name.

'Just the man. You busy?'

Langham held up his case. 'Just collected some review copies.'

'Still churning out the column?' He clapped Langham on the shoulder, his breath stinking of drink.

'Well, it does keep the wolf from the door.'

'You still with that pretentious old queer, Elder?' Lassiter asked.

'I know you had your differences,' Langham

68

said, 'but Charles is a good man.'

Lassiter laughed without humour. 'Differences? You'd have "differences" if he'd dumped you as he dumped me back in 'thirty-nine. Biggest mistake of his career – not that I'm worrying! Anyway,' he went on, 'how're the Sam Brooke books doing these days?'

Langham pushed open the door, inviting Lassiter through before him. He followed and emerged into dazzling sunlight.

'I'll forever be a stalwart of the mid-list, Nigel. But I can't complain.'

Lassiter paused on the busy pavement, lit up his habitual Pall Mall cigarette, and blew out a cloud of smoke. 'Well, that's what I want to chat to you about. A business proposition.'

Langham was surprised. 'Business?'

'Over a drink?' Lassiter looked at his watch. 'Three, dammit ... How about Tolly's? Charge through the nose but I'll stand the pints.'

'An offer I'd be a fool to refuse.'

They crossed the road and cut across Leicester Square. Lassiter peered at Langham's bandage. 'Looks nasty. What happened there?'

'Stupid accident. I fell down the front steps the other day. And before you ask, I was sober.'

They turned down a narrow alley to Lassiter's Soho drinking club, a subterranean dive sandwiched between a cheap Italian restaurant and a Chinese laundry.

'Grenville told me about Sidley,' Langham said.

'Just delivered the copy of his obit. Ghastly business.'

69

They descended a flight of greasy steps and pushed through into a twilit corridor. Lassiter signed them in and led the way to a small room packed with dedicated afternoon drinkers.

Tolly's was the haunt of indigent artists and writers, every square foot of the walls plastered with gaudy canvases traded for drinks in lieu of cash. The effect was claustrophobic and somewhat disorienting, Langham thought, a little like being trapped inside the nightmare of a crazed abstract expressionist.

Lassiter pushed his way to the bar. The only beer on offer was bottled Double Diamond or Guinness. Langham opted for the latter while Lassiter ordered a double whisky.

They found a table near the bar. Lassiter called out over the din of chatter and raucous laughter, 'Fortuitous bumping into you, Donald. Just read your latest.'

'Oh, dear...'

'Don't be so modest, man. I loved it. Had heart.' He swallowed his drink, accounting for almost half the short.

'Well, cheers,' Langham said, hoisting his Guinness.

Lassiter stubbed out his first cigarette and lit up a second. 'How many have you done now?'

'Twenty-two mysteries, twenty of them featuring Sam Brooke.' He didn't own up to the early westerns.

'Feeling jaded?'

Langham shook his head. 'Miraculously, I'm still enjoying the job.'

'Then you're a better man than me.' Lassiter's

broad, meaty face looked pensive. 'How do you do it, Donald? I mean, keep up the enthusiasm? Your latest ... Bloody hell, it was as fresh as your first. The writing ... crisp, sharp. I could tell you loved writing it.'

Langham shrugged. 'I did. I do. Each book is different.'

'But bloody hell ... Twenty books about the same private detective?'

'Ah, but the trick is to introduce major new characters which Sam can bounce off in every book; learn things about himself as he works on the mystery.'

Lassiter listened silently, staring down at his drink. 'I've just finished my fortieth thriller, Donald. Between you, me and the gatepost, it's sheer baloney. Every sodding day was a chore. Woke up thinking, Christ, do I really have to hack out another thousand words of this meaningless run-around?'

Langham shrugged. 'How about taking a break? You're not short of a bob or two...'

Lassiter laughed; a sound utterly without humour. 'Good idea. Only trouble is, I'm contracted to my publisher for another three of the wretched things. They take me three months to write, another couple of months to rewrite, and then I have some time off to recover my sanity. Christ, I'll be at it for another two years.' He rose to his feet, leaned over to the bar and called out, 'Another double in this one, Rosie!' Then he slumped back down beside Langham, rocking the precarious table. 'I had a nightmare the other night. All I could hear was someone reading out

71

my prose ... It was just: "He said, she said, he nodded, she opened the door and ran, he was aware of his heartbeat as he raised the gun..." Jesus Christ! I awoke in a sweat, terrified. Think it was my subconscious, telling me something.' He twisted his mouth around another slug of whisky and looked at Langham. 'How do you do it, Donald? How do you wake up in the morning and face another ruddy day at the typewriter?'

Langham shrugged. 'We're different people, Nigel. I...'

Lassiter focused on him blearily. 'What do you mean by that? "We're different people". I know that, man! But what do you *mean*?' He was tipsy, and a note of aggression had entered his studied Oxbridge tones.

Langham wondered how to explain what he meant without depressing, or insulting, the man. 'I think it's something to do with our backgrounds, Nigel. I left school at sixteen. I never made it to university. To me, writing books was always something other people did, people with an education. So when I began writing and getting published ... well, I didn't think it my *right* ... And I still don't.'

Lassiter held up a fleshy hand. 'Stop. I know what you're saying. You're saying ... I'm privileged, Winchester, Oxford and all that. I tossed off my first novel when I was twenty-two and it did well, and since then it's always come easily. And now I'm still cranking them out without care or concern, and I hate myself for doing it ... hate my lack of integrity. Is that what you're saying?'

72

Langham frowned. 'Well, I wouldn't phrase it quite like that.'

Lassiter stared at him. 'And you know what?' he said. 'You're exactly right. Spot on. Comes easily because it always has, and in consequence it means nothing to me ... Nothing. Christ, I need another drink.'

'Let me get these.'

'You're a gentleman and a scholar, old man.'

Langham took the empties and escaped to the bar. Only when he was easing himself back through the press of bodies did he recall what Lassiter had said about a business proposition. What on earth had he meant by that?

A depressing thought dawned. What if Lassiter wanted him to write the next Nigel Lassiter title?

He slid Lassiter's whisky across the table and sat down. 'You mentioned something about a business proposition?'

'And so I did! Old brain's grinding to a halt.' Lassiter leaned back and regarded him. 'Occurred to me the other day, reading your latest ... I had an idea.'

Here it comes, Langham thought. How do I say that I'm quite happy writing my own books, and really don't want to ghostwrite the latest 'Nigel Lassiter'?

Lassiter leaned forward and said with the maudlin sincerity of a seasoned drunk, 'Why don't we – you and I, Donald – why don't we collaborate?'

Langham's heart sank. If anything, the thought of collaborating with Lassiter was even more dreadful than the idea of writing a 'Lassiter' novel solo. 'You mean, write a book together?'

Lassiter guffawed. 'Not together! Not together *as such*, Donald. Christ, it's hard enough living with my wife these days. The thought of shacking up with another writer ... no offence meant. What I mean is, I use Sam Brooke in my next book, and you use my detective, Sergeant Hamm? They make guest appearances, as it were. Work together on a case.'

Langham felt relieved. He considered the idea, and it had mileage. The publicity would do his sales no end of good. That was, of course, if Lassiter really meant what he was saying and it wasn't just some drunken notion forgotten with the onset of his hangover in the morning.

'I like the idea, Nigel. I think it'd work.'

'You do? Excellent. Let's meet up later this week, over lunch – and I'll try to go easy on the old booze.'

Langham raised his glass. 'Let's do that.'

'Capital, Donald! I think this calls for a celebratory drink.' He swayed to his feet and bought another round.

When he eased his bulk back down, Lassiter said, 'Must admit I've been hitting the old bottle of late. The last novel was a bastard, and then yesterday I heard about old Sidley.'

Langham nodded. 'As I was telling Grenville, he was my very first editor.'

'I worked with him just before the war,' Lassiter reminisced. 'Douglas and Dearing bought the three collaborations I did with Frank Pearson. Remember old Frankie?'

'I met him a few times. Wasn't he with Charles

Elder for a few books in the thirties? Prickly customer, I recall. He rather fell out with me over a review I did of one of his books.' It was one of the acerbic reviews Grenville had alluded to earlier.

'"Prickly" hardly describes the man,' Lassiter said. 'We got on fine in the early days – the mid-thirties, that'd be. We were both youngish, ambitious, interested in the same kind of fiction.'

'How did you come to collaborate?'

'Don't get me started!' Lassiter laughed and took a gulp of whisky. 'Well, it seemed like a good idea at the time – like many a marriage, and look how most of them end up!' He fell silent, gazing into his glass. 'I liked Frankie, back then – before we fell out.'

'What happened?'

Lassiter shrugged. 'Frankie had energy. Came up with ideas ten a penny, and they were often good ones. What he lacked was human empathy. His characters were cardboard cut-outs totally subservient to his convoluted plots. He thought that plot, twists, cliffhangers ... he thought they alone kept the reader hooked.' He belched. ''Scuse me ... My argument was that readers would ... would only engage with a story if they believed in the characters, if they empathized with the human element. Make your characters real, believable, sympathetic, and you've got the reader. They'll keep turning the pages.'

'Let me guess. It was his idea to collaborate, right?'

Lassiter nodded. 'I was doing reasonably well. I'd sold three books to Hutchinson's and they

75

were selling OK. Frankie ... well, he'd sold a few to Hubert and Shale, a third-rate outfit whose books went straight into the lending libraries. They sank without a trace and Frankie was despondent. Over a few pints one night I tried to tell him, tactfully, where I thought he was going wrong. The upshot was that he suggested we write a crime novel together. He'd do the plot, I'd do the character sketches and we'd take it in turns to do the writing.'

Langham took a mouthful of Guinness. 'It worked?'

Lassiter puckered his liverish lips. 'Up to a point. The novel – though I say so myself – was better than anything he could have done alone, but not up to what I'd been doing until then. I hope that doesn't sound arrogant. Wasn't meant to.' He shrugged. 'But it's true. It was a second-rate book. I was amazed when Max Sidley took it for Douglas and Dearing.'

'Frankie must have been pleased. How did it do?'

'He was, and the book did well enough for Sidley to want two more ... Which I was loath to commit to. Truth be told, I did it for Frankie. He needed the money and the kudos the books gave him in the publishing world. So we did two more, each one worse than the last.'

'Let me guess – Douglas and Dearing didn't want a fourth?'

Lassiter shook his head, a distant look in his eyes. 'That's just the thing, they did. The books sold reasonably well and Sidley approached us for another one. I'll never forget the meeting with Frankie when I told him I didn't want to do another collaboration. He looked like a puppy I'd just kicked in the balls.' He shrugged. 'Fact was, my own books were taking off, the advances on the collabs weren't that great, and career-wise it just wasn't a good move for me to churn out these potboilers.'

'How did Frankie react?'

'How do you think? Distraught, then angry. He got raging drunk and it would've ended in a fight if I hadn't legged it.' He shook his head sadly. 'I saw him once or twice after that, just before the war. He did the fourth book alone. Apparently it was appalling.'

Langham said, 'I think that might have been the one I slated in the *Herald*.'

'Well, Douglas and Dearing dropped him like a hot coal after that one. He did a dozen or so crime novels for some fly-by-night outfit ... even scribbled during the war – he was exempt from military service on account of his eyesight or something. Wrote romances and school stories to keep body and soul together.'

'What's he doing these days?'

'Still scribbling, would you believe? He does westerns for the people he started with in the thirties, Hubert and Shale. Potboilers, believe me.' He fell silent, then looked at Langham as if wondering whether to tell him something. 'I bumped into him about three, four years ago in a pub in Camden. Didn't look well. He'd hit the bottle in a big way. Made my drinking look amateur by comparison. I tried to be friendly, offered to buy him a drink for old times' sake.

77

But he wasn't having any of it. Would've attacked me if he hadn't been legless.'

'Poor Frankie...'

'And then yesterday ... hearing about old Max Sidley, it brought it all back. Jesus!' he exclaimed. 'The damned thing is, Donald, the stupid thing is, I feel so damned guilty.'

'About Frankie?' He started to reassure Lassiter that he shouldn't burden himself with guilt over something he had done – with all justification – almost twenty years ago, but Lassiter interrupted: 'No, not about Frankie, damn him! About old Max.'

'Max Sidley? I don't see...'

Lassiter sighed, drained his whisky and said, 'Do you know how he did it? How he killed himself?'

'Grenville didn't say.'

'The poor man took a hand-held electric drill and pressed...' He mimed holding the tool to his ear.

Langham winced. 'Good God,' he said, then shrugged. 'But why the guilt?'

'Because,' Lassiter said, 'that was exactly the method I devised in *Murder Will Out*, the first book I did with Frankie. We needed to get rid of one of the minor characters, so I thought up a gory suicide. How the hell was I to know old Max would remember it and use it twenty years later?'

'Exactly,' Langham said forcefully. 'You weren't to know. Nothing could have stopped Max from killing himself, if that's what he wanted. If he hadn't done it in the way you described,

78

he would have found another way. Nigel, every time we put pen to paper we can't worry that people might copy whatever death we describe. We'd never write a word.'

Lassiter looked up from his drink. 'I know, I know. It's irrational. But ... but nevertheless I feel ... guilty is the only word for it. Poor old Max.'

'When did you last see him?'

Lassiter thought about that. 'A month ago at a publishing do at the Douglas and Dearing offices. He seemed fine, for someone knocking on seventy-five.'

'Not at all depressed?'

'Not at all. As bright as a button, extolling the virtues of some young new writer whose first novel they'd just acquired. So when I heard about ... Well, it knocked me sideways.' He smiled, sadly. 'I did the obit as a tribute. Hell, I put more work into it than I did my last novel – and I know, that isn't saying much.'

Langham smiled. 'Would you like another drink?'

Lassiter looked at his watch. 'Christ, it's almost five. Better not, old man. Wifey'll be wondering where the hell I am. I'm like this.' He mimed thumbing a drawing pin into the tabletop.

'How is Caroline these days?'

Lassiter winked. 'I complain, but I shouldn't. She keeps my feet on the ground, keeps my alcohol consumption under control, damn her. Bless her. I'd better be on my way. Lovely seeing you, Donald. And I'll be in touch about the collab, OK?'

'I'll look forward to that.'

'Oh – you're going to the Crime Club dinner next week, I assume?'

'Forgotten all about it,' Langham said. 'But yes, I haven't missed one for years. I'll be there.'

Lassiter saluted, climbed unsteadily to his feet and wended his way through the crowd towards the exit.

Langham remained at the table, half a glass of Guinness before him. He'd finish his drink, then find a phone box and ring Charles to see if the blackmailer had written with his next demand.

Five minutes later he drained his glass and pushed through the crowd, climbing the steps into the fresh air like some troglodyte creature emerging from hibernation. He had the typical light-headedness, and the odd sense of being removed from reality, common after an afternoon session.

He hurried across Leicester Square, found a phone box and got through to the agency. Seconds later Maria answered. 'Donald, where have you been all day? I've been phoning your flat again and again.'

'Something's happened?'

'This morning another letter arrived. This time he wants even more money.'

Langham swore. 'How's Charles taking it?'

There was a hesitation at the other end of the line. 'Badly, I'm afraid. Please, could you possibly come over? He's been asking for you.'

'I'm on my way.'

'Thank you so much, Donald.'

As he stepped from the phone box and made

his way across the square to where his car was parked, he tried to see a way out of this for Charles. The fact was that his agent was in a double bind: he couldn't go to the police for fear of prosecution and a prison sentence – and if he didn't accede to the extortionate demands of the blackmailer, then the result would be the same. Charles was not short of the odd thousand or two, he suspected, but his resources were finite.

He eased his Austin into the busy flow of traffic going north on Charing Cross Road, then turned along Oxford Street and headed west. The traffic was light today, and in due course he pulled into a parking space across the road from the agency.

The door to the street was unlocked, but when he reached the door to the outer office he found it barred. He knocked, and seconds later Maria let him in. She had a strand of jet-black hair nervously nipped into the corner of her mouth, and only when he stared did she remember herself and remove it, self-consciously.

'I closed the office just after the letter arrived,' she explained. 'Charles was so very upset. He said he couldn't possibly concentrate on work. I've been with him all day. Thank you for coming.'

'It's the least I could do. Where is he?'

'In his rooms...' She indicated the stairway and followed him up.

Charles was pacing the sitting room, waving a sheet of paper before him. Even in distress he had the look of a seasoned thespian hamming it up. 'Thank God you're here, Donald! Five hun-

81

dred! Would you believe it, the wretch wants five hundred!'

'Let me see...' Langham crossed the room and took the letter.

'Can I get you a drink?' Maria asked.

'A brandy for me, my dear,' Charles said. 'Make it a double.'

'I'm fine,' Langham told her. He took the letter to the window and angled it into the light.

Dear Charles,

It was a rather foolish thing for you to do, allowing a man to do a lady's job now, wasn't it? Your messenger deserved that cosh on the head. This time, you will do the delivering. I want five hundred in used ten-pound notes. Follow these instructions to the letter and the judiciary will be none the wiser. Tomorrow, Tuesday the 15th, take your Bentley and drive down to the village of Chalford in Sussex. From there follow the lane to the village of Hallet. A mile out of Chalford you will pass a derelict farm building on the right, and a hundred yards further on, to your left, you will see the opening to a field, barred by a gate. Stop there at two p.m. exactly, get out of the car and leave the money in an envelope propped against the gatepost. This done, return to the car and drive back to London. I have no need to stress that you should come alone.

Langham read the note for a second time. He looked across at Charles, who was regarding him with tear-filled eyes.

'The envelope?'

Charles passed him a long manila envelope identical to the others. This one also bore a

82

Streatham postmark.

'What should I do, my dear boy?'

'Can you get hold of the money by tomorrow?'

'Just about, though it will clear out my current account. I have funds, of course, investments ... But this just cannot go on! Where will it end, Donald? My nerves are shattered.'

Maria passed Charles a brandy. Langham took Charles's elbow and guided him across to a settee before the hearth. His agent flopped into the seat, sloshing the brandy, and closed his eyes in an expression eloquent of despair.

'Do you have a gazetteer of Sussex?' Langham asked.

Charles waved a languid hand. 'In the bookshelf, bottom shelf.'

Maria fetched the road atlas and passed it to Langham, then sat on the edge of an armchair, stockinged legs crossed, watching him.

Charles wailed, 'I have half a mind to hand myself in now, confess all, make a clean breast of the situation and trust in the inherent fairness of my country's legal system.'

Langham eyed him sceptically. 'You'll do nothing of the sort, Charles. The "inherent fairness" you speak about will see you sent down for a year or more.'

'And the alternative? Allow the cad to bleed me dry?'

Langham looked up from the gazetteer. 'The only incriminating things the blackmailer has in his possession are the photographs, am I right?'

'Does he need anything *else*, my boy – a signed confession, perhaps? Donald, Donald, what

83

else *does* he need? The wretched photographs are evidence enough!'

'Hear me out, Charles. It occurred to me earlier that it would be to our advantage if we could find out who's blackmailing you.'

'You're making rather a habit of stating the obvious without the foundation of logic, Donald. Forgive me, but I am at my wits' end!'

Maria said, 'What do you suggest, Donald?'

Langham looked from Charles to Maria. 'I intend to be there when the blackmailer picks up the money. I'll follow the motorbike, or whatever vehicle he's using this time. I have contacts who can loan me a pistol—'

'But what if he himself is armed?' Maria exclaimed.

Langham recalled the sensation of something cold being held to the back of his head, and what the bomb site kids had said, but refrained from telling Maria.

'I can look after myself,' he said. 'The only way we can defeat the blackmailer is to find his copies of the photographs, along with the negatives, and destroy them. And the only way to do that is to confront the...' He was about to say 'bastard', but stopped himself. '...the blackmailer.'

'Donald, Donald...' Charles said. 'I don't like this one bit! The risk at which you are placing yourself ... and all because I was weak and foolish.'

'Let's consider it research for the next book, Charles.'

He found the page showing the roads and lanes

of East Sussex, and after a minute located the village of Chalford. Maria came and joined him on the settee, leaning against him and peering at the page. Langham indicated the village, and the lane to Hallet.

He said, 'You, Charles, will approach from the north, leave the envelope, and continue until you come to the A22, from where you'll drive back to London.'

Maria said, 'You said you would be "there", Donald. But where is "there"? What if the blackmailer sees you?'

'I intend to arrive an hour or so earlier and park in the derelict farm mentioned in the blackmailer's letter.'

Maria interrupted. 'But how do you know you can see the gate from the farm? What if you cannot?'

'I don't have to see the gate, do I? All I have to see is the motorbike passing—'

'If he does arrive on a *motorbike* this time—'

'—either having picked up the envelope, or about to pick it up,' he went on. 'Then I drive from the farm and follow him.'

'I think it will not work out,' Maria said. 'Too much could go wrong. If you do not react fast enough, or you fail to see the motorbike or whatever...'

He smiled. 'Well, what do you suggest?'

She pursed her lips and tipped her head to one side as she regarded him. 'Now, if there were two cars,' she said, 'stationed here, and here' – she indicated points at each end of the lane – 'then one of us would be bound to see the

85

motorcyclist – or whatever – passing at the appointed time. Then we follow at a distance when the blackmailer picks up the envelope. That way we cannot fail.'

He stared at her. '*We?*'

She was indignant. 'Do you think we cannot drive in France?'

'Are you sure you want to get mixed up in this?'

She shrugged. 'Do you think me incapable? Did you know that French women, and for that matter English women, fought for the Resistance in my country?'

'There is something I haven't mentioned,' Langham said a little sheepishly. 'The blackmailer *was* armed.' He told them about the gun being held to the back of his head.

Maria's lips were firm with resolve. 'I will merely follow the motorcyclist to see where he goes. I will not confront him.' She looked to Charles. 'Will you make Donald see sense, please?'

'My friends,' Charles said, reaching out and grasping their hands, 'I feel as if I have been transported to the pages of a Bulldog Drummond adventure. My head spins and my heart swells at the thought of the lengths to which you, my dears, would go to save my considerable bacon ... I would plead with you to allow me to go alone, but I fear my pleas would fall on deaf ears. Am I right?'

Maria looked at Langham and laughed. 'Right,' they said in unison.

Fifteen minutes later, after arranging the details of their expedition to Sussex, Maria looked at her wristwatch and excused herself. She had an errand to run for her father, she said, and was meeting him for dinner later that evening.

Langham saw her to the door and watched her hurry down the stairs.

Charles sighed. 'Now, my dear boy, I demand you join me in a drink! And I will not take no for an answer.'

Langham accepted a shot of whisky and sat back on the settee.

Charles narrowed the folds of flesh around his piercing blue eyes and squinted at Langham. 'It is only when one finds oneself *in extremis*, shall we say, that one learns the true nature of not only oneself, but also of those around one. You are proving a true ally, Donald.'

Langham smiled and sipped his whisky. 'It's the least I could do.'

'But may I ask, my dear boy, why are you going to such lengths? I have friends of long standing who would throw their hands in the air, run a mile, and let me stew in the juices of my own making.'

Langham thought about it. 'You're a friend, Charles, and what's happening here is appalling. It's bad enough that some twisted hypocrite is threatening you like this. But what truly angers me is the system that allows him to do so.'

Charles detonated a derisive laugh. 'The system! But such has always been the case, and when will it change? And before you spout that we need a change of government, let me say that the problem goes much deeper than the prejudices of those in power. There will be no change until the people of this benighted land see me and my kind as fellow human beings, not some minority to be mocked and derided. Mark my word, there will be no change before the end of the century!'

Langham gestured with his glass. 'I think it'll come sooner than that.'

Charles sighed. 'I am fifty-five this year, Donald, as old as the century, and I have been waiting most of my adult life for the decriminalization of homosexuality ... I doubt it will happen in my lifetime.' His face took on a wistful aspect. 'I've had a good life, Donald. Winchester was bliss, and Oxford a happy continuation. Odd to say, but it didn't occur to me then that I was in a minority. Good Lord, we were all at it! What hedonistic times those were, after the war and into the twenties.' He finished his drink with one swallow and poured himself another. 'It was only later, when I came down from Oxford and dipped my toes in the muddy waters of publishing that I first encountered the prejudiced and petty-minded piranhas, if you will allow me the somewhat far-fetched piscine metaphor.'

Langham smiled, sank into the cushions and gestured that such oratory was eminently permissible. When Charles was in full flow, his mellifluous eloquence was more than a little entertaining.

'I learned to pull in my horns, ahem, as it were, and practise circumspection. In the circles in which I swam, my secret was open. I surrounded myself, and still do, with those of like mind and similar persuasion, writers and actors who, if not actually *active*, then are open-minded enough to accept me and my kind.'

'And then something like this happens.'

'I have found reserves of strength within me enough to withstand whatever slings and arrows are cast my way.' He looked sheepish. 'Even if I was in a bit of a flap earlier.'

Langham laughed. 'That's the spirit.' He finished his drink and glanced at his watch. 'I must be off. I'll call around here at eleven tomorrow and we'll go through what we have to do.' He regarded Charles. 'You'll be all right tonight?'

'I have a dinner engagement with friends at eight, dear boy. I shall be sparkling and eloquent ... and I might even get a little squiffy.'

Langham laughed and clapped Charles's meaty shoulder. 'You do that. I'll see myself out.'

'Bless you, dear boy.'

As he drove home slowly through light traffic Langham considered eating that evening at the nearby Lyons' Corner House, but the thought didn't appeal. When he arrived at his flat he made himself a cheese sandwich and ate it accompanied by a bottle of Worthington's best bitter while listening to the Third Programme on the wireless: a talk by a writer recounting his travels in Argentina.

Later he sat in his armchair, switched on the standard lamp and sorted through the titles he'd selected at the *Herald* that morning. He chose what looked to be the best of the bunch, a classic whodunit by a writer whose novels he'd enjoyed in the past. He was ten pages into it when he realized that his attention was drifting: he'd taken in nothing of the opening scenes. He set the book aside and contemplated what tomorrow might bring, and then found himself thinking back to Maria seated beside him on the settee, her elegant legs crossed, emanating a heady perfume of powder and eau de cologne, a vision of beauty and sophistication in her twinset and pearls.

SIX

Maria left the agency at four o'clock and drove into the West End. She found a parking space along New Bond Street and sat in a café across the road from Sotheby's. She ordered tea and cake and glanced at her watch. It was four fifteen, and the statuette was due to be auctioned at five.

In the meantime she sipped her Darjeeling and nibbled at the Bakewell, wishing that the English were as competent at making the latter as they were the former.

Her mind drifted, and she found herself thinking about Charles and his predicament. How puritanical and petty-minded the English were when it came to affairs of the heart! Which was entirely the problem, she thought: the English did not count Charles's predilections as an affair of the heart, but rather as a weakness of the flesh, and thus punishable by law. And yet they considered themselves a civilized people!

It was not long before her thoughts strayed from Charles to his client, Donald Langham.

A greater contrast to the conceited, self-absorbed Gideon Martin she could not imagine. Langham was self-effacing to the point of being almost self-erasing. She had known him for almost five years, though the term 'known' did not quite describe their acquaintance. They had met perhaps four or five times a year, exchanged pleasantries and occasional witticisms, but always it seemed that there was something holding Langham back, a diffident reserve, almost a shyness, that would not allow him to show his real self.

For a long time Maria had assumed he was married. She'd read some biographical information about him on the back of one of his earlier novels which stated that 'Donald Langham is married and lives in London', and Maria had been curious about what kind of person his wife might be. Langham himself was tall, thin and upright, with the bearing of the soldier he had been. He was good-looking in a quiet, English, pipe-smoking kind of way, and she had imagined his wife as around his age, early forties, elegant and attractive.

One day she had asked Charles about Mrs Langham.

'Mrs Langham, my dear? There is no Mrs Langham.'

91

'But I thought...'

'Ah ... Well, he *was* married, but Mrs Langham died during the war. I don't know what happened. Donald never speaks about it.'

'He is very ... reserved, no?'

Charles had laughed. 'Well, I suppose he is. I've never thought about him like that. I rather thought of him as having good manners and breeding – for a provincial grammar schoolboy, that is.'

'Oh, you English! You are so obsessed with class!'

'Guilty as charged, Maria. But why do you ask about Donald?'

'Oh, I don't know ... But he is rather handsome, don't you think?'

Charles had stared at her over his pince-nez. 'I would agree, he is – in a very quiet, staid, English way.'

Maria liked Donald Langham; she liked the quiet reserve that came over as him being comfortable with himself, and which suggested that he had no need to impress others. She liked his habit of clenching his empty pipe between his teeth while absorbed in thought, and the way he absent-mindedly stroked the scar at his temple.

'That scar,' she had said to Charles just yesterday, 'how did he get it? It would be ugly anywhere else on his face, but at his temple it rather suits him.'

Charles laughed. 'That, my dear, irony of ironies, was thanks to a French bullet.'

'A *French* bullet?'

He amended, 'Well, a Vichy French bullet. He saw action in Madagascar. Not that he speaks of that, either. All he told me was that an inch to the left and the world would have been spared a dozen Sam Brooke novels. Which pretty well sums up Donald's self-deprecating manner, don't you think?'

She wondered if tomorrow, on the jaunt down to Sussex, she might get to know Donald Langham a little better.

She sipped her tea and pushed the half-eaten Bakewell – which was *not* baked very well – to one side and concentrated on the street beyond the window.

Fifteen minutes later an old Rolls Royce pulled up outside Sotheby's and Monsieur Savagne alighted, the sight of so small a man stepping from so large a vehicle somewhat comical. He adjusted his cravat, arranged his thinning hair, then crossed the pavement and entered the building. Maria looked at her watch. It was four forty-five, and there was no sign yet of Gideon Martin.

Five minutes later the man himself, clutching a rolled copy of the *Express* in one hand and his swordstick in the other, stepped from a taxi cab and trotted into the auctioneer's. She gave him a few minutes to ease his way to the front of the crowd – as *he* would not skulk at the back of the room, she thought – then paid the bill and left the café.

She dashed through a gap in the traffic, one hand holding her hat to her head as she did so, then hurried into the auction rooms. The sale was to be held in the main room, and the place was packed. As she eased her way through the throng at the door and stationed herself at the rear of the room next to a mock-marble pillar, she heard a medley of European voices – mainly French and Italian – and one or two American accents. To a man, everyone was dressed as if for a formal engagement. Maria had outfitted herself likewise in a body-hugging silk two-piece and a dainty little hat by Lilly Daché.

A Rembrandt miniature was on the easel next to the auctioneer's podium. The auctioneer himself was scanning the gathering and indicating the bidder with a languid hand. 'Three thousand four hundred to my right ... I have three-five. Do I hear three-six? Thank you, sir. Three-six bid. Three-seven, Three-eight...'

She glanced at the catalogue. The Rembrandt was lot two; the Italian statuette was lot four.

She peered over the heads of those before her and caught sight of Gideon Martin. As she had suspected, he was near the front, leaning nonchalantly against a pillar to the right. She wondered if his entire life was a carefully thought out and staged event, each elegant pose designed for maximum theatrical effect.

She looked for M Savagne, but the little man was lost in the crowd.

The Rembrandt went for six thousand pounds, and the painting was taken from the easel by two buff-coated members of staff and replaced with a landscape by Sisley.

'Lot three, an early piece by Alfred Sisley, very collectable. A considerable work by this

94

fine English artist. Do I have a starter at one thousand? Thank you, sir. One thousand to my left. One thousand one hundred. One-two. One-three ... Thank you, sir. One-four. One-five. Do I hear one-six...?'

Towards the front, Gideon Martin turned his profile to the crowd as if seeking their appreciation. His hooded eyes took in his surroundings and Maria slipped behind the pillar as his gaze swept her way. When she emerged, Martin's attention was once again on the auctioneer. The Sisley had sold for three thousand and was being replaced by the statuette.

'A fine example of eighteenth-century silver-ware...' The auctioneer began his spiel. 'Do I have a bid to start off proceedings at one thousand five hundred?'

Maria saw a big, silver-haired man raise his folded catalogue. 'Thank you, sir,' the auctioneer said.

Gideon Martin raised his swordstick.

'One thousand six hundred.'

The catalogue went up.

'One-seven,' said the auctioneer.

Martin bid.

'One-eight.'

The silver-haired gentleman bid and the auctioneer indicated him. 'One-nine.'

This, Maria thought, is where I step in.

She raised her catalogue fractionally and the auctioneer's eagle eye saw the movement. 'I have two thousand at the back. Two thousand one hundred, anyone?'

The silver-haired man raised his catalogue.

'Two thousand one hundred bid in the centre.'

Gideon Martin lifted his swordstick imperiously.

'Two-two to my left.'

Maria waited to see if silver-hair would bid; he refrained. She raised her catalogue, her heart thumping in her chest.

'Two-three.'

Martin gave a tight, angry nod.

'Two-four.'

Maria bid.

'Two-five.' She was ready to duck behind the pillar should Martin turn in order to see who might be bidding against him, but his attention remained focused on the auctioneer. He hoisted his swordstick.

'Two-six.'

Maria raised her catalogue.

'I have two-seven at the back of the room ... Two-eight...'

Maria kept her eyes on Martin lest he turn; he appeared irritated. She smiled as she considered his words at the party, to the effect that he had saved three thousand to spend on the statuette.

She wondered how much beyond that he would be prepared to bid. Her father had indicated that he was prepared to foot a bill of no more than three thousand five hundred: he had contacts in Paris museums who might be persuaded to show the piece and, over time, reimburse him the fee.

Martin bid again.

'Two-nine...' the auctioneer intoned.

She lifted her catalogue.

'Three thousand. I have three thousand at the back. Do I hear ... Thank you, sir. Three-one.'

Maria bid.

'Three-two.'

Martin hesitated visibly, then lofted his swordstick almost angrily.

'Three-three,' said the auctioneer.

One more bid, Maria thought. She indicated three-four, and the auctioneer said, 'Three-four at the back. Do I have three-five, sir?'

Martin's gaze remained fixed on the statuette, his expression rigid. She could see that he was deliberating. *Don't do it*, she urged. A trickle of perspiration coursed down the side of her neck.

Gideon Martin seemed to wait an age before he shook his head.

'Three-four at the back. Do I hear three-five? No ... Then, at three thousand and four hundred pounds, going once, going twice ... Sold!'

Maria almost collapsed with relief. She gathered herself and slipped from the auction room, but not before appreciating the look of barely suppressed rage on Gideon Martin's face.

She paid for the statuette and arranged for its delivery to her father's house, considering it a job satisfactorily concluded. *Voila!* She had avenged herself for Martin's buying the very watercolour she had intended for her father's birthday present.

She returned to her apartment, made herself a bowl of minestrone soup, and ate it while listening to Radio France.

Later she tried to read a manuscript – a literary

novel by one of the agency's authors – but was unable to concentrate. She considered what she had planned with Donald Langham for tomorrow; she liked the way he had listened to her suggestions earlier today, and had quietly agreed to them. She could not imagine Gideon Martin being that fair-minded.

And thoughts of Martin made her ask herself if, perhaps, she did not feel a *little* guilty at the ruse she had played today?

Then she thought of his arrogance at the party the other evening, and she realized that she felt not the slightest prick of conscience at all.

SEVEN

Langham sat in his Austin and raised the binoculars, taking in the surrounding countryside and the network of narrow lanes.

Hallet was a tiny hamlet clinging to a hillside in the folds of the South Downs. One lane meandered through it, leading to the village of Chalford a mile away. From his vantage point, tucked behind a wall at right angles to the lane, and hidden from the sight of any motorist who might approach from the north and London, Langham had a bird's-eye view of the lane along which Charles was due to drop the money. At this time of day – an hour before the scheduled drop at two – not a soul stirred in the hamlet. Intermittent birdsong filled the air and a herd of Friesians pastured negligently in a nearby field.

It was a perfect English summer's day in the country, and Langham felt sick with apprehension.

He swung the binoculars in the direction of the drop-off point along the lane. The gap in the hedge sprang into view a quarter of a mile away. The gate was open, and the churned mud between the gateposts looked like a muddy goalmouth after a particularly one-sided football match. He couldn't help smiling at the thought of Charles's reaction to the quagmire. It would be just like him to toss the envelope in the general direction of the gatepost and have done.

He sighted along the lane until he spotted Maria, half a mile further on from the gate. Her maroon Sunbeam saloon was parked on the grass verge, facing him. As planned that morning she had propped open the bonnet and was peering at the revealed engine, ostensibly attempting to repair some imaginary fault. From time to time she straightened up, backhanded hair from her eyes, and looked around.

If the motorcyclist passed her, she would slam down the bonnet and give chase; if he came from the other direction, passing Langham, then Langham would initiate the pursuit while Maria drove to the gate, turned and duly followed.

That morning he had mooted the possibility that some passing motorist might take it upon himself to play St Christopher and offer her assistance. Maria had replied promptly, 'In that

99

case I'll close the engine and say that I've repaired the fault all by myself. How that will astound the superior Englishman!'

Langham considered a more advantageous scenario, that the blackmailer himself might exhibit contrary altruism and stop to offer his assistance, affording Maria a good look at the man. He thought this unlikely in the circumstances, however.

As a sop to his nerves, perhaps hoping to impose a sense of normality on the events, Langham had brought along one of the books he was due to review. It sat on the passenger seat beside him, more a talisman of his quiet, bookish life than anything that might be read now as a diversion. It was nine years since he'd worked for Ralph Ryland's investigative agency – and then most of the work had consisted of trailing suspected unfaithful husbands or wives – and he had to admit that he was out of his depth here. He would much rather write about foiling blackmailers than actually attempting to do so.

His stomach clenched at the sound of an approaching engine. It was still only one thirty, so Charles would not be passing just yet. Seconds later a battered, mud-splattered tractor grumbled into view, bouncing along the lane. A minute later the vehicle crawled past the gate and approached Maria.

He raised his binoculars. In the distance Maria saw the tractor, lowered the bonnet and slipped in behind the steering wheel. 'Good girl!' Langham said.

When the tractor passed, Maria swivelled

herself from the driving seat and resumed her fictitious inspection of the Sunbeam's engine.

He tried to envisage all the possible outcomes of their actions here, much as he looked ahead when plotting a book. The preferred result, of course, would be that he and Maria followed the blackmailer back to wherever he lived; then he would stake out the place until such time as the man left the house. All that would remain, then, was the small matter of breaking in and finding the incriminating photographs and negatives ... which would be no small feat in itself.

And so much could go wrong along the way, he thought.

The blackmailer was armed, but would he resort to shooting anyone who might follow him? Well, last week in the ruins of the mill he'd seemed willing to blow Langham's brains out, but for the timely intervention of the bomb site army.

And the recollection of that close call turned his thoughts to the blackmailer's motives in wanting him dead, if indeed he had. Langham had spent long hours wondering if the gesture, the placing of the gun to the back of his head, had been nothing more than the blackmailer's nervous reaction to the situation. He'd wanted to ensure that Langham was unconscious, and was merely covering the possibility that he, Langham, might leap up and attack him before he escaped with the envelope.

But the very fact that the blackmailer carried a gun suggested that he would not be averse to using it.

He reached into the pocket of his overcoat and gripped the service revolver he'd borrowed – with the exchange of a five-pound note – from Ralph Ryland that morning. The weapon was cold and heavy in his hand, and afforded him little reassurance.

His thoughts were interrupted by the distant sound of an engine. He glanced at his watch. It was three minutes to two. He laid aside the binoculars and gripped the steering wheel nervously, his palms wet with sweat. The distinctive, dull throbbing of a Bentley Continental's engine preceded the appearance of the car itself. Seconds later it flashed by, a blaze of electric blue in the sunlight.

He watched the car motor along the lane, his heart thudding. He raised the binoculars. The Bentley slowed as it approached the gate. He looked at his watch. Charles's punctuality was impeccable: it was one minute to two.

Charles opened the car door and stepped into the lane, clutching the envelope. He rounded the nose of the car, then stopped in his tracks as he took in the state of the ground between the gateposts. While his agent vacillated, Langham swept the binoculars along the lane: there was no sign yet of the blackmailer.

At considerable risk to the shine of his brogues, Charles stepped forward and tentatively placed a foot in the mud. Heartened by the fact that he didn't sink in up to his knees, he took a further step, and then another. A yard or two from the gatepost, he stopped and tossed the envelope the rest of the way. The rectangle of paper planed aerodynamically through the air and lodged itself against the timber post.

Charles dashed his hands together, looked right and left along the lane, then turned and high-stepped back to the car. He wiped the mud from his shoes on the grass verge and seconds later was driving towards Maria. She stood next to the Sunbeam's gaping bonnet, and glanced up as the Bentley sped past.

Langham listened for the sound of the black-mailer's vehicle. He hoped it would come from his right, so that it would be he who would give chase first; at least then he would be active and the intolerable wait would at last be over.

In the event, the motorbike passed neither him nor Maria.

He heard the rapid throb of its engine and looked along the lane past Maria, but there was no sign of the motorbike. In which case, it had to be coming from his right. He started the engine and released the hand brake, readying himself to set off.

Only then did he see the motorcycle – not flashing past before him as had Charles's Bentley, but coming across the crown of the field down below and approaching the open gate from the north. At the far end of the field was a copse, and Langham wondered how long the black-mailer had lain in wait. Had he seen the two cars stationed suspiciously at either end of the lane?

The motorcyclist stopped as he came to the gate, reached over and plucked up the envelope. Langham tried to get a view of his face through the binoculars, but the rider was wearing goggles and the lower half of his face was concealed by a scarf. He caught sight of the motorcycle's logo on the fuel tank – Triumph – and recognized the model as a Thunderbird.

As he watched, the blackmailer tucked the envelope beneath his khaki-coloured greatcoat, then steered the bike from the field and turned right, heading towards Langham.

Maria was already in pursuit, perhaps a hundred yards behind the motorcyclist. Langham would have insufficient room to pull out between the blackmailer and Maria, so he elected to let her pass and then give chase.

Seconds later the motorcyclist sped past in a dazzle of flashing spokes, and ten seconds later Maria's Sunbeam roared by. Langham eased the Austin out into the lane, turned right and followed.

He kept a couple of hundred yards between himself and Maria's car. He had no idea what kind of rear view the motorcyclist might have, but he didn't want to alert him to the fact that there were two cars on his tail. For her part, Maria was likewise hanging back, maintaining two hundred yards between herself and the rider. Langham just hoped he wouldn't suddenly accelerate and give her the slip.

Langham had assumed that the blackmailer was resident in London, but he had no definite evidence that this was so. The Streatham postmark meant nothing, he knew, unless the blackmailer was supremely stupid, and something about his modus operandi so far suggested that that was far from the case.

104

If he did live in London, then that might pose something of a problem when they reached the capital. It was all very well following a motorcyclist out in the uninhabited wilds of the Sussex Downs, but trailing him through the streets of London, keeping the rider in sight while negotiating busy traffic, might be their undoing.

He found himself wishing an accident upon the blackmailer: a slick of oil on the road or a tight bend ... anything which might unseat the rider. And then what? If the man survived, would Langham be up to the task of confronting him, disarming him, and threatening him sufficiently to get the details of where the photographs and the negatives were concealed?

Perhaps if the imaginary accident were to prove fatal, then that would solve all their problems...

He realized he was spinning fantasies and told himself to concentrate on the road.

Ahead, he made out the tiny shape of the motorcyclist as he slowed and turned north on the London road. Fortunately the traffic was light here too, and Maria managed to turn right without another vehicle interposing itself between her car and the motorbike rider.

Langham was not so lucky.

A dawdling charabanc passed from left to right on Maria's tail. Langham pulled out behind the coach and waited for a stretch of straight road that would allow him to overtake in safety.

Minutes seemed to crawl by before the opportunity arose. The bend unwound and he sighted a long, up-curving stretch of road ahead. The

105

motorcyclist was a distant figure, having put perhaps a mile between himself and Langham. Maria was three hundred yards behind the blackmailer.

Langham indicated, pulled out and accelerated.

He sped past the coach and tucked himself in behind Maria's car. The rider seemed to be increasing his speed and Langham wondered if he was becoming suspicious. Maria accelerated so as not to be left behind. The road levelled out and passed through a plantation of fir trees. He put his foot down in order to keep Maria in sight, and glanced at the speedometer: he was pushing fifty. All he needed now was the attention of a passing police car.

The plantation petered out and was replaced by rolling hills. They drove north, and soon the land flattened as they left the Downs and approached Surrey. Would it be too much to hope that the blackmailer lived in some quiet suburban backwater to where he could be followed with ease?

His daydreams came to an abrupt halt when, a mile ahead, he made out a railway crossing. That might not have set the alarm bells ringing, but what did cause him consternation was the fact that the signals were flashing red. He watched as the motorcyclist sped through the warning, ducking as the barrier dropped across the road. Maria was right behind him as she attempted to catch up. Langham winced as she swerved into the middle of the road in order to give herself a better chance of passing beneath the falling barrier.

She made it with just inches to spare, and on the far side of the railway line the chase continued.

Langham braked and came to a halt, cursing his luck as the barrier clanked down before him. Now he would have to drive like a maniac if he were to make up the ground.

A goods train crashed into his field of vision, an alternating cavalcade of dark wagons and daylight. It seemed to be the longest goods train in the history of railway transportation, a deafening barrier rattling by a matter of feet before the bonnet of his Austin. He gripped the wheel, urging the train to pass and attempting to see between the interstices of the wagons and glimpse the road on the far side.

And then, with a suddenness that was shocking, the train passed and Langham saw that Maria had come to a halt perhaps thirty yards from the crossing. For a second he assumed that the motorcyclist had sped ahead and escaped her, and she had stopped to wait until Langham caught up. Then his heart leapt sickeningly as he saw that the motorcyclist had stopped too – stopped, he saw, dismounted, and was walking casually back towards where Maria waited in the road.

Langham willed the barrier to rise, but it remained obdurately in place before him. He fumbled the car door open, found the revolver in his pocket and pulled it out as, beyond the railway line, the motorcyclist did the very same thing.

Langham watched, frozen, as the rider stopped

107

ten yards before the Sunbeam and raised his pistol with both hands. He willed Maria to get out of the car and run.

He cried out and stepped back, shocked, as something thundered by within feet of him – a train speeding in the opposite direction to the first. This one was a passenger train, and only later did he wonder at the reaction of anyone who might have looked out to see a distraught man waving a pistol.

All he could think about was what might have happened to Maria, and he cursed himself for his not being the leading car.

Then the train passed by, leaving in its wake a silence that was almost as startling as its arrival. He stared across the railway line at the Sunbeam and saw with disbelief that Maria was slumped against the steering wheel. He looked desperately for the motorcyclist, but the blackmailer had fled the scene.

The barrier rose. Shaking, Langham climbed back in and started the car. At the third attempt the engine kicked into life. He bumped across the railway line and eased the Austin forward, coming to a halt behind the Sunbeam. Automatically, dazed and disbelieving, he climbed out and approached Maria's car.

As his shadow fell across her, she raised her head from the steering wheel and looked out at him with tear-filled eyes.

He hauled open the door and she stumbled out and fell into his arms.

She was shaking. 'I thought he was going to shoot me, Donald! I thought ... Oh, my God...'

She wept against his chest, and Langham felt a surge of relief, quickly followed by anger.

'When he fired...' She looked up into his eyes. 'I *knew* I was dead, and the fear I felt...'

'He fired?'

She gave an odd half-laugh, half-sob, and pointed to the front offside wheel. The motorcyclist had shot the tyre, effectively ending her pursuit.

'Do you have a spare?'

She shook her head. 'No. And anyway, he shot both tyres.'

'Very thorough,' he commented.

He led her back to the Austin and eased her into the passenger seat, then climbed in and held her in silence, murmuring comforting words while feeling thoroughly sick.

Five minutes later he started the engine. 'We'll drive to the next town and find a garage. I'll get them to tow your car back and fix the tyres. It might take a while.'

She nodded, sniffing, and dabbed at her eyes with a tiny handkerchief. 'I couldn't see the man, Donald. He was wearing a scarf over his mouth, and these things...' She made circles of her thumbs and forefingers and placed them over her eyes. 'What do you call them?'

He glanced at her, smiling. 'Goggles.'

'I did see he was short, though, and ... how do you say ... portly?'

He nodded. 'We live to fight another day, Maria.'

She looked at him. 'You sound so very calm and ... unflappable, yes?'

109

He had to laugh at that. 'Unflappable? That wouldn't really describe me five minutes ago when I saw him get off the bike and draw his gun. I thought...'

He couldn't get the words out; something was blocking them. He felt shaky now with the closeness of the call.

Maria reached out and squeezed his hand.

They drove on, and a sign indicated that Lingfield was just two miles away.

Ten minutes later Langham located a garage and instructed a mechanic to fetch the Sunbeam. He found a phone box and tried to get through to Charles to tell him that they'd been delayed by a breakdown, but there was no reply: evidently his agent had not yet got back.

They sat in the garden of a public house across the road from the garage and waited for the tow truck to arrive with the Sunbeam. The pub was closed, unfortunately, as it was after three o'clock. Langham could have murdered a pint.

Maria said, 'What are we going to do?'

Loath though he was to admit defeat, he shook his head. 'To be honest, I don't know. Charles can't go on paying out like this, and if he doesn't pay...'

'Damn this stupid country and its primitive laws! You English pride yourself on your judicial system and fair play, but it's barbaric.'

He said, 'And in France?'

'In my country, Donald, while the ignorant man in the street might ridicule Charles for what he is, at least the law would recognize his desires, his homosexuality, and not criminalize

110

him for them.'

'Perhaps we have a lot of catching up to do.'

'Yes, perhaps you have,' she said.

He pointed along the high street to where the tow truck was labouring under the weight of the Sunbeam. It came to a halt outside the garage and the mechanic jumped from the cab. He sauntered across the road, wiping his hands on an oily rag.

'Not good news I'm afraid, guv. We don't have the tyres in stock. We'd have to order them from London. They'd come in later today or tomorrow. Either way, the car wouldn't be ready until tomorrow afternoon.'

Maria shrugged. 'There is nothing else for it. Will you order the tyres, please?'

The man nodded. 'Odd, though – that they both went at the same time like that.'

'Very odd,' Langham said. 'Will you put the old tyres to one side? I'd like to look them over.'

As they returned to Langham's car, Maria said, 'The bullets, right?'

'If we can retrieve them, I know someone who'd be able to identify the weapon they came from. You never know, it might help.'

They set off, and Langham considered what he was about to say. 'Do you think Charles will give you some time off tomorrow?'

'I'm sure he would.'

He hesitated, then said tentatively, 'In that case, why don't we make a day of it? I'll drive you down here, we'll have lunch somewhere, and then you can pick up the Sunbeam and we'll drive back in convoy.'

She smiled at him. 'That sounds like an excellent idea, Donald. Let's do that.'

Charles was beside himself by the time they arrived back at the agency.

He leapt from the settee as they climbed the stairs to his apartment. 'My dears, you've been an age! My fevered imagination leapt to all manner of dire scenarios!'

'He lost us,' Langham reported. 'I'm sorry.'

Charles waved this aside. 'I'm just glad that you both survived the ordeal. I ... What's that behind your back, dear boy?'

Langham flourished the bottle he'd bought for Charles. 'To soften the blow,' he said.

His agent took the bottle as if presented with a coveted award. 'Laphroaig ... The very finest, my boy. You are kind. Should we indulge?'

Maria laughed. 'Not for me. I'll make myself a cup of tea.'

'Help yourself. Donald?'

'Just a finger.'

'A finger it is, dear boy!'

Maria arranged herself on the settee beside Langham and gave Charles the story they'd concocted on the drive back, so as not to alarm him. 'My car broke down, Charles. Donald offered to drive me down to collect it tomorrow.'

'Do that, my dears. A day in the country, why not? You should find a nice little place and perhaps stop for lunch.'

Maria tipped her head and smiled at him. 'Thank you, Charles.'

'And speaking of food, my dears – I take it

you're both doing nothing this evening?'

Maria shook her head and Langham said, 'I'm free.'

'In that case the treat is mine. We shall dine in luxury, I shall regale you with fabulous tales of London between the wars, and not a word about this beastly affair shall pass our lips!'

EIGHT

Langham picked Maria up outside her Kensington apartment at eleven the following morning. He moved the box Brownie camera from the front seat and placed it in the glove compartment.

'Are you going to photograph me, Donald?'

'Do you know something? I might just do that.'

She laughed. 'I must warn you that I take a terrible photograph!'

'Now that,' he said, easing the Austin into the road, 'I cannot believe.'

The sun was shining and he was looking forward to a day in the country. The reviewing, for a day, could go hang.

'Seriously, Donald, why the camera?'

'Ah ... wait and see. All will be revealed.'

'Mysterious.' She pulled off her hat and gloves and said, 'Anyway, Charles seemed to enjoy himself last night.'

113

'I think the meal helped to take his mind off things.'

'I wish I could forget about it. I hardly slept a wink.'

'We'll sort it out. These things take time.' Even as he said the words, he knew they were platitudes.

She turned in the passenger seat, gazing at him. 'I know Charles. I think I know him well. I have been working for him for almost five years now.'

He glanced at her. 'And?'

She made a pretty bud of her rouged lips. 'His gaiety is often a show. He makes light of things, puts on an act. I think that is because over the years he has had to do this, because of what he is, no?'

'Hiding his true nature?'

She nodded. 'Exactly. The thing is ... I worry about him. I fear he will do something silly.'

He gripped the wheel as they headed south. 'Silly?'

'I don't know ... I might be wrong. But I would not be surprised if Charles turned himself in.'

'What makes you think that?'

'It would be entirely in keeping with Charles's character, I think. He might do it to spite the blackmailer – admit to his liaison with this boy, and suffer the consequences rather than go on paying the blackmailer.'

'And face a jail term?'

She shrugged. 'I think it's not so much paying the money that he detests, as the principle ... along with the idea that the blackmailer is like

114

him, too – homosexual.'

'I see.'

'I think he sees people like himself as a ... a fraternity, no? And that someone would break the unspoken trust and blackmail him like this...' she smiled, '...it offends his English notion of fair play.' She was silent for a time, and then said, 'How long might he be jailed for, if the police find out?'

Langham thought about it. 'Well, a few years ago a friend of mine – the crime writer Leo Bruce – did six months in Wormwood Scrubs for a trumped-up charge of gross indecency. So ... if the police got hold of the photographs, and according to Charles they're pretty graphic, then I wouldn't be surprised if he were sent down for a year or more.'

'A year! But that's medieval! What if he turned himself in, Donald? Might that work in his favour?'

Langham released a long breath. 'Knowing the draconian views of the current Home Secretary,' he said, 'I doubt it. Anyway, I'd rather we sorted the affair out without involving the police.'

'Oh, Donald!' Maria exclaimed. She beat her fists against the dashboard in a funny, panto-mime display of rage, then laughed. 'Let's try to forget about this and enjoy the day, no?'

'Capital idea!'

They left London in their wake and motored through the fields of Surrey. 'Before we stop at Lingfield, I want to go on to Chalford and Hallet, or rather the lane where Charles dropped the money.'

'Why?'

'Take a peek at the mud in the gateway.'

'Ah, that explains the camera, no? You wish to photograph the motorcyclist's footprints?'

'It might lead us nowhere, but you never know.'

'Donald,' she said with censure, 'I thought we agreed to talk about something else!'

He laughed. 'My fault. OK, let me see ... Very well, tell me how you came to live in England.'

She laughed and said, 'Oh, that is a very boring story, but if you really want to know...'

'I'd like nothing more.'

They bowled through the countryside, the windows down to admit the cooling breeze and the scent of wild flowers in the hedgerows. She told him about how she and her father had fled to London a few days before the Nazis marched into Paris, and how, while her father set up a government in exile with De Gaulle, she was packed off to a girls' school in Gloucestershire.

'I thought I would hate it, Donald! Away from my father, in a foreign country in wartime...'

'And did you?'

She laughed. 'I had the most wonderful time. All the real teachers had been called up, and their replacements were elderly and retired and didn't really want to get back into teaching. We had a few basic lessons, and the rest of the time we were allowed to do what we wished, which was smoke cigarettes and play cards in the tumbledown greenhouse behind the school.'

'You obviously learned enough to get into university, though.'

'One day my father arrived at the school. He was angry. I don't know how he found out about what was going on, but he threatened to send me to an aunt in Canada if I didn't apply myself. *Mon Dieu!* He hired a private tutor and I stayed at the school and, as you English say, "put my head down".'

They sped through Lingfield and into the rolling countryside beyond. Over the low thrum of the engine, Langham made out the trilling of skylarks. He gripped the wheel, listening to Maria's lilting contralto as she described her time at Cambridge. 'I studied politics and history and graduated in 'forty-six.'

'Your father must have been delighted.'

'I think he was. But he was far from happy when I decided I wanted to work in publishing. You see, he wanted me to go back to France and work as a political researcher for a government minister. The thought of it!' she exclaimed. 'Anyway, I worked for a couple of publishers in London for a while, then met Charles at a launch party for one of his authors, and he offered me a place at his agency.'

'And the rest, as they say, is history.'

'The agreement,' she went on, 'was that I should work for Charles for five years, learning the business, and then become a joint partner in the firm.'

'Five years? Isn't that now?'

She nodded. 'We were about to discuss the details when all this business began. So,' she said, 'that is my life in a little capsule. Now it is your turn. Where did you go to school?'

117

He smiled. 'You really don't want to know the boring details, Maria. Life growing up in 'twenties Nottingham, at a dull, second-rate grammar school ... Ah, I do believe this is Chalford.'

They passed through the tiny village and turned along the lane to Hallet. A couple of minutes later he slowed down and drew to a halt beside the gate.

They climbed out and stretched. The sun beat down, and after the noise of the car engine the countryside seemed preternaturally silent, interrupted only by birdsong and the distant barking of a farm dog. He decided he should get out of the city more often.

'I didn't come equipped for a hike through the mud,' Maria said. 'Do you mind if I just stand here and laugh while I watch you?'

'Not at all, but before you start laughing could you pass me the camera?'

She obliged, and he squelched through the mud and located the deep rut the motorbike had made. Beside it, next to the gatepost, was the imprint of the rider's left boot.

He squatted, squinted through the viewfinder and snapped. He stood, moved to gain a different angle and took another photograph of the footprint along with the tyre mark.

He was taking a third picture when he made out the chunter of an approaching tractor.

'Donald,' Maria called out. 'I think we have company.'

The tractor pulled into the verge behind his car, its engine ticking over. The farmer peered down at him, scratched his head and said, 'Know

118

this might be a silly question, sir, but why are you photographing my field?'

Maria sidled off behind the Austin, hiding her mouth behind a cupped hand.

'Ah ... well,' Langham temporized, 'as a matter of fact I'm making a documentary record of the rural gateways of England, and today I'm concentrating on East Sussex.'

The farmer regarded him without expression. 'Rural gateways?'

'That's right,' Langham replied. 'Rural gateways.'

The farmer stared at him, then asked, 'From London, are you?'

'We are,' Langham replied.

'That'd explain it, then,' the farmer said, slipping the tractor into gear and bucketing off down the lane.

Maria was doubled up beside the car. 'Oh! A documentary record of the rural gateways of England! Oh!' she gasped.

'Well, it worked, didn't it?'

'The look on his face! He ... he must have thought you were a lunatic!' She wiped a tear from her eye. 'And when ... when you told him you were from London and he said, "That'd explain it, then". Oh!'

Langham laughed. 'Perhaps I am a lunatic,' he said, wiping his muddy feet on the grass and climbing in behind the wheel. 'Come on, let's get some lunch. I spotted a likely-looking little tea room when we passed through Lingfield.' He glanced at her. 'Do you think you could stop laughing long enough to have a spot of lunch?'

119

She wiped tears from her eyes and shook her head. 'Oh, Donald! Probably not!'

Fifteen minutes later he pulled the Austin into the forecourt of the garage and climbed out. Maria's Sunbeam stood in the shadow of the building, equipped with two brand-new front tyres.

The mechanic strolled out to meet them, rubbing his chin. 'I put the old tyres in the boot. You said you wanted them.'

'Excellent.'

'Strange thing was,' the mechanic went on, 'I found these...' He pulled a hand from his pocket and opened a grease-stained palm, bearing two small grey bullets. 'God knows how they got there.'

He tipped them into Langham's hand.

'Mysterious,' Langham said. 'Who on earth would take pot shots at two tourists innocently passing through the Downs?'

Maria linked an arm through Langham's. 'We are safer in London, Donald. Come on!'

They left the mechanic scratching his head and strolled from the forecourt, along the high street to the tea room.

They sat at a tiny window table and ordered ham and lettuce sandwiches, Earl Grey tea and fruit scones. Langham stood the bullets upright on the tablecloth, both dented from the impact with the wheel hub. 'It's a .38 calibre,' he said. 'Possibly fired from a service revolver. There were thousands of them that were never handed in after the war, or stolen from barracks up and down the country. The underworld is flooded with them.'

Maria shrugged. 'Do they tell you anything?'

He shook his head. 'Not really – other than the fact that our blackmailing friend *might* have been in the services himself, stolen it, or has criminal contacts.' He pocketed the bullets. 'Ah, here comes lunch.'

As they ate, Maria asked him about his war service. 'Charles told me you were in Madagascar. How exotic!'

'It was, the little I saw of it. I was only there a month, before being shipped off to India. I was there for four years, and I came to love the place. Truth be told, I had a rather enjoyable war, though I feel guilty for admitting it.'

He told her about his work in field security, administering an area of central India the size of Great Britain, monitoring rumours of espionage and keeping tabs on nationalist unrest. He'd travelled a lot as an officer with the rank of captain, liaising with divisional commanders and hobnobbing with the occasional maharajah. When one of the latter found out he'd written crime novels before the war, he invited Langham to stay at his palace during a period of leave and even provided him with a typewriter so that he might begin a book.

'So while I was smoking cigarettes in the greenhouse at school,' Maria said, 'you were taking sundowners with Indian royalty.'

'And now here we are in a quaint English tea room drinking Earl Grey from bone china cups.'

'How strange is the world, Donald!'

After lunch they strolled around the town, inspected the ancient churchyard, then returned to their respective cars. She took his hand. 'I've had a wonderful time, Donald. Let's do it again, soon, no?'

'That would be wonderful.'

'So ... back to the city. I'll pop in and check that Charles is OK,' she said.

He hesitated, his mouth suddenly dry. 'Perhaps ... I was wondering, maybe we could go out for dinner one evening later this week?'

She smiled. 'Yes. That would be nice, Donald.'

He followed her as she drove from the garage forecourt and headed north on the London road. This time, the journey home proceeded without event. He passed Maria's Sunbeam before Hammersmith Bridge, waved and turned off towards Notting Hill. He was still grinning like a lovesick schoolboy when he arrived at his flat fifteen minutes later.

That evening he poured himself a Scotch, sat in his armchair by the window and tried to read for review. He found it impossible to concentrate; the story seemed trite, the characters one-dimensional. He laid the book aside and poured another drink, telling himself that he could still smell the heady scent of Maria's eau de cologne.

NINE

Two days later Langham drove south to Wandsworth and parked outside a shabby row of premises which consisted of a run-down betting office, a fish-and-chip shop and a tobacconist's.

The Ryland and Hope Investigative Agency had its headquarters – as Ralph Ryland liked to call the poky, flyblown office – above the chip shop. It was the cheapest place for rent along the row, on account of the smell of fish and stale dripping that drifted up through the cracked linoleum, though Ryland had never stopped claiming that it was only a temporary measure. When the agency made it big, he said, they would move lock, stock and barrel to the West End.

They had occupied the current premises for as long as Langham could recall.

The same blue carpet adhered to the soles of his shoes as he climbed the steps and rapped on the door.

Ralph Ryland sat behind a desk, his chair tipped back and his winklepickers lodged on the blotter. He was a whippet-thin, balding man in his mid-forties, with the shifty, sharp look of an East End spiv. He kept a meticulously clipped moustache and a Woodbine continually burning beneath it.

123

He quickly removed his feet from the desk when Langham pushed open the door. 'Oh, it's you, Don,' he said, replacing his feet. 'Thought I had a punter for a second there. Cuppa?' His cigarette waved in time to his words like a conductor's baton.

'Earl Grey?'

Ryland laughed. 'You'll have Typhoo like the rest of us plebs, mate.'

Langham sat down on a rickety chair while Ryland poured strong tea into a chipped mug. He drew the revolver from his overcoat pocket and slid it across the desk. 'Thanks for this, Ralph.'

Ryland resumed his tipped-back position against the wall. 'Now, you going to tell me what malarkey you've been up to?' He pinched the Woodbine from his lips with fingertips stained the colour of cockroaches and flicked the accumulated ash on to the carpet. 'I take it the shooter was for more than research purposes, right?'

'You're sharp, Ralph. Ever thought of opening a detective agency?'

'Thought about it, but heard there's no money in the lark.'

Langham sipped his tea, which was dreadful. 'A good friend of mine is being blackmailed.'

Ryland grimaced and the cigarette stood up like a flagpole. 'Nasty. What's he done?'

'Gross indecency. I suppose the legal term would be pederasty.'

'And just how good a friend is this friend, Don?'

He wouldn't be drawn, either to refute the

124

degree of his friendship, or to divulge his agent's name. He trusted Ralph, but he didn't trust the investigator not to talk when he hit the bottle, which was often these days.

'He's someone I know in publishing, and he's a good man. Anyway, someone photographed him with a rent-boy.'

He gave Ralph the broad outlines of the case, detailing the delivery he'd made to the bombed-out mill and then the abortive trailing of the motorcyclist.

Ryland whistled. 'A hundred for starters and then upped it to five hundred? The guy means business.'

'He has my friend between the old rock and a hard place.'

'And you thought you could handle it your-self?'

Langham shrugged. 'I thought I'd give it a go. But after what happened in Sussex ... and something else.'

'Yes?'

He thought back to the minutes after the blackmailer had coshed him in the mill. He gave Ryland the details. 'Then he placed a gun to my head. My impression was that he was minded to shoot me ... but some kids saw him and he scarpered.'

Ryland's shoulders, as slim as a ferret's, lifted in a shrug. 'Why would he do that?'

'Anger that I, instead of my friend, had delivered the cash? But why escalate his crime from blackmail to murder? It worried me.'

'You want me to see if I can find out who the

geezer is?'

'Well, you're the professional. I just write about these things.'

Ryland nodded and tipped his chair upright, suddenly businesslike. 'OK, so what have you got so far?'

Langham recounted everything, from his encounter with Kenneth at the Hackney baths to the shooting out of Maria's tyres. He described the blackmailer from Kenneth's description of him, then gave Ryland the bullets and the pictures of the footprint and the tyre track he'd had developed yesterday.

Ryland examined the bullets. 'They're from a service revolver, a .38. Most likely an Enfield. Leave them with me. I'll get an expert to check them out.' He looked at the photographs. 'You said he was riding a motorbike? Catch the make?'

'A Triumph Thunderbird.'

'CC?'

Langham shook his head. 'I never got that close. There's one other thing – he smokes Camel cigarettes. For what it's worth, one of the envelopes containing a blackmail demand had a Streatham postmark.'

Ryland nodded. 'Not a lot to go on.' He thought about it. 'There's not much I can do until your friend gets the next demand. As soon as he does, get it to me, OK? How do you want this played?'

'Well, the main thing is that the police don't get wind.'

'Understood. The way I see it...' Ryland nip-

126

ped the tab end from his mouth, ground it out in a full ashtray, and immediately lit another. 'Way I see it, we need to get hold of the evidence. The photographs and the negatives.'

'That's what I thought.'

'I'll try to trace the bastard and put the frighteners on him until he blabs where the stuff is,' Ryland said. 'It'll cost your friend, though.'

'I'm sure it won't be as much as the next demand.'

Ryland grinned. 'I'll do it for fifty, plus expenses.'

Langham reached out and shook Ryland's thin, cold hand. He took another sip of tea, decided that it really was too foul to finish, and left the cup on the desk.

'Oh—' Ryland gestured to a bookshelf stuffed with tatty paperbacks, many of them copies of Langham's titles. 'When's the next one out?'

'Just before Christmas. I'll send you a copy.'

Ryland saluted with three fingers. 'Nice one, Captain.'

'I'll be in touch, Ralph.' Langham left the office and hurried down the sticky stairs.

He drove home slowly, satisfied that he'd done the right thing. He wondered if he'd been a fool to have thought he could handle the problem himself. Perhaps ... but he wasn't such a fool to ignore what had happened to Maria's Sunbeam the other day. He had every confidence in Ryland; the man might not look like everyone's idea of a private detective, and he did like his drink, but he was respected in the business as someone who worked doggedly on a case till he solved it or could take it no further.

It was five by the time he reached his flat, and he wondered if it was too short notice to ring Maria and suggest dinner that evening. He poured himself a beer and stood by the window, staring out on the busy street. Late sunlight slanted through the elms spaced along the pavement, and pedestrians hurried like film extras past the shops on the far side of the road. He saw another old codger in a sandwich board, this one advertising Oxo cubes.

He was still wondering whether it would be wise to call Maria when the phone rang.

He hurried into the study and picked up the receiver. 'Hello?'

'Donald...'

'Maria, I was just about to—'

'Donald, I've just had a call from Charles's solicitor.'

Langham sat down quickly. 'What's happened?'

'Charles was arrested earlier today. He's at Bow Street police station.'

'Arrested?' His heartbeat sounded loud in his ears. 'He gave himself up?'

'No...' There was a catch in her voice. She gathered herself and went on: 'No, he didn't. His solicitor said that the police had "been in receipt of certain incriminating documents..." That can only mean one thing.'

Something as cold as ice turned in his stomach. 'But that doesn't make sense. Why would the blackmailer...?'

'I know, I know. It's crazy ... I'm going to the station now to try and see Charles. The police are opposing bail, but his solicitor said he'd apply anyway when Charles goes before the magistrate in the morning. He'll be in custody until then.'

'Did he say how much bail might be, if it were to be granted?'

'No. I'm sorry, I didn't ask. Donald, I was wondering ... I feel sick. I don't feel up to driving. Could you possibly...?'

'I'll pick you up in ten minutes,' he said. 'I want to see Charles myself, if they'll allow visitors.'

'Oh, Donald, Donald ... what's going to happen?'

The misery in her voice made him want to hold her. 'I'll be right over, Maria.'

He pulled on his overcoat and hurried from the flat, wondering why the blackmailer would staunch his source of income by turning in the goose that laid the golden eggs.

TEN

Langham pulled up in front of Maria's apartment, leaned over and opened the passenger door. She appeared at the top of the steps wearing a belted fawn mackintosh and a tiny hat that clung to the side of her head like a limpet. She hurried down the front steps and ducked into the car.

He had wondered how to greet her, but his dilemma was solved when she reached for him. They hugged. She pulled away and dabbed at her eyes, drying tears.

Langham started the engine and pulled out into the street, heading towards Bow.

'It was such a shock, Donald, when the solicitor called. All I could think of was poor Charles, locked in a police cell.'

'With luck he'll be out in the morning.'

'I hope so.' She opened her compact and powdered her cheeks, peering intently at her reflection in the tiny mirror.

'I've been trying to work out why the blackmailer might have turned him in,' Langham said.

'Does it make sense to you?'

'On the face of it, no. Why would the blackmailer put an end to a potentially lucrative and indefinite source of income? I came up with two

130

possible reasons. One is that he thought he'd get out while he was ahead. He's made six hundred from Charles, and so he's happy with that – especially after we tried to trail him the other day.'

Maria thought about it. 'But it still doesn't make sense. Very well, so he thought he would get out while he was ahead, perhaps fearing that next time we might trace him or whatever. But surely if that were so, then he'd merely stop making the demands – but leave himself the option of threatening Charles in future.'

Langham sighed. 'That's what he'd do, logically. But what about this: perhaps this isn't so much about making money, but destroying Charles. The demands were just a way of making a bit of cash before he did what he always intended to do: turn Charles in and watch him suffer.'

Maria pulled a pained face. 'But who would do such a terrible thing?'

'Someone who bears a hell of a grudge against Charles.'

'But Charles is a sweetheart, Donald. Surely no one could bear such a grudge?'

'Who knows?'

He told her about his visit to Ryland that afternoon. 'I thought it best to get a professional on the case. I was hoping there'd be another demand so that Ryland could investigate. This latest turn of events isn't going to make his job any easier.'

She smiled at him. 'I'm pleased you did that.'

He glanced at her. 'You are?'

131

'It shows that you know when you're beaten. Many men would have ... what is the phrase? ... ploughed on regardless. At least you had the humility to engage a professional.'

He smiled. 'I admit I'm not Sam Brooke,' he said. 'Perhaps a small part of me thought I was, for a while.'

She reached out and squeezed his arm. 'You're a good writer and a fine friend to Charles.'

He parked in a side street off Bow Road and they hurried round the corner to the ugly Victorian building that housed the police station and magistrate's court.

Maria linked arms with him, then paused at the foot of the steps to the police station. 'One moment.' She took a deep breath. 'I am not looking forward to this, Donald. I just hope Charles is bearing up.'

He squeezed her hand. 'Come on, let's show our support.'

They climbed the steps and passed through a tiled atrium that reminded Langham, in its stark functionality, of the entrance to Hackney Public Baths. The only difference here was that the tiles were not white but sky blue and navy, and the posters on the walls exhorted citizens to lock their cars and beware of pickpockets.

A beefy sergeant was on duty behind the desk, and he eyed Maria as she strode towards him.

'Mr Charles Elder's solicitor contacted me earlier this evening, Sergeant.'

He consulted a log book. 'Mr Winstanley is with the accused at the moment. He should be out presently.'

'Do you know if Mr Elder will be granted bail?'

'That's really not for me to say, Miss...?'

'Dupré. Maria Dupré. Will we be able to see Charles when—?'

The sergeant looked surprised. 'I'm afraid not, Miss Dupré. Mr Elder has been arrested on a serious charge. Visits are out of the question. I'm sorry. Now if you'd care to take a seat, Mr Winstanley should be finished shortly and he'll brief you...' The sergeant indicated a bench facing the desk.

Langham took her arm and led her away. They sat side by side on the uncomfortable wooden bench and Maria whispered, 'This place depresses me.'

He looked around. 'It's not exactly the foyer of the Ritz, is it?'

She removed her gloves and smoothed them out on her lap.

He steeled himself and said, 'I hope you don't mind my saying, but you're looking rather wonderful tonight.'

She favoured him with a half-smile. 'And if you don't mind my saying, my dear boy, as Charles would say, you're looking like something the cat has dragged around.' She reached out and rearranged his collar, then plucked a shred of golden tobacco from his sleeve. 'This overcoat has seen better days, Donald.'

The sergeant cleared his throat, caught their attention and pointed with a biro pen to a door that had just opened along the corridor.

A stooped, greying man in his sixties stepped

133

out, impeccably attired in a grey suit and homburg. He was carrying a briefcase and a cane, a distant expression on his thin face as if absorbed still with the intricacies of his client's case.

Maria stood quickly. 'Mr Winstanley? Maria Dupré. We spoke earlier.'

Winstanley raised his homburg. 'Enchanted.' He shook Langham by the hand as Maria introduced him.

'How is Charles?' Maria asked.

'Forgive me one moment. Sergeant, might I bother you for a room where we might conduct our business in private?'

The sergeant showed them to a tiny, tiled room with two chairs and a desk, and obligingly fetched a third chair. 'Under the circumstances,' Winstanley began as they settled themselves, 'Mr Elder is bearing up remarkably well. He was arrested at noon on a charge of having perpetrated an act of gross indecency, and it seems on the evidence of the photographs now in police possession to be a pretty incontrovertible charge. Mr Elder will appear before a magistrate at eleven in the morning, if you would care to be present. My educated guess, and I must stress that this is only a guess, is that he will be granted bail, but that really depends on the magistrate himself. If we get a petty-minded stickler, then I might be wrong.'

'Do you have any idea how much bail might be?' Langham asked.

Winstanley gestured with an elegant hand. 'Again, this is an educated guess, but I would say in the region of two hundred and fifty pounds. A banker's draft would suffice, deposited at the court in order to secure Charles's release.' He looked from Maria to Langham. 'You could raise this amount?'

Langham glanced at Maria and said, 'Between us, certainly.'

'Very good.' Winstanley paused, then said, 'One more thing. Mr Elder mentioned the fact that he was being blackmailed. This might – and I stress *might* – have a bearing on proceedings when the case comes to trial. His defence will certainly bring up the matter, which might engender a more sympathetic attitude from members of the jury. It is certainly a card his defence will play. Now, Mr Elder told me about two letters sent by the blackmailer.'

Maria nodded. 'He kept them under lock and key in his office.'

'And I understand you have access to the premises, Miss Dupré? In which case I'll arrange for the police to meet you there later this evening and collect the letters.'

'We'll go there straight away,' Maria said. 'Do you know when Charles will come to trial?'

'That is usually two to three months after the initial hearing,' Winstanley said.

Langham asked the question he would rather have avoided. 'And if he is jailed, do you know how long the term might be?'

'Again, to a certain extent I think it depends on the judge, but I would guess at between a year and eighteen months. Now, I'll talk to the sergeant about collecting the letters.'

Maria linked an arm through Langham's as

135

they left the station, and she shivered as they hurried down the steps. 'Donald, a year to eighteen months...?'

He considered what Winstanley had said and wondered if Charles would survive that long in jail.

'I just hope he's granted bail,' Maria said. 'At least then he will have a little freedom before...'

He patted her arm. 'We'll make it the best couple of months he's ever had, Maria.'

'One big party, no?' She tried to invest the words with levity, but Langham detected the despair that underlay them.

They arrived back at the car and Langham drove west to Pimlico. On the way he asked, 'Have you eaten tonight?'

She shook her head. 'I was about to make something when Mr Winstanley rang.'

'What say we go out for something when the police have collected the letters?'

'That will be nice. I will drink an entire bottle of wine, I think.' She laughed. 'I have never felt like murdering someone, Donald, but if I could get my hands on the person who...'

Langham smiled. 'You'd have to stand in line behind me.'

He pulled into the quiet tree-lined street and parked across the road from the agency. Maria ran up the steps before him and unlocked the door. She did the same with the door to the outer office, reached out to switch on the light, then halted in her tracks.

'Oh,' she said.

'What?' Langham began, a yard behind her.

136

The French window at the far end of the room stood open six inches, admitting the warm evening breeze.

She turned and looked at him. 'Surely Charles would not have left them like this?'

Langham hurried across the room and was about to reach out for the handle. He stopped, his hand in mid-air. The small pane of glass beside the handle bore jagged fangs of glass.

'Donald?'

'Someone broke in,' he said. 'Try not to touch anything. There might be prints.'

He elbowed the door further open and looked out. The windows gave on to a raised patio, and steps from the patio led down to a long, lawned garden. At the far end of the garden was a high brick wall, and beyond that a quiet back street.

Maria swore in French and hurried over to a picture on the wall. She swung it aside and said, 'They haven't touched the safe.'

'Do you keep any loose cash lying around?'

She shook her head. 'And there's not that much in the safe. Why would anyone...?'

She stopped suddenly and pointed to the door leading to Charles's office. The white gloss paint was splintered, raw timber showing where the lock had been forced.

Langham pushed open the door with his forearm. Maria was beside him, a hand to her lips.

Papers littered the floor in foolscap drifts as if a madman had been let loose. Langham picked his way through the mess, careful not to stand on the books that had been pulled from the shelves, and approached the desk. The top drawers on each side of the kneehole had been forced and hung open.

He knelt and peered into the top right drawer, where Charles had left the blackmail letters. There was no sign now of the long manila envelopes.

'Donald?' Maria stood beside him, pulling her bottom lip with a quick, worried gesture.

'The blackmailer,' he said. 'He came for the letters...'

Maria swallowed, clearly fighting the urge to cry. 'I don't feel safe, Donald. The blackmailer, he might be anyone, anywhere...'

He held her. 'He's got what he wanted. He won't be back.'

'It's just the thought of him being in *control*, Donald, and we are so powerless...' She pulled away from him. 'Would you like a drink?'

'Actually, I'd love a cup of tea.'

'You English and your tea,' she said. 'I need a brandy.'

She fetched a bottle of Courvoisier from Charles's flat and made Langham a strong Earl Grey. Langham found a phone book and got through to an emergency glazier.

They sat on the settee in the outer office and drank for a while in silence.

'I don't like looking ahead like this,' he said at last, 'but it must be a relief to Charles to know that you'll be here to run the agency while he's...'

She pressed a finger to his lips. 'Please, don't say the word. I get angry when I think about it. But yes, I'll run the agency and when he comes out everything will be back to normal. *Voila!*'

'Have you told your father about what's been happening?'

'I have told no one, not even Papa. We are close, but I thought it best to keep quiet.'

'Because he doesn't like the idea of his daughter working for a...?'

She pulled a scandalized expression. 'Of course not! My father is a man of the world, no? He is civilized and tolerant. It is the idea of his only daughter working as a *literary agent* that causes him distress! He would rather I was in politics.' She pulled a sour face. 'But politics in France is a game for cut-throats and robbers—'

'I'm sure your father would be delighted to hear that!'

She laughed. 'Why do you think he got away from all that and became the cultural attaché here in London? Ah, the door.'

She leapt to her feet and hurried down the stairs to answer the doorbell. A minute later he heard gruff male voices, then footsteps approaching the outer office.

Maria appeared with a plainclothes detective and a uniformed constable. She introduced Langham to the detective, Evans – a big northerner in a crumpled suit and a battered trilby.

'I was due to collect some letters for use in evidence in the Elder case,' he said. 'But Miss Dupré informs me that there's been a break-in?'

He showed Detective Evans the smashed French window and the forced inner door. The detective stood over the desk, peering down at the open drawers.

'And you say this is where Mr Elder kept the letters? So the theory is, the blackmailer breaks in, finds the letters and makes off with them?'

Maria said sharply, 'Do you have an alternative suggestion?'

'I'm merely trying to establish the facts, Miss.' Detective Evans looked from Maria to Langham. 'I'll take a brief statement from each of you, if you don't mind.'

'You'll be sending fingerprint experts out?' Langham asked.

Evans frowned. 'As busy as we are at the moment, and for this kind of crime? I doubt it, Mr Langham. It'd be a waste of time, in my opinion. The thief wouldn't have been foolish enough not to wear gloves, would he?'

Langham conceded the point, and for the next fifteen minutes they gave an account of their discovery of the break-in, which Evans took down with laborious exactitude. While their statements were being taken, the uniformed constable let the glazier in. By the time Evans was ready to go, the glazier had installed a new pane of glass and presented Maria with the bill. Langham showed the detective and the constable to the door.

Five minutes later they stood alone in the outer office, Maria staring aghast at the sheet of paper. 'Ten shillings and sixpence for a *tiny* piece of glass?' she said.

Langham smiled at her horror. He eased the bill from her fingers. 'I'll take care of that,' he said. 'Come on, let's go for dinner. I know a nice little Italian place around the corner.'

140

ELEVEN

Maria gave Langham a kiss on each cheek, French fashion, thanked him for a wonderful evening and slipped out of the car. She ran up the steps to her apartment as if moving on a stairway of clouds, then turned and waved goodbye at the top.

She let herself into her rooms and leaned against the door, smiling inanely to herself.

The meal had been perfect. Donald had insisted that they talk about things other than Charles's predicament and the break-in, and had even opened up and talked a little about himself. She had asked him about Madagascar and his scar, and he had described the skirmish in which he'd received the wound. 'To be honest I didn't notice it at the time – and that had nothing to do with bravery. I thought it was an insect bite. I didn't realize I was bleeding till the shooting stopped.'

But for the most part she had talked about herself. Donald had the writer's ability to draw one out of oneself, and to listen with interest to every word she spoke. She told him about her mother, a shadowy figure she hardly remembered, who had died of cancer when she was four. She'd described being brought up by a

141

series of nannies, some more loving than others, and the constant affection and support of her father. The one regret of her childhood was that he had not been around as much as she'd wanted.

Donald had asked her why she had remained in England, and she had answered truthfully that, by the end of the war, she considered it home. She had friends in the capital, and her father had decided to remain there. It made sense to make London her base. Then Charles had offered her the job and for a while life had seemed perfect.

She wondered if her dissatisfaction of late had been less to do with her job and more to do with the fact that she had no one with whom to share her life.

Her thoughts were interrupted by the chime of the doorbell. She hurried down the stairs to the front door, her heart hammering.

She should have known that it would not be Donald. Pressing himself upon her like this would be a very un-English – a very un-Donald – thing to do, but nevertheless a part of her hoped that she would find him standing on the doorstep, a little sheepish, when she opened the door.

A man *was* standing on the step when she answered the summons, but it was not Donald.

Gideon Martin pushed past her, reeking of drink, and characteristically did not catch her furious glare.

'Gideon!' she began, fearful he'd discovered that it was she who had bid against him the other day.

142

He took the stairs to her rooms two at a time. Maria followed. By the time she caught up with him he was striding up and down the length of the front room as if it were a stage and he the principal actor.

'Who is he?' he demanded.

She felt an immediate wave of relief. His presence was the result of jealousy, then, not rage.

She stood her ground, staring at him. 'Who is who?'

He reached the far end of the room and turned dramatically. He swayed, tipsily, and his eyes burned at her. 'Don't try to deny it, Maria. I saw you get out of his car. I saw you ... saw you kiss him. Who is he?'

She controlled her anger. 'If you must know, he's an agency author and I dined with him to discuss business.'

As soon as the words were out of her mouth, she regretted them. She regretted her spinelessness. Why couldn't she simply tell him the truth, that she had at last found someone whom she liked a lot?

Then she knew why she had not told him. It was not because she feared hurting Gideon Martin, far from it. She feared *him*; she feared his strength, but more than that she feared his mercurial mood which, if pushed, she had no doubt might easily tip into physical rage.

He approached her slowly and said, 'An agency author? And do you kiss *all* your authors like that?'

'Like what? I'm French. Or hadn't you noticed? We kiss when saying goodbye to friends.'

Then she knew what was so unsettling about Gideon Martin tonight: he was actually looking straight at her, staring at her with the full intensity of his dark, storm-filled eyes.

'I know you're lying, Maria. Since when have you dined in the evening with agency clients?'

She stared at him, then shook her head very slowly. 'Oh, go to hell! Who are you to question me like this? Who are you to say who I should and shouldn't see?' She approached him, trembling with anger now. 'What is *wrong* with you?'

His response surprised her. He walked to the end of the room and turned to face her. 'I love you, Maria.'

She continued to shake her head, despairing. She wanted to tell him to go away, to get out of her life.

He said, 'I am angry because I love you.' He stepped forward, reached inside the jacket and withdrew a neatly packaged parcel. He held it out to her.

'What is it?' she asked suspiciously.

'The first of two surprises,' he said.

'Two?'

'I have another, in here...' he touched his jacket, 'if you refuse this one.'

The package was perhaps a foot square and as thin as a paperback book. She stared at it without reaching out.

'Take it,' he said.

She was reluctant to do so, as if by accepting the gift she might be acceding to something which, in his eyes, was far greater.

144

He thrust the parcel into her hands. She stared at him, then down at the parcel, and only then fumbled with the gold wrapping paper.

'Oh...' she said.

It was the watercolour she had intended to buy for her father's birthday. 'I know how much you wanted it for your father,' he said.

She looked up at him. Why had he made a point of telling her, at the party the other evening, that he had rather liked the same watercolour and had bought it for himself?

He said, 'Maria, I'm going away to Paris next week. I would like you to come with me. We could go to restaurants that make those here look like soup kitchens. I know a romantic little place in Montmartre...'

She held the watercolour out to him, rage boiling within her. 'Is this a bribe?'

He smiled his insufferably arrogant smile. 'A bribe, no. Merely a token of my esteem.'

She threw the painting at him and cried, 'I don't want it and I don't want to spend time with you in Paris!'

His response was to stride to the far end of the room, then turn and stare at her. 'In that case you may have the second gift.'

She felt like weeping. *Just go*, she thought; *go...!*

'I don't want *anything* from you! I don't want your gifts. I don't want your offers of holidays ... I don't want you! Can't you understand that?' She was close to weeping, but fought the impulse.

He pulled a small parcel from his jacket,

wrapped like the first in gold paper.

'Here.' He tossed her the packet, and she caught it instinctively. It was far heavier than she thought it would be.

'Go on,' he barked, 'open it.'

She stared at him, knowing what was within the wrapping paper from its shape. She said, 'You're mad...'

'I said open it!'

With trembling fingers she pulled off the ribbon that bound the parcel, then unfolded the paper.

She stared at the revealed object lying on her palm and looked up at him. 'I don't understand...'

His smile could be cruel as well as arrogant. Her heartbeat was thundering. She wanted to sit down, but there were no chairs nearby and her legs would not move. She stared at the small silver pistol in her hand.

He said, quietly, 'There is one bullet in it, Maria.'

Her vision swam, and his features became Mephistophelian. She wondered why he would want her dead, why he just didn't shoot her himself.

Then all was explained. He said, 'Shoot me.' His voice rang with theatrical intensity.

She wondered if he'd planned this for days, weeks – planned what he might do if she spurned him. A part of her wanted to laugh, but the fearful part of her would not grant that release.

I must be very careful, she told herself: he *is* mad.

'I said shoot me!' he yelled at her, spittle flying.

'Gideon...' was all she could manage.

'Do it! You obviously hate me, despise me. Go on – shoot me!'

'This is...' She had been about to say 'insane', but something stopped her. If she intimated to Martin that she thought him insane, might that be the very thing that tipped him over the edge?

Startling her, he leapt forward and grabbed the pistol from her hand. He backed off, smiling at her, then stopped and raised the weapon to his head. He lodged its barrel against his temple. 'Well, Maria, if you refuse to do it, then I will.'

She wanted to tell him to grow up, to look at himself. Why the theatrics? she wondered. Why the grand gestures that, when analysed, were nothing other than a manifestation of a self-centred petulance?

He said, 'I've contemplated life without you for months, Maria, and I can't bear the thought.'

She cried, 'But you've had years without me! For God's sake, we've never really been to-gether!'

'But we could be. You could grant my wishes, and I could show you how happy you would be. All you have to do is say yes.'

She shook her head, tears coming freely now. She stared at him. 'I will not be blackmailed!'

And it was as if a tide of rage was released in her at the utterance of the word. She saw his finger tighten on the trigger and, surprising herself, she strode towards him, raised her right hand and slapped him across the face.

147

The blow almost knocked him off his feet. She grabbed the gun from his fingers and flung it across the room with a cry.

He fled, but not before stooping to pick up the watercolour from the floor.

Her heart beating madly, she followed him down the stairs. He disappeared through the front door, leaving it wide open. She slammed the door shut and fell against it with a sob, then locked it and ran back up the stairs.

She saw the gun, small and malignant, lying on the carpet. She picked it up as if it were something poisonous, carried it across the room and locked it in her writing bureau.

Weeping, she pulled the telephone towards her and cradled it in her lap. She wanted to ring Donald, to hear his reassuring voice, but at the same time she didn't want to lay the fact of her weakness before him.

She set the phone aside, then poured herself a brandy and sat crying quietly to herself, wishing Gideon Martin dead.

TWELVE

Charles Elder went up before the magistrate at eleven fifteen the following morning, the session heard in a small court to the rear of Bow Street station. A local reporter and two members of the public occupied the narrow public gallery along with Langham and Maria.

Charles was led into the room by a uniformed constable, staring ahead without expression. His usual ebullient, expansive self appeared reduced, physically smaller, as if just one night in custody had taken its toll.

A detective sergeant read out the particulars of the case, and Charles's solicitor, Mr Winstanley, applied for bail.

The magistrate deliberated with a clerk, and their *tête-à-tête* seemed to last an age. Maria found Langham's hand and squeezed. 'Please,' she implored. 'Please...'

Minutes later the magistrate cleared his throat and granted bail at two hundred pounds, to be stood by Mr Donald Langham and Miss Maria Dupré. At the sound of their names Charles seemed to expand and become himself again. He looked up for the first time, raised his fingers to his lips and blew them a kiss with a mimed, *'Bless you.'*

149

Langham glanced at Maria. Tears tracked down her face, at odds with her overjoyed smile.

'Let's go and meet him,' he said.

They were escorted into a small office where Langham handed over a banker's draft for the sum of two hundred pounds, then signed a declaration binding him and Maria to abide by the stipulations required as Charles Elder's bailers. Only then was Charles escorted into the room by a uniformed officer and officially granted his freedom in accordance with the terms of his bail.

Langham shook his hand. 'Donald!' Charles exclaimed. 'You cannot imagine my pleasure at seeing such friendly faces! Maria, my sweet child.' They embraced, only for the intimacies to be cut short by the throat-clearing of the presiding officer.

Charles comported himself in exemplary fashion. He signed a release form with a flourish, handed the pen to the officer with a gracious smile, and on the way from the station thanked the desk sergeant for his supply of copious and excellent tea.

He paused in the foyer and smiled. He looked around the tiled room as if with fondness. 'I followed hallowed footsteps, my friends. Hallowed! Did you know that, almost sixty years ago to the very day, this is where Oscar was brought when he was so foully arrested?'

Langham smiled. 'Come on, Charles...'

They left the station and Langham escorted Charles to his waiting car. 'Is it vain of me,' Charles said while inserting himself into the

150

passenger seat, 'but I was rather hoping that there might be a posse of pressmen encamped outside the station, awaiting my emergence.'

Maria smiled. 'You had a small column in this morning's *Express*, Charles.'

'Just a *small* column? I wanted the leader and nothing less!'

Langham said, 'We'll get you home. You can refresh yourself, and then we're taking you out for lunch.'

'Lunch? Now there's an offer! While the judiciary's tea was ambrosial, breakfast was revolting. I hope it isn't a harbinger of the fare on offer in the Scrubs, my dears. I don't know how I might survive incarceration without at least one cordon bleu meal a day.'

Maria laughed, and Langham wondered if Charles's *savoir faire* in the face of adversity was nothing more than a show to reassure them.

As Langham parked outside Charles's office, his agent said, 'And the estimable Mr Winstanley informed me of the burglary, so please don't fret that you need to break the news.'

Maria smiled. 'Well, I *was* worrying.'

'Compared to the rest of my trials and tribulations, my dear, what does a little petty larceny matter? Just so long as the fiend did not outrage my aspidistra.'

'The monster is fine,' Langham reassured him.

Once in the flat, Charles excused himself while he attended to his toilette and exhorted them to make merry with the drinks. They compromised with Earl Grey and sat side by side on the settee.

'That went a lot better than I feared,' Maria murmured. 'Charles seems in good spirits, no?'

Langham tipped his hand. 'I'm not so sure. I was just wondering if it wasn't an act for our sakes. We'll just have to make sure we're around for him.' He shrugged. 'He seems fine now, but I'm not even sure the reality of a prison sentence has fully hit him yet. And when it does...'

Maria stared into her tea. 'Your friend, the writer, how did he cope in prison?'

'Leo fared very well, but he's a strong, self-reliant character.' He smiled. 'He even got a book out of it. I fear Charles won't cope half so well. Some of the hardened criminals in there don't take kindly to Charles's type. And he's no fool. He must know what to expect.'

'Oh, Donald...'

He took her hand.

Charles sailed into the room, magnificent in tweed plus-fours.

Maria released Langham's hand quickly, and Charles twinkled a smile. 'You don't know how much it delights me to see you two getting on so well. If nothing else, my little contretemps has brought you closer together, am I correct?'

Maria blushed. 'Charles, you are terrible!'

Charles flourished his cane. 'To lunch! I have an appetite to sate and good friends with which to share the experience. Could one ask for more?'

They dined at Bartholomew's in Knightsbridge, where Charles was known and respected as a regular and discerning patron. He was brilliant and sparkling throughout the meal, and

152

Langham sat back, metaphorically, and enjoyed the experience.

His agent regaled them with tall stories of his time in the trade, the famous names he had known and represented and some of their more risqué behaviour. 'Did I ever mention that I briefly represented Noel? I didn't? How remiss! He was on my books before he hit the big time. I recall one famous lunch we had together...'

They ate grilled trout followed by fresh cream meringue, accompanied by a white wine. 'A vintage *par excellence*!' Charles carolled, 'and from a vineyard regarded as the greatest in Bordeaux. Which reminds me, did I ever tell you of the time I entertained Conrad in the little pied-á-terre I had in Antibes in the twenties?'

He attacked his meal with gusto, a large napkin reduced to the size of a kerchief tucked beneath his multiple chins. His belly bulged like a tweed spinnaker and it seemed that only the gold chain of his fob-watch held the swelling in check.

He accounted for most of the wine himself, and then insisted on brandy to follow the coffee. By the end of the meal his face was a crimson beacon, his tiny eyes rheumy with unshed tears.

Towards four o'clock, with the debris of the meal littering the tabletop and Langham for his part feeling decidedly replete, Charles gripped their hands and declared, 'You, my children, have made an old and foolish man very happy. Do you realize what a boon your friendship is to a man of my nature? All the money in the world cannot buy what you fine people give me. Now, let me settle the bill and flee before I embarrass

153

myself and burst into tears.'

Charles was quiet during the drive back to his apartment, and Langham wondered if, after the excitement of the lunch, and in the maudlin aftermath of so much alcohol, the consequences of that morning's hearing were finally dawning.

They escorted Charles from the car and installed him on his settee with a cup of Earl Grey.

Maria knelt before him and took his hand. 'I'll be in tomorrow morning, Charles. Business as usual.'

'Business as usual...' he repeated somewhat sombrely.

'And we'll take you out for dinner later this week,' Langham said.

Charles looked up. 'I have a capital idea, my friends. I rather think I've had my fill of the metropolis for a while. What say you come up to my place in Suffolk for the weekend? I'll phone Mrs Carstairs to prepare the food, and we'll walk the countryside to give us an appetite.'

Maria looked at Langham. 'Well, I'm free this weekend.'

Langham nodded. 'That sounds wonderful.'

'Oh, excellent, my friends. Excellent!'

'Are you sure you'll be OK if we go now, Charles?' Maria asked, patting his hand.

'You children go and enjoy yourselves. Go! If you pass me *The Complete...*' he gestured to a buckram-bound volume on a nearby occasional table, 'I will console myself with his sonnets.'

They took their leave and descended to the street in silence. As Langham drove Maria to Kensington, she said, 'My father is hosting an awful drinks party tonight, and he really wanted me to show myself.'

'Will you?'

'I'll phone him and make some excuse. I really couldn't face my father's political friends right now. I need to sleep. And you?'

'I've a pile of wretched thrillers to review, so I'd better burn the candle.'

He pulled up outside her apartment. She reached out and took his hand. 'I'm so glad you've been around for the past few days, Donald. I don't know what I would have done without you.'

'The feeling is mutual,' he said, and kissed her fingers.

'Goodnight, Donald.'

'Goodnight. Sleep well.'

He watched her climb from the car and run up the front steps. At the top she turned quickly before letting herself in, paused and waved.

He returned her wave and pulled out into the road.

THIRTEEN

Langham poured himself a whisky and settled into his armchair by the window. He tried to read but found it hard to concentrate for thinking about the events of the day, the iniquity of Charles's situation, and Maria. She filled his thoughts as no one had for years, and he found the fact oddly ambivalent: on one hand he welcomed her sudden presence in his life, but on the other he was disconcerted by the distraction it brought. He was forty years old, for God's sake – surely too old to be falling in love. The helpless sensation brought to mind the last time it had happened, almost twenty years ago now, and the slew of painful associated memories.

He was saved further introspection by the summons of the phone.

'Don? Jeff Mallory here. I'm in the Bull and wondered if you'd care for a pint?'

'You've saved me from a dull evening of reading for review,' Langham said. 'I'll see you there.'

He'd known Mallory for twenty years, having met the tall, tanned South African at a literary soirée in Hampstead. Mallory had just stepped off the boat from Cape Town; he'd sold his first detective novel to Jarrolds and was starting a new life in Britain. They'd hit it off immediately, helped by the fact that they both felt uneasy with the faux intellectual chatter and pernicious backbiting of the publishing world represented by the gathering.

They'd kept in contact over the years. Mallory had written that one novel and no more, struck by a block that Langham, as a big producer, found as alarming as the diagnosis of some dread disease. Mallory had joined the police force, and over the years worked his way through the ranks to the post of Detective Inspector at Scotland Yard. Langham found him an indispensable source of inside information when it came to researching his novels.

The sun was going down and the street lights coming on. Notting Hill was quiet, inhabited only by the occasional dog-walker. Even the high street was almost deserted, and quiet but for an oasis of light and revelry that was the Black Bull. A tangerine glow spilled into the twilight, along with the tinkle of a piano and bursts of raucous laughter.

He pushed through the door into a fug of warmth and cigarette smoke. It was a Wednesday night and the main bar was packed with drinkers marking the mid-point of the working week.

Detective Inspector Mallory waved from a booth at the back of the room, a big man in a rumpled, navy-blue pinstriped suit. Langham mimed drinking and Mallory lifted an almost empty glass. He eased his way to the bar, bought two pints of Watney's and carried them to the booth.

'Aren't you a bit out of your usual stamping ground?' Langham said.

'Just finished an interview around the corner. Popped in for a quick one. Cheers.' Three empties on the table before Mallory testified to the extent of the 'quick one'.

'Good health,' Langham said.

Mallory was not as tanned these days, and his blond thatch of old was thinning while his jowls were thickening.

'It's been a while?' Mallory said. 'Before Christmas?'

'It must have been. You had the manuscript of my last one, and a bunch of notes almost as thick.'

Mallory laughed. 'That's right. Scads of procedural errors. How's the work going?'

Langham always felt a little uneasy talking about his writing to Mallory, and found himself downplaying his success. 'Can't complain. Still one a year, still popular with the old dears who patronize the lending libraries.'

'I see you're still reviewing.'

'For my sins.' He winced as the familiar line came out. 'It makes up for the pitiful advances.' Which was another self-deprecating line: his advances were not that bad, and he continued the review column to keep his name in the public eye between book releases.

He took a mouthful of beer and changed the subject. 'How's Dorothy?'

Mallory mock-flinched. 'God, I haven't seen you since it happened?'

158

'*What* happened?'

'Well, things hadn't been too good between us for a while, and then I met someone...'

Mallory's gaze became distant. 'Alice was ... lovely. A bit younger than me. Twenty-five, in fact. Blonde, bubbly ... An actress.'

Langham lifted his pint and drank. '"*Was?*"'

'That's right. Was. I thought things were going well, thought I knew her, as you do. Then she buggers off. I found out later she'd been seeing someone a lot younger than me all the time we'd been together.'

Langham pulled a face. 'I'm sorry.'

Mallory laughed bitterly. 'Anyway, Dorothy wouldn't have me back. Serves me right. Dorothy was ... is ... a good woman. Hell, we'd been married for fifteen years. I was a damned fool to do what I did, and I got what I deserved when I tried to crawl back.'

'Christ, Jeff.'

'Yeah, well. That's water under the sodding bridge now, isn't it?' He saw that Langham's pint was almost empty. 'Another?'

He drained his glass and passed it to Mallory.

He sat in the comfortable warmth while his friend was at the bar and looked around at the assorted faces. What surprised him was the variety of people who sought refuge in the Bull and in the balm of liquid anaesthesia it provided: middle-aged men in bowlers and suits who looked like city financiers, working men in flat caps playing cards and darts, casual bohemians who looked like artists, and blowsy, overdressed women who sat on high stools at the bar, smoking cigarettes and waiting for gentlemen customers to offer to replenish their gin and tonics.

He considered what Mallory had told him, and inevitably his thoughts strayed to Maria.

Mallory returned, sloshing their pints as he lodged them on the tabletop. He stared at Langham and said, 'You've changed, Don.'

Langham lowered his pint. 'I have?'

'There's something about you tonight. Just before Christmas you were sozzled when we met and proceeded to get drunker. And you were grizzling about being alone. Now you seem much ... dare I say it? ... happier. What's happened?'

Langham smiled. 'Is it that obvious?'

Mallory tapped his head. 'Years of observing suspects trying to lie their way out of tight spots. You hone your observational senses, even if you don't know you're doing it. You're acting like a cat with the cream, Don. Who is she?'

Langham smiled. 'Well, it's early days yet. I'm still not sure if she feels the same towards me. I've known her for years, but recent events have thrown us together. We get on tremendously; being with her just seems natural.'

'You've got it bad. Looker?'

'I'll say. And brains. Thirty, French, very ... what's the word? *Chic*?'

Mallory concealed his grin with a long draught of beer.

Maria filled his mind's eye, and he found himself wondering what she was doing now.

'Penny for them?'

Langham smiled. 'I was just considering my

160

good luck.'

'Well, enjoy it while you can, Don. Nothing lasts for ever.' He shook his head. 'Spoken like a true bleeding cynic. Ignore me. I'm happy for you.'

Langham changed the subject, asked Mallory about his work, and the detective wiped his mouth with the back of his hand and pointed at him. 'Glad you asked. When I found myself in the area I thought I'd call on you, kill two birds with one stone. Thought you might be able to help me with an investigation I'm working on.'

'I write mysteries, Jeff; I don't solve them.'

'I'll do the detective work – you just supply me with details.'

'Fire away.'

'You knew a writer chap called Gervaise Cartwright? Wrote under the name Gerry Carter. Didn't you collaborate with him on a few short stories just after the war?'

Cartwright was a rum character, an Old Etonian who affected a working-class accent and was never happier than when slumming it with criminal East End types, all in the name of research.

'Go on, what's he done?'

'Just gone and got himself murdered.'

'Murdered? Christ, Poor Gervaise. When was this?'

'Three days ago,' Mallory said. 'How well did you know him?'

'Not that well, really. I met him after the war at a dinner of the London Crime Club. We got talking about writing, batted a couple of ideas

161

back and forth, and decided to collaborate on a few short stories. We sold five or six, as far as I recall.'

'Why did you stop?'

Langham shrugged. 'We were both busy with other projects. Gervaise churned out potboilers under his pen name and wrote reviews for the mainstream press under his real name. And to be honest, I didn't like the man that much.'

'Why was that?'

'He was a two-faced creep who was always very pally one to one, but wasn't averse to talking behind your back. He was notorious for giving competing writers bad reviews.'

'So he made lots of enemies?'

Langham shrugged. 'Only very sensitive, neurotic types would bear a grudge. But ... yes, I suppose he wasn't well liked in the trade. He also hobnobbed with the criminal fraternity, so he might have made enemies there, too.'

'Do you know if he still reviewed?'

'He gave up his *Times* column about five years ago, as far as I recall.' He sipped his beer. 'What happened?'

'He was found by his housekeeper, sitting at his typewriter. He'd been stabbed through the back of a rattan chair. An eighteen-inch stiletto, straight through the ribs into the heart. Died instantly. An odd thing about the killing, though: he was wearing a hood over his head when he was found, like a black bag with holes cut out for the eyes—'

Langham raised a finger. 'Like a hangman's hood?'

'Yes, I suppose it was.'

'That ties in. He had a nickname in the trade, for doling out those acid reviews. The Hangman.'

'Ah...' Mallory said, lifting his pint. 'Cheers. So ... Maybe someone in the field was cut up about a bad review they'd received?'

Langham frowned. 'But that would have been years ago.'

'It's a line worth following,' Mallory said. 'We reckon he died around midnight on Sunday. At seven the following morning his housekeeper went into his study and found him.' He shrugged. 'We're working on the assumption that Cartwright knew his killer. There was no sign of a struggle or forced entry. He let the killer in late that night and was stabbed through the back of the rattan chair. Then the killer placed the hood on his head.'

'Nasty,' Langham said.

'I didn't know he was known in the trade as The Hangman,' Mallory said. 'You've given me an interesting lead.'

'I'll charge you at Sam Brooke's rate.'

Mallory smiled. 'I'll pay you in pints, starting now. Fancy another before last orders?'

'You've twisted my arm.'

The Gervaise Cartwright killing, he thought, sounded like something from a Golden Age whodunit: the body in the study, the stiletto, the hangman's hood ... He wondered if it were these elements which gave it an air of familiarity, or if he had read of a similar murder somewhere before.

163

Mallory returned with the Watney's and Langham dismissed the notion as the product of inebriation.

For the last half hour, until throwing-out time, they chatted about Churchill's resignation and Eden's succession, and were united in agreeing that nothing much would change for the better until the Tories were ousted. Langham admitted that he hadn't kept up with much else in the news of late, being too busy finishing the latest novel ... among other things. Mallory clapped him drunkenly on the shoulder and left him with the parting shot that he was a lucky man.

Langham wended his way home, a little tipsily, under a full moon racing through silvered clouds, and wondered if he'd ever felt happier.

FOURTEEN

He spent the next day reading for review.

It was almost four o'clock and he was coming to the end of the third of the four novels, having polished off the first two and typed up the reviews. The second book had been a shocker – in every sense – and he'd ended up skim-reading the last hundred pages. If he finished the third book this afternoon and did the review, then began the fourth book and read all evening, he might just be able to file the reviews within the deadline of noon tomorrow. After that he had a weekend in the Suffolk countryside with Charles – and more importantly, Maria – to look forward to.

He set aside the book he was reading and thought about Maria. He wondered if he should ring her, perhaps suggest dinner tonight – and to hell with the deadline – or if that might seem too presumptuous. He was still deliberating when the phone rang. He leapt from his chair, hoping that this might be Maria now, pre-empting him.

'Donald? Nigel here.'

'Oh...' He tried to conceal his disappointment. 'Nigel, good to hear from you.' He recalled Nigel Lassiter's suggestion that they should collaborate, and assumed that that was what he was calling about.

'Not interrupting the old muse am I, Donald?'

'Of course not. I'm between books at the moment.'

'Lucky swine. I've just started the latest with sod all – I said sod all – idea where it's going.' The way he slurred his words suggested to Langham that he'd been hitting the bottle a bit early. 'But I s'pose I'm lucky.'

Langham humoured him. 'Lucky?'

'Lucky,' Lassiter repeated. 'I could be dead.'

'Dead?'

'Dead as in stone cold. Deceased. Kicked the bucket. D.E.A.D.'

'Ah...' He assumed, then, that Lassiter had heard about Gervaise Cartwright.

Lassiter continued, 'He shouldn't have done it, Donald. I mean, what makes someone do something like that?'

'Sorry, Nigel, I'm not with you,' Langham said. 'Like what?'

'Kill yourself. Take your own life. SUI ... shit, I've forgotten how to spell the bloody word. I mean, what makes you throw yourself under a train? That's serious. No messing about. That's no cry for help. That's "Right, let's get the job done".'

'Nigel...' Langham said with forbearance, 'what on earth are you talking about?'

'Horrible thing is, it happened a fortnight ago and I've only just heard about it. We were talking about him the other day and he was already stone cold dead.'

'Talking about who?' Langham dredged his memory, to no avail.

'You know, Frankie Pearson. The hack. Little Frankie. The snivelling little shit I collaborated with on three dreadful potboilers and then kicked in the balls. That Frankie.'

'He's dead?' Langham said stupidly.

'As the proverbial. Poor little bastard threw himself under the London train down in Kent. Didn't stand a chance. Meant business.'

'God, they're dropping like flies...'

A pause. Lassiter hiccupped. 'They are?'

'I heard last night – Gervaise Cartwright was murdered on Sunday.'

'Cartwright? The Hangman?' Lassiter laughed. 'Well, the shit had it coming to him. But Frankie...' He stifled what sounded like a sob. 'Poor Frankie.'

Langham said, as tactfully as he was able, 'But I thought you didn't like Frankie Pearson?'

166

'I didn't, Donald. Frankie was an annoying little twerp and he couldn't write to save his life ... but that isn't the point. I felt *sorry* for him, d'you see? I feel ... I feel I let him down, back before the war. Maybe I should have gone on collaborating with him, helped him to build his name up. But I was only thinking of number one.'

'You shouldn't blame yourself.' Langham had a sense of déjà vu. Hadn't he said something similar last week when Lassiter had admitted feeling guilty over the method of suicide chosen by old Max Sidley?

'Christ, Donald. Frankie had a hell of a time of it lately. He was dossing in a flea pit of a bedsit down in Hackney. Churning out cowboy books for Hubert and Shale at twenty quid a throw and no royalties, thank you very much. No wonder he wanted to end it all. I was talking to his agent earlier today, Dorothy Crawley. She rang to tell me about what'd happened. And guess what? She told me that she only kept Frankie on her books because no other agency would touch him. She felt sorry for him. Poor sodding Frankie.'

Langham glanced across the room to where his book was beckoning. 'That's terrible, Nigel. Tell you what, let's meet sometime next week? Have a pint, talk about the idea you mooted the other day?'

'The idea?' Lassiter sounded perplexed.

'About our using each other's detective?'

'Oh, that. Yes, yes ... But what I actually rang you about, Donald ... Dorothy Crawley has arranged a memorial service for Frankie in the morning. Saint Mary's Church, Clerkenwell.'

'A memorial service?' Langham said. 'I'm surprised she found a church that'd conduct a service for a suicide.'

Lassiter grunted. 'Well, she had to ring round a few places. Eventually found Saint Mary's, talked the parson round with a hefty donation to his organ restoration fund ... Where was I? Oh, yes. Dorothy – she was having trouble drumming up customers, as it were. Y'see, old Frankie had no family. Not a soul. Only child, parents dead, no aunts or uncles. And the poor sod had no friends, come to that. So I thought I'd go along, let bygones be bygones, pay my last respects, say sorry and all that. And I was wondering – seeing as how you knew Frankie – if you'd come along. Swell the ranks kind of thing.'

'Ah...' Langham quickly tried to think of a convincing excuse.

'For me,' Lassiter wheedled. 'Just to make up numbers so it doesn't look too pathetic.'

Langham sighed. 'What time?'

'Eleven, Saint Mary's.'

If he got the bulk of the fourth book read tonight and in the morning, and rushed off the review before eleven, he could attend the service and deliver the copy to the *Herald* just after midday.

He sighed. 'OK, Nigel. I'll be there.'

'Good man!' Lassiter said. 'Frankie'll be looking down on you.'

More likely looking up, Langham thought. 'I

168

seriously doubt that, Nigel. See you in the morning.'

He replaced the receiver, returned to his book, and hurried through the last thirty pages.

He was sitting at the Underwood an hour later, having just finished the two-hundred-word review, when the phone rang. He moved to the hall, praying that it wouldn't be Lassiter again, even more lachrymose and maudlin over the death of the man who, in life, he'd detested.

'Donald?'

'Maria! I've been thinking about you.'

'You have? You're kind, Donald. I was wondering ... Charles seems a little, how do you say, "under the weather" today. I think everything is on top of him all of a sudden. I thought it might be nice if we took him out for an early drink, and then go on for dinner.'

So much for getting the last book read tonight, but there was no way he was going to pass up the opportunity of seeing Maria. 'That sounds wonderful. What time?'

'Say six – would that give you enough time?'

'I'm on my way.'

He washed and changed into his best suit, then left the flat and drove to Pimlico.

He bought a bunch of daffodils at the florists and presented them to Maria when he entered the outer office.

'And they're for you, not the office,' he told her.

'Oh, how lovely!' She buried her face in the blooms and emerged looking radiant. 'Thank you so much.'

'How are you feeling today?'

'I'm fine, but a little worried about Charles. I think he's been dwelling on what might happen when...'

'Have you told him we're taking him out on the town?'

'He's upstairs changing right now. He's excited. Shall we go up?'

Charles was adjusting a flamboyant yellow bow tie in a full-length mirror, turning this way and that to better admire the effect. He was dressed in a silver-grey suit and, sporting a carnation, looked the epitome of haute couture.

'My boy, Maria is a veritable treasure to suggest an outing. Now come and regale me with the doings of the world in order to lighten my mood.'

Langham sat on the arm of the settee while Charles made minor adjustments to his attire. Maria belted herself into her mackintosh and secured a tiny hat on the side of her head with three lethal-looking pins.

'Well, I've just heard today that Frankie Pearson took his own life a couple of weeks ago.'

Charles turned, his big face a picture of theatrical shock. 'No! Frankie? Frankie Pearson?'

'I've just had Nigel Lassiter on the phone for twenty minutes, giving me the gory details. Frankie threw himself under a train in Kent.'

Maria pulled a face. 'Did I know him?'

'Before your time, my dear,' Charles said. 'He was once one of my authors, before drink got the better of him and the quality of his work became

170

so bad that I was left with no option but to suggest a parting of the ways. It was rather sad, Donald, because I felt responsible for introducing him to the writing game in the first place.'

'So you're to blame!' Langham said.

'Mea culpa!' Charles pressed fingers to his chest. 'It's a long story, and I shall bore you with it over drinks. Are we ready?'

They descended to the street and Charles inserted himself into the rear of the Austin, the process somewhat akin to the genie's emergence from Aladdin's lamp – only in reverse, and accomplished with less finesse.

'Where to?' Langham asked.

'Claridge's,' Charles declared, 'and the drinks are on me.'

Langham drove into the West End and fifteen minutes later they strode three abreast and arms linked into the cocktail lounge. Charles ordered pink gins and led the way to a table beside a window.

'Now I do recall threatening you with a story,' he said as they settled into their seats.

'Frankie Pearson,' Maria reminded him.

'Ah, yes, Frankie ... Now this was in the days of yore, way back in the late twenties, if I remember rightly. Probably before you were even born, Maria. I can't recall first meeting Frankie – he was a hanger-on to a group of tearaways I knew while at Oxford, though Frankie hadn't schooled anywhere with distinction. I think we rather patronized him. He was still wet behind the ears, and barely out of his teens – and not, I repeat *not* – the nasty little cad he turned out to be in later life. If truth be told, and my memory is to be trusted, I do think he was rather sweet.'

Langham smiled to himself. Sweet did not describe the jaded, washed-up hack, running to fat and vindictive, he'd known just after the war.

'He was bisexual – a sexual opportunist, I thought of him at the time – with neither the guts to commit to *our* side, nor the decency to settle down with a good woman. He was full of braggadocio about his conquests, but with little hard evidence. I felt rather sorry for him, and decided to play cupid.'

'You said you introduced him to writing?'

'I'm coming to that, dear boy. Do curb your impatience. I introduced him to Nathaniel De Silva and to the writing game in one fell swoop.' Charles sipped his drink, declared it divine, and continued, 'I was in thrall to Wilde and Bosie and Swinburne at the time, and I harboured the desire to pen immortal lines myself. I swam in literary circles and paddled at the feet of the greats. I also knew a lot of pretenders and literary dilettantes. Nathaniel was one such, a sweet child of Jamaican extraction who was quite devoted to me. When I suggested he bestow his favours upon Frankie, he fell to the task like a man possessed. They had a torrid affair, so I heard; quite torrid. Frankie was besotted; Nathaniel less so, and it ended in tears. They had a blazing row when Nathaniel informed Frankie that their affair was over, and in the ensuing mêlée Nathaniel pulled a knife and ran it through Frankie's midriff. The affair was hushed up and Nathaniel fled the country. Frankie made a full recovery and sported a horrendous scar, rather like a starfish, just under his ribcage, which he was forever wont to exhibit when in his cups.'

'But how,' Langham asked, smiling to himself, 'did this introduce him to writing?'

'Oh, you doubt my skill as a raconteur, my boy? I am coming, somewhat circuitously I must admit, to the meat of my story. You see, Frankie had always fancied himself with the pen, but had shown little talent for any genre. It occurred to him, in his hospital bed, that he might use his experiences and write a purple tale of skulduggery and knife crime. And I must admit the resulting shocker did, while admittedly a potboiler, show promise. I was starting the agency around this time – this was back in 'twenty-eight – and took Frankie on as one of my first clients, more I think now through a sense of duty than with any expectations of fostering his literary talents. In the end I was proved correct. Each book he produced was far worse than the last one, and the day came when enough, as they say, was enough, and I told Frankie straight that his latest effort was unpublishable. I think I also added that he would be better suited to less cerebral work.'

'He should have taken your advice,' Langham said, 'though one or two of his books in the thirties were OK.'

Charles peered at him over his pince-nez.

173

'Your judgement shows the same failings as your reviews, Donald. You are just *too* kind.'

Maria said, 'Do you know why he took his life, Donald? He left a note?'

'Nigel didn't say. He did mention that Pearson was living in squalor towards the end, drinking too much and churning out cowboy books.'

'A sad final chapter to a sad life,' Charles said.

'Anyway, the reason Nigel rang was to twist my arm to go to Frankie's memorial service in the morning. I said I'd attend, to make up the numbers.' He looked at Charles. 'I don't suppose...?'

'Do you know,' said Charles, 'I think I might just do so. It will take my mind off things, and I might bump into a few old faces.'

'From what Nigel said about the likely attendance, we might be the only faces there. Frankie didn't have many friends towards the end.'

'All the more reason to attend,' Charles said gravely. 'Now, who is for another drink?'

While Charles swanned off to the bar, Maria moved her chair closer to Langham's. She took his hand and smiled into his eyes. 'Thank you for the flowers, Donald. I've been meaning to ring you, but I've been so busy in the office.'

He squeezed her hand, wishing they had the evening to themselves.

'I'm looking forward to the weekend at Charles's,' she said.

'I'll pick you up around eleven on Saturday morning. We could always stop somewhere for lunch.'

'That would be magnificent.'

They pulled apart as Charles approached with the drinks, and his agent proposed a toast. 'To friends!' he declared.

'To friends,' they laughed.

FIFTEEN

A dozen sombre individuals – Langham found it hard to think of them as mourners – kicked their heels outside St Mary's Church the following morning. It was a better turnout than he'd expected and he wondered if the majority had attended because, like him, they felt sorry for Frankie Pearson and harboured not a little residual guilt. He recalled his acerbic review of Pearson's novel *Death on the Farm* and wished he'd shown the same disinclination to lambast bad novels then as he did now.

He was entering the church when he saw Charles's silver Bentley pull up with a jolt. Charles struggled out and hurried up the path, puffing and sweating like the last runner across the finish line in a particularly gruelling cross-country marathon.

'Nearly didn't make it, my boy,' he panted as they filed through the porch. 'Roadworks in Knightsbridge, would you believe!'

Langham felt solemnity descend on him as they passed into the cold environs of the church. Morning sunlight exploded through an enfilade of stained-glass windows, sending a display of polychromatic light dancing across the pews. Organ music droned mournfully.

He glanced around at the men and women quietly seating themselves. There were three representatives from Frankie Pearson's last publisher, Hubert and Shale, and a writer from the same stable. Langham recognized Pearson's agent Dorothy Crawley, her mouse-like assistant, and three other mystery writers. He was surprised to see the eminent crime writer and critic Justin Fellowes in attendance, and wondered at his association with Pearson. The Grand Old Man of crime smiled at him sadly and murmured, 'Good to see you here, Donald. Frightful business.'

Everyone present, Langham thought as he slipped into a pew beside Nigel Lassiter, knew Pearson through his work. There was not one mourner here who wasn't in some way associated with the trade – no family member or loved one. What a send off: not a loved one in sight and a gathering of stage mourners who'd rather be elsewhere. It seemed morbidly appropriate that even Frankie Pearson himself was not present.

Langham leaned over and whispered to Lassiter, 'Why a memorial service and not a funeral?'

Lassiter said, 'Police haven't released his body yet.' His breath reeked of beer.

Langham thought of Pearson's cold corpse, lying in a mortuary somewhere, while thirteen reluctant mourners acted out this meaningless charade.

176

A palsied, geriatric clergyman climbed into the pulpit, gripped the oak rail and declared in a frail falsetto, 'We are here today not to mourn the passing of Frank Edward Pearson but to celebrate his life...'

The service was a travesty, and like others he'd attended seemed to be a false representation of the life it purported to commemorate. He looked around at the stony faces and wondered if they, too, were embarrassed on the dead man's behalf. The parson, clearly knowing nothing about the quality of Pearson's work – only that he was a published writer – commended the man for his contribution to the hallowed literature of the land.

'In his industry down the years – and Frank Edward Pearson was publishing for almost thirty years – he was an inspiration to us all. He provided not only entertainment for tens of thousands of eager readers the length and breadth of Britain, and I daresay across the world, but an insight into the human condition and the working of the human mind...'

Lassiter grunted, 'Obviously hasn't read *Ambush at Cooper's Gulch.*'

Langham closed his eyes and wished he was elsewhere. The clichés rolled on, and ten minutes later the parson culminated his eulogy with, '...and while Frank Edward Pearson's passing was by his own hand, and who knows what pressures moved him to the act, his life was in its own way heroic and he left us a corpus of work for which we can all be thankful...' He cleared his throat and said, 'Please turn to page three

177

hundred and fifty-two in the hymn book and be upstanding for *Weep not for a Brother Deceased.*'

The hymn was followed by an address by his agent, Dorothy Crawley, who stood hesitantly before the congregation. 'I for one would like to echo the sentiments of the Reverend Jones. While it cannot be said that Frankie, as his colleagues knew him, was a great writer, what he lacked in talent he more than made up for in industry. It is a little-known fact that he published over a hundred books in his lifetime – many pseudonymous, it is true – but among the titles written under his own name one or two stand out as examples of excellent storytelling...'

A hundred books, many under pen names, alcoholism, death by suicide at the age of fifty-two, and a memorial service more farcical than commemorative ... Langham stared at the beauty of the stained-glass windows and wished the service over and done with.

Crawley went on: 'Frankie wrote me a letter just before his death, which I received shortly after I heard about his passing. It was not a suicide note as such, but certain passages do read like the musings of a man contemplating the end. I would like to read out a few lines.' She coughed decorously, unfolded a sheet of paper, and continued, '"I have never feared death," Frankie wrote, "seeing it as the start of possibilities at which we cannot even guess. As a philosopher once said, Death is but a sleep and a remembering..."' She lowered the paper and smiled. 'Thank you.'

Another hymn was sung, the Lord's Prayer intoned, and the parson uttered a final anodyne few words before allowing the captives to flee into the sunlight.

Charles breathed deeply of the fresh air. 'Poor old Frankie. He even misquoted Gandhi. I think the line should have gone, "Death is but a sleep and a forgetting".'

A representative from Hubert and Shale made the rounds and invited the mourners back to their offices for drinks. Charles accepted with fulsome thanks. Langham declined, citing the pressures of work.

Nigel Lassiter buttonholed him as he was about to slip from the gathering. 'Donald. Fancy a quick pint? The Fox and Hounds is just around the corner. I'd like a word.' He lit up a Pall Mall.

Langham capitulated. 'But just the one. Still haven't finished the bloody reviewing.'

He said goodbye to Charles, shook hands with Dorothy Crawley and Justin Fellowes, and left the churchyard with Lassiter.

'Well, how did a man of your atheistical sensibilities find that, Donald?'

'Meaningless and terribly sad, to tell the truth. I applaud Dorothy for her thoughtfulness. I thought her address struck the right note. But I should have ignored your arm-twisting and stayed away.'

'I'll buy you a pint in compensation.'

The public bar of the Fox and Hounds was busy with lunchtime drinkers. Lassiter and Langham carried their pints out to a cobbled yard behind the pub. They sat at a table in the

179

sunlight and Langham loosened his tie.

Lassiter tipped half the contents of his glass past his liverish lips. 'There's something I'd like your opinion on, Donald.'

'Fire away.'

Lassiter shook his head. 'Who can work out what goes through the human mind?'

Langham smiled, eying Lassiter warily. 'Are you turning philosophical in your old age?'

'Hardly,' Lassiter grunted. 'Just wondering what went through Frankie's head in the days before he topped himself.'

'We'll never know, and it's probably just as well.'

'Had a letter, arrived just this morning. From Frankie's solicitor. Frankie made a will and left me something.'

Langham lowered his pint and stared. 'Left you something?'

'I know, bizarre.'

'I thought you parted on terms worse than acrimonious?'

'You said it. Far worse. Did I tell you I had a phone call from him a couple of years ago, just after I won the Silver Dagger? He was pissed, almost incoherent. Ranted for a while, asking me how it felt, how Mr Big-Shot-Award-Winner felt while "the rest of us are swimming in piss in the gutter?" I just hung up on him and took the phone off the hook when he tried to call again.'

'And you say he's left you something?'

Lassiter gestured with his cigarette. 'When I read the letter, and the first line or so said I was a beneficiary of Frankie's will, I thought he'd

180

left me his author's copies of his entire opus. Kind of an ironic parting shot. Typical spiteful thing he'd do.'

'But?'

'Frankie had a place in the country. Tiny cottage in Kent. Back in the thirties, when we wrote those three collabs together, that's where we wrote them. Get away from the rat race, hole up in solitude. Write during the day, go to the pub in the evening. Anyway, turns out Frankie left me the cottage.'

Langham blew in surprise. 'That *is* strange.'

'Exactly what I thought. Thing is, I can't accept it, can I? One, I really don't need a dilapidated cottage in the middle of nowhere, and two, without bragging, I really don't need the money if I were to sell it. And I don't want to keep it. Too many bad memories. Too many reminders of how I treated the poor sod.' He stared into his drink, morose.

'So, what are you going to do?'

'It occurred to me I could sell the place and put up the proceeds to fund some kind of award. I don't know – the Frank Pearson First Novel Award or something.'

Langham sensed a note of doubt in his voice. 'Only?'

'Only, Donald, to be honest what kind of credibility would an award have that bore Frankie's name? Let's face it – he was a fifth-rate hack of unreadable potboilers. No poor first-timer would want to be saddled with the bloody accolade!'

'You're right. It wouldn't be a good idea. Why not just donate the proceeds to charity? The

Writer's Hardship Fund.'

Lassiter laughed. 'Is there such a thing? Well, it'd be appropriate.'

'Just made it up,' Langham said. 'But for what it's worth, that's what I'd do. Donate the lot to charity.'

Lassiter nodded. 'Good idea, Donald. I'll think it over.' He sighed and drained his pint. 'I'm meeting the solicitor down there tomorrow morning to sign a few papers and pick up the keys.' He smiled. 'It'll bring back memories. The time we wrote those damned novels ... To be perfectly honest, I quite enjoyed the fortnight we spent on each book. Frankie was tolerable company back then, before ... Well, before I did the dirty on him.'

Langham clapped his friend on the shoulder. 'Don't be hard on yourself. Anyone would have done the same thing. How about another pint?'

'Thought you only wanted one?'

'I'm in no real hurry, and that one slipped down without touching the sides.'

He collected the empties and made his way inside.

It was four o'clock by the time he arrived home, four pints worse off and wishing he'd never gone to the bloody service. He made himself a strong pot of Earl Grey and began reading the fourth review book. He found himself skimming, then skipping. Towards six o'clock he read the last ten pages to confirm that the dénouement was as predictable as he'd expected, then dashed off two hundred words commending the author's readable prose while criticizing the formulaic finale. Harsh, for him. Grenville at the *Herald* would be pleased. He'd deliver the copy in the morning before he picked up Maria.

The thought of her warmed his evening. He made himself a plate of beans on toast and ate it slowly, with a bottle of Double Diamond, while listening to the news on the Third Programme.

That night he slept badly, his dreams haunted by images of Charles. His agent was behind bars, striding back and forth and declaiming, with the eloquence of a thespian born, at the injustice of his incarceration.

SIXTEEN

On Saturday morning Langham woke late with a throbbing head and a sand-pit mouth. He told himself that he should never have indulged in the Double Diamond on top of yesterday's lunchtime session. He washed down a couple of slices of toast with three mugs of strong tea, then ran himself a hot bath.

That morning's post brought a pleasant surprise, which occasionally – very occasionally, he thought – befell the freelance writer. The proprietor of a hotel near Felixstowe was an avid reader of the Sam Brooke books. His late wife, he wrote, had also enjoyed the novels, and the

183

last six months of her life had been 'brightened by your expert storytelling'. In acknowledgement of the pleasure Langham had brought to her last months, the proprietor – he glanced at the letter heading – a Mr Sellings, would be honoured if he would accept an expenses-paid weekend for two at the hotel. Enclosed with the letter was a leaflet showing a white-painted Victorian building overlooking a picturesque cove.

The unexpected rewards of pounding the keys, he thought.

He set the letter aside as an idea formed. Perhaps in a few weeks, if his relationship with Maria developed as he hoped it might, he would suggest a quiet break on the Suffolk coast. He would write to Mr Sellings on Monday morning, thanking him for his kindness and gratefully accepting the offer.

A second letter proved to be the official invitation for the annual spring London Crime Club dinner at the Albemarle Club, Pall Mall, next Wednesday. He hadn't missed a meeting since the war, and he made a mental note to reply to the invitation.

He packed a suitcase in excellent spirits, remembered to pick up the envelope containing the reviews, and headed into the city.

He found a parking space just along the road from the *Herald*, left the engine turning over and ran up the steps into the building. The newsroom was as hectic as usual and there was no sign of Grenville at the review's desk. Langham left the envelope propped against a telephone and got out fast, before Grenville appeared and chastised him for late delivery.

He motored to Kensington, whistling a dance band tune he'd heard on the wireless and which seemed to be lodged in his head like a virus. Rain had fallen during the night, but now the sun was shining and the forecast for the rest of the weekend was good: sun over the east of England with temperatures in the low seventies.

He left the car outside Maria's apartment and took the steps two at a time. Still whistling, he rang the bell and waited. A minute later the door opened and Maria stood framed in the entrance, stunning in a flowing red gingham dress.

She laughed at his mute reaction. 'You like, Donald? Papa bought it for me.'

'You look wonderful.'

'Good. Now please stop gawping and help me with this case, would you?'

He obliged, and a minute later they were motoring north. 'This is exciting, Donald. To be leaving London and heading into the country.'

'I'll say. I've known Charles for twenty years, Maria, and I've never once seen his country pile.'

'Never? I have been only once, when he held a party and invited me and my father. It's a rather nice place, I think Georgian, in beautiful grounds. Did you know that it's the Elders' family seat, and has been in the family for almost three hundred years?'

'Someone once did tell me that Charles's forbears were minor aristocracy. He certainly acts the part.'

'Charles is a dear. Oh—' She laid confiding

fingers on his arm. 'I haven't told you. Charles came back to the office from the service at five o'clock yesterday and he was rather merry. He said he went back to the publishers for drinks afterwards.'

'Hubert and Shale were hosting a do. I ducked out.'

'Well, Charles didn't, and he was in such a good mood when he returned that he made me an offer.'

Langham put on a mock-horrified expression. 'Not of marriage?'

She hit him. 'Silly! Of course not. He made a long speech, as only Charles can, about how indispensable I was to the running of the agency and how, as he would soon no longer be around to oversee the business, he wanted to do more than just leave it in my hands. So he said that now was the time to make me a business partner. He said he'd have Mr Winstanley draw up the papers.'

Langham slapped the steering wheel. 'That's magnificent, Maria. Well done.'

She was beaming to herself. 'The strange thing is, just a few days ago I was wondering where my life was going. I liked working for Charles, but a part of me wanted to move on ... and yet I felt reluctant to let him down. And then, *pfff*! All this happened, and...' She stopped suddenly.

He felt his mouth go dry. He stared ahead, gripping the wheel. 'Yes?'

She was silent. They were barrelling along a quiet stretch of road through Epping Forest. He turned to look at her.

She was regarding her impeccably manicured fingernails, pressed against the material of her dress, and said in a soft voice, 'And then you became more than just a face, more than just one among many of Charles's authors. You became someone ... *real*. Oh, that sounds silly, but you know what I mean. You became someone who showed that he cared for Charles and would stand by him whatever, someone who was brave and...'

He said, 'Go on, I'm rather liking this.'

She laughed. 'What I'm trying to say is, how could I leave the agency now that all this has happened...?'

He was unable to find the appropriate words in response, so he just reached out and squeezed her fingers.

She sighed happily and said at the top of her voice, 'Oh, I want to take long walks in the countryside and then eat wonderful meals – and maybe even beat you at tennis!'

'Charles has a court?'

She nodded. 'I played with my father when we came up last year.'

'Then we'll have a game, and you'll no doubt beat me because I'm rubbish.'

'How about croquet?'

'Never played. The only game I could play with any skill was cricket.'

'Oh, what a silly English game!' she laughed.

He wound down the window, now that the city was behind them, and admitted the fragrance of the countryside.

One hour later they arrived at the sleepy town

of Bury St Edmunds, and Langham pulled into the car park of the Midland Hotel. He'd read somewhere that they did decent lunches.

'Hungry?' he asked.

'I could eat a horse.'

'I doubt *cheval* is on the menu, my dear. You'll have to make do with ham salad.'

They ate in the plush dining room overlooking the cathedral, and Maria did opt for a cold meat salad while Langham ordered whiting with chips and peas.

He smiled as he recalled something she'd said the other day, and he decided that now was as good a time as any to broach the matter. He pointed a fork at her. 'Last week you asked me if I'd ever written anything other than mystery stories, with the implication that I could do better.'

She assumed an expression of prim innocence. 'The implication? *Non.* That is entirely your presumption. Perhaps, Donald, *you* think you should be writing something better than mysteries?'

He had to laugh at her arch expression. 'You're playing psychological games with me, Maria.'

She leaned forward, lodged her chin on the back of her hand, and said, 'Why *do* you write only mysteries?'

He finished the whiting and pushed the plate aside. 'Well, there are a number of reasons. The first is that I enjoy writing them. The second is that that's what I'm known for, and changing horse midstream in this game is always a bit risky. And third ... third ... I'm not a literary snob. I put a lot of work into the novels and I think they're as good as I can make them.' He shrugged. 'I grew up in a family which wasn't at all bookish. I discovered novels late, when I was around fifteen – picked up a Bulldog Drummond in the public library ... and the rest, as they say, is history.'

She pulled a face. 'Bulldog Drummond?'

He laughed. 'Well, I wasn't politically aware back then. I just wanted a rattling good yarn.'

'But you've never thought of writing a real novel?'

'Never. I'm happy doing what I do.'

She finished her salad. 'Do you know, I think you should write a literary novel about ... about a young man who falls in love.'

He stared into her eyes, something preventing the glib reply that sprang to his lips. He just stared at her, and she returned his gaze, smiling to herself, and he had never felt more like kissing anyone than he did at that moment.

The magic was broken by the waiter enquiring, 'Will that be all, sir? Dessert?'

'Oh...' Langham said. 'No, not for me. Maria?'

'Nor for me either, thank you.'

'Just the bill, please.'

As they were leaving the hotel she slipped her hand into his, and the gesture felt like the most intimate he had experienced in a long, long time.

They set off on the last leg of the journey, and Langham indicated a road map in the passenger footwell. Maria retrieved it and found the relevant page. 'Where are we now?' she asked.

189

'Coming out of Bury St Edmunds and heading towards Thetford.'

'Ah, *oui*. Here we are. And Charles's house is just outside a village called ... here it is. Meadford. We are about five miles away.' She gave him directions. 'The house is set back from the lane and hidden behind lots of trees.'

Fifteen minutes later they passed through the chocolate-box village of Meadford and Langham turned right after the church. He slowed down as Maria placed a hand on his arm and said, 'Somewhere around here, to the left. Ah, there...' She pointed.

He braked quickly and turned into a wide driveway. It had evidently rained here during the night as the drive was patched with silver puddles, reflecting the sunlight. He splashed through the rainwater and followed the drive as it swung around a stand of rhododendron.

Charles's Bentley stood before the brilliant white façade of the Georgian mansion.

Langham whistled. 'I never realized it would be quite this grand.'

'Fifteen bedrooms, a ballroom, and a library you will love, Donald.'

'I should be appalled.'

She looked at him. 'And are you?'

He laughed. 'I would be if it belonged to anyone other than Charles. So much for my political credentials.'

'Come on, let's go and see the Englishman in his castle.'

They climbed out of the car and Langham carried their cases to the imposing front door. He rang the bell. 'I wonder what they make of Charles in the village?' he mused.

'I think they see him as a rather loveable uncle. He's forever opening church fêtes and flower shows.'

'The bigwig London agent playing the squire.'

Maria regarded him shrewdly. 'You're so very different from Charles, but you like him a lot, don't you?'

'I've known him for twenty years. He's always been kind and supportive to me. And he's the soul of generosity. How could I not like him?'

'Even though he represents minor aristocracy and privilege?'

Langham shrugged. 'He can't help what he is ... on many levels.' He peered through the etched glass at the chessboard-tiled hallway and rang the bell again. 'Come on, Charles!'

A minute later he said, 'I'll take a wander ... try the tradesman's entrance.'

He left the plinth of steps and walked along the front of the building, peering into the house; he must have passed four sets of rooms before arriving at the corner. In London, Charles lived in his rather modest Pimlico apartment, but this was an order of luxury on an altogether different scale.

He turned the corner and walked until he came to a door beside the kitchen window. He peered through, but the room was empty. He knocked on the door, then tried the handle. The door was locked.

He returned to Maria, who was still kicking her heels before the main entrance.

191

'No luck?'

He shook his head. 'You don't think Charles has forgotten that he invited us, do you?'

She bit her lip worriedly. 'That would be quite unlike Charles,' she said. 'Perhaps if we try the door, yes?'

'Right-ho.' He approached the imposing door and turned the big brass handle, and to his surprise the door opened. 'Well, what do you know?'

He stepped into a big hallway, deposited the cases by a hatstand, and followed Maria along the corridor, marvelling at the sumptuous decorations as he went. Carved marble figures and swelling Chinese vases occupied alcoves set into the wall, which was hung with oil paintings depicting rural scenes.

'He might be in the conservatory,' Maria said. 'This way.'

They came to a pair of double doors at the end of the corridor. Maria opened them and peered in. A riot of potted palms and assorted vines gave the room an incongruous jungle aspect. 'Charles!' she called out.

Langham made out a wicker armchair next to a small table bearing a tray of drinks; a second table was loaded with bound manuscripts. He imagined his agent enjoying a sundowner while reading and imagining himself in Africa.

'We could try the library,' Maria suggested. 'It's the next room.'

They retraced their steps along the corridor to the next door. Langham was about to knock when he heard a sound from within the room.

192

Maria cocked her head. 'There is someone in the library, Donald.'

The voices were faint at first, but as they listened the conversation became louder.

'If you think...' Charles's unmistakable tones declared.

He was cut off by someone replying in a low, gruff voice.

'Absurd!' Charles cried.

Alarmed, Langham rapped on the door. 'Charles?' He reached out and turned the handle, and to his frustration found the door locked.

He knocked again, this time with urgency. 'Charles!'

Maria clutched his arm, staring at him with massive eyes.

Langham heard Charles's cry from within the library, quickly followed by a curse from whoever was in there with him.

He turned to Maria. 'Stand back...'

He backed across the room, took a run at the door and hit it with his shoulder. He felt the lock give a little, backed up and tried again. A second before he impacted with the door, a startlingly loud gunshot rang out. Maria screamed. Langham hit the oak panel with his shoulder and the lock gave way. The momentum of his charge carried him staggering into the library.

He saw two things at once: Charles, lying in a quickly expanding pool of blood before the hearth, and a mackintoshed figure fleeing through the French windows and racing across the rear lawn.

He dashed across the room and knelt beside

Charles, stifling a cry of rage. His agent lay on his back, eyes closed, a great red mark staining the front of his waistcoat. Langham felt for his pulse and found the faint suggestion of one in Charles's padded wrist.

He looked up at Maria, advancing into the room with her fingers to her lips. 'Call an ambulance and the police!' he called. 'Quickly!'

She was sobbing. 'There's a phone in the hall...' She stumbled away in shock.

As soon as she was gone, Langham looked around in desperation and snatched an antimacassar from a nearby chair. Anything, he thought, to staunch the flow of blood. He wadded the material and pressed it to the wound.

Maria appeared a minute later. 'They're on their way.'

'Come here and take over,' Langham ordered. 'There's nothing we can do but try to stem the bleeding.' As Maria knelt beside him and took the rapidly soaking material, he rushed across to a small bar in the corner of the room and found what he was looking for. He returned to the hearth with a handful of bar towels and dropped them beside Maria.

She looked up at him, tears in her eyes. 'Donald?'

He moved to the French windows and peered out. The gunman was at the far end of the vast lawn, disappearing into the shrubbery. Without a thought as to the possible danger Langham gave chase, sprinting from the library and across the lawn and ignoring Maria's faint cry behind him. With luck he would have surprise on his side, and might even succeed in running the gunman to ground in the woods.

He came to the border of shrubbery and dived through. He stopped and listened intently, making out the crash of someone running through the undergrowth to his right. He set off, following the sound and wishing that he was still armed with Ralph Ryland's revolver. Failing that, he should have thought to pick up a poker from beside the hearth. Though, on second thoughts, a poker would be little use against a killer armed with a pistol.

He was beginning to flag, his breath ragged and painful. Twenty yards further on the wood was bisected by a muddy lane. Langham remained in the cover of a laurel tree and peered out. Fifty yards to his left the gunman was mounting a motorbike. As Langham watched, impotent, the man kicked the bike into life and skidded off down the lane. Seconds later he passed from sight around a bend and Langham felt an odd sense of relief and frustration that he had been unable to apprehend the gunman.

He turned and ran through the woods, fearing that when he returned to the library he would find Charles Elder dead and Maria beside herself with grief.

A minute later he came to the French windows and stepped inside. Maria was still on the floor beside Charles's body, and when Langham entered she looked up with vast brown eyes veneered by tears. She pressed down on Charles's massive chest, holding one of the bar towels which was quickly turning red as it

195

blotted the blood. The pathetic sight of it, and Maria's desperate efforts to save his agent's life, brought tears to his eyes.

He took up another towel and knelt beside her. She removed her sodden one and instantly blood pooled. He applied the second towel and pressed, knowing in his heart of hearts that the gesture was futile.

He stared down at Charles's waxy face. His agent seemed unconscious, unaware of what had happened and hopefully in no pain.

'It was the same gunman,' Langham murmured. 'He got away on a motorbike.'

Maria stared at him. Big tears tracked down her cheeks. She shook her head. 'I don't understand,' she sobbed. 'Why would he do this?'

Langham stared down at Maria's hands, which appeared to be wearing gloves of dripping crimson. He glanced at his own hands, feeling the heat of Charles's lifeblood.

He experienced a succession of very intense, rapid emotions: sorrow and anger, visceral repulsion at the physical effect of one small bullet, followed by a numbing sense of shock which seemed to crash through him, rendering him speechless.

He found himself thinking: no more grandiloquent monologues, no more expansive, trademark stories of his younger days; no more heartfelt soliloquies praising the finer things of life; no more wonderful, frivolous, generous queer old Charles Elder.

He had the sudden vision of Charles at breakfast a few days ago, singing the praises of the humble kidney...

He felt a sensation in his throat like acid and tears stung his eyes. His hands otherwise occupied, he was unable to do anything other than let the tears flow.

It seemed like an hour later, though it might have been just minutes, when he heard the sound of vehicles crunching gravel in the drive.

He looked at Maria. 'The ambulance, with luck. Hurry and tell them where we are.'

She nodded and dashed off, and he turned the towel in order to find a dry section with which to soak up the blood. It was still pumping out, which he supposed was a good sign as it signalled that Charles was hanging on to life.

Two ambulance men, followed by Maria, a sergeant and a constable, hurried into the library. The ambulance men crossed to Langham and knelt beside Charles. One of them swore pithily and the other told Langham, in unceremonious terms, to give them room.

Langham stood and backed away, looking down at his blood-soaked hands. Maria passed him a towel, already stained with blood from her own hands. They crossed to a chaise longue and sat down while, across the room, the ambulance men cut away Charles's waistcoat and worked on the wound.

The next ten minutes passed in a blur. He was aware of recounting what had happened to the sergeant, who took down his statement in a tiny notebook. The ambulance men loaded Charles on to a stretcher and manoeuvred him – with difficulty – from the library. As they passed, Maria stood hesitantly and approached them. 'Do you think...?' she began.

The leading ambulance man didn't spare her a glance as he eased the stretcher through the door, but said, 'Never can tell, love. But I'd pray, if I were you.'

She returned to Langham's side, clutched his hand and asked the sergeant if they would be allowed to follow the ambulance to the hospital.

'I'm sorry, miss. I've called in an Inspector Bryce from Bury St Edmunds. He should be here in five minutes. By all means, after he's taken your statements...'

Maria nodded and dried her eyes on a small lace kerchief.

The sergeant moved to the door, where he stationed himself next to the constable.

Maria said in barely a whisper, 'But, Donald...' She pressed her fingers to her temples and screwed her eyes shut. She opened them and stared at him. 'It doesn't make sense!'

Numb, he said, 'What doesn't?'

'Why would the motorcyclist – the very same man who blackmailed Charles ... why would he murder him? It just doesn't make sense!'

'I know,' he said. 'It's the same question we asked ourselves earlier, when we wondered why the blackmailer sent the incriminating photographs to the police. Why would he terminate a potentially lucrative source of income? Now we're asking ourselves why would the blackmailer want to *kill* Charles?'

Maria shook her head. 'I don't know. I just don't know!'

Langham thought about it. He had the inkling of an idea, and said tentatively, 'Perhaps we've been looking at it from the wrong angle.'

She pouted her lips at him in a typically French gesture. 'We are?'

'Perhaps the blackmail was just a ruse. Perhaps the blackmailer designed the entire charade, the photos, the blackmail, to...'

She was watching him with big eyes as he formulated his thoughts. 'OK,' he went on. 'I'm thinking aloud here ... But what if the gunman never planned to shoot Charles in this way?'

She shrugged. 'I do not understand.'

'We interrupted the gunman, didn't we? How about this – the gunman shot Charles in panic because we'd arrived on the scene and I was battering the door down. But he never intended to shoot him *like that*.'

Maria said, 'So ... what did he intend to do?'

Langham stared at the blood-soaked rug and murmured, 'He intended to kill Charles, but stage the killing so that it appeared to be a suicide. He'd rig it so that the police, and everyone else, would take it as the suicide of a man depressed about the fact that he would soon be sent to jail.'

Maria stared at him. 'But who would do that, Donald?'

'Someone who had such a grudge against Charles that they wanted him dead, but dead in such a way as to make it appear at first glance like suicide. Then the killer would not be implicated in the death.'

She was silent for a while, then said, 'Poor,

poor Charles.'

'What I'd like to know,' Langham went on, 'is who might bear Charles such a grudge that they would want to kill him? He doesn't have an enemy in the world, does he? You work with him – you know his contacts in publishing.'

'Charles is well liked. I've never met anyone who has a bad word to say about him. I know this is a cliché, but he was – *is* – a good man.'

Five minutes later Inspector Bryce from Bury St Edmunds arrived, a thin, dour-faced Lancastrian in his forties. He questioned Langham and Maria in much greater detail than the sergeant had, and Langham gave him the background details concerning the blackmail and the motorbike-riding gunman.

Bryce looked up from his notebook. 'But why would the blackmailer resort to murder?'

Langham repeated what he'd told Maria about his suicide theory.

'Well, it's a possibility, I suppose,' Bryce said grudgingly. 'I'll liaise with my London colleagues on the matter. I'd like you to accompany me to the station where I'll take a more formal statement, if you don't mind.'

Langham glanced across the room at the blood-soaked rug on which Charles had lain.

Inspector Bryce said, 'Do you know if Mr Elder had next of kin who need informing, miss?'

'He had no one,' Maria said.

They left the house and followed Inspector Bryce and his colleague back to the station at Bury St Edmunds.

It was getting on for eight later that evening when Bryce concluded that he had all the necessary information and allowed them to go. The inspector gave Langham the directions to the hospital to which Charles had been admitted, and the sun was going down in a gorgeous laminate of tangerine and pewter as they left the police station and made the short drive to the infirmary.

Five minutes later, after giving their names at reception, a matron told them that due to the severity of his wounds Charles had been transferred by ambulance to the Chelsea Royal Hospital in London, where he was due to undergo an emergency operation upon arrival.

'We'll go straight to the hospital,' Langham said as they returned to the car. 'I'd rather be there, for all the good it'll do, than go straight home.'

Maria nodded. 'I agree, Donald.'

They set off on the long drive south to London.

They were silent for what seemed like an age, in contrast to earlier in the day when they had talked non-stop. At last Maria said quietly, 'I'm not sure, Donald, that I want to spend the night alone in my flat.'

He nodded. 'I have a spare bedroom at my place, if you'd care to...?'

She smiled at him. 'If you don't mind, that is.'

'Of course not.'

Another, longer silence settled between them.

They drove through Epping Forest, with dark and encroaching trees on either side. Oddly the lights of London, when they drove through Walthamstow thirty minutes later, seemed equally as threatening, as if their gaudy brightness did nothing but emphasize the surrounding darkness.

One hour later they were back at Langham's flat, having stopped at the Chelsea Royal only to be told that Charles had just gone into the operating theatre and would be under the knife for a couple of hours – and then would be in no fit state to receive visitors. They had decided to go home and return first thing in the morning.

Langham made a pot of Earl Grey and carried the tray into the front room overlooking the quiet street.

Maria stood and, cup and saucer in hand, moved to the hearth. He watched her as she examined the photographs lined up on the mantelshelf: sepia prints of his mother and father in their younger days, one or two of himself as a child, and wartime photographs taken by colleagues in Madagascar and India.

She placed her cup on the mantelshelf and picked up the photograph of Langham and his wife, taken shortly after their wedding in 'thirty-seven.

'Who is this, Donald?'

He said, 'Susan, my wife.'

She looked him. 'Charles told me that...'

Langham moved to her side. 'She died, back in 'forty-one.'

'I'm sorry.'

'I was stationed up in Fife. On exercises with field security. I had a telegram from her sister.

202

Susan had collapsed at work – the sorting office at Hackney post office. Apparently she died instantly. Cerebral haemorrhage.'

He would never forget the train journey south from Edinburgh, the intolerable delays at every station between there and King's Cross. He would never forget the pain of knowing that Susan was dead, nor the guilt that underlay the sadness: guilt at the fact that he could not help but feel an incredible sense of being freed from a terrible incarceration.

A guilt that resurfaced still, from time to time, and kept him awake at night.

'Things hadn't been well between us for years,' he said. 'Looking back, I realize it wasn't a successful marriage.' He smiled. 'She was my very first girlfriend, and Susan wasn't much more experienced. My father advised against it, but I was only twenty-one when we met.'

He often wondered what might have happened had Susan not died back in 'forty-one, if their marriage would have stumbled on, each of them too weak and hidebound by convention to suggest separation; if they would have remained together in the mutually, emotionally injurious union ... The thought appalled him, and only increased his guilt at the sense of liberation he felt then and still felt to this day.

'She was very pretty.'

He found himself saying, 'I can't really see that. All I recall when I look at the picture is the argument we had immediately after it was taken ... and I can't even remember what we argued about.'

'And yet you still keep her picture?'

He shrugged. The guilt, he thought. One day, he hoped, he would know Maria well enough to explain how he felt. 'More tea?'

She returned to the settee and he refilled her cup. She looked at him. 'Donald, I want you just to hold me, OK?'

He set down his tea cup and stroked a tress of jet-black hair from her cheek.

SEVENTEEN

Maria awoke suddenly and found herself staring up at a strange ceiling in a strange bedroom. Then she recalled the events of the day before and she experienced a quick surge of despair at what had happened to Charles.

Her thoughts were interrupted by a tap on the door. Donald called, 'Breakfast, Maria?'

'I would love some,' she said. 'Just give me a few minutes.'

She found the bathroom, washed and changed into a new dress she'd brought with her for the weekend at Charles's, and then joined Donald in the living room.

He was wearing a bear-coloured dressing gown over striped pyjamas, and she couldn't help but laugh.

'What?' he asked.

She pointed. 'You're wearing striped flannel pyjamas.'

He smiled. 'Well, perhaps it's not the most fetching apparel.'

'I'm surprised you're not gripping that funny old pipe of yours in your teeth,' she teased.

He made breakfast – fried eggs and toast and Earl Grey tea, and they ate at the table in the bay window of the front room, splashed with sunshine. 'What do you normally do on Sundays?' he asked.

'Nothing,' Maria said. 'That is, I get up late and have a leisurely breakfast, then maybe wander out and pick up a paper and come back and have a cup of tea and read ... and by that time it's mid-afternoon. Sometimes I go for afternoon tea with my father, and others I might catch up on a little reading for work. Sometimes I see friends, but not so often these days. They all seem to be married with children, and...' She stopped, suddenly self-conscious, and said, 'And you?'

'When I'm working on a book, I write. I don't see it as a day any different from the others. When I'm not writing I buy a paper, read, occasionally see friends.' He gestured. 'More tea?'

'Please.'

How pleasant it was to be in his company, she thought. She felt as though she ... *belonged*.

'What?' he said. 'You're smiling. Does my boring routine amuse you?'

She reached across the table and took his hand to reassure him. 'Of course not. Nothing of the kind. I was just thinking...' She smiled. 'Well, I was just thinking how safe I feel with you.'

He laughed at that. 'Safe? That speaks volumes about the kind of company you must keep.'

'Well, the last man who was interested in me did pull a gun and asked me to shoot him if I refused a date.'

'By Jove.' He stared at her above his toast. 'You didn't shoot him, I take it?'

'I refused, though I was tempted. So he turned the gun on himself.'

He lowered his toast, looking enthralled. 'What did you do?'

'Oh, I just slapped him across the face and told him to get out.'

'Attagirl! Well, I promise I won't pull any such theatrical stunts to win your heart.'

She smiled at him and almost said, 'You don't need to do anything to win my heart...' but stopped herself just in time.

She glanced across at the mantelshelf, to the photograph of his ex-wife. 'Has there been anyone since...?'

He finished chewing his toast and said, 'I met someone a few years ago. A sub-editor at my publishing house. We went out a few times.' He shrugged. 'I think she found me dashed boring and refused a fourth date.'

'Silly woman.'

'Well, the truth was I found her a tad dull, too. Not the type of woman to slap a gunman's face and order him to get out.' They finished breakfast and he looked at his watch. 'Ten o'clock. Shall we motor over to the Chelsea Royal and see how...?'

She smiled brightly. 'Perhaps Charles has managed to pull through?' she said.

He smiled reassuringly. 'Perhaps,' he said.

They drove to the hospital and Maria spoke to a blue-uniformed nurse on reception. She referred to a stack of paperwork and said, 'Mr Elder was admitted late last night and underwent an operation at ten. He's currently on ward five and not receiving visitors.'

'But he pulled through?' Langham asked.

The nurse glanced at a sheet of paper. 'He did, though I'm unsure as to the patient's condition at the moment. However, even though it isn't strictly visiting time, if you go to reception on ward five someone there might be able to tell you a little more.'

Maria thanked her and they made their way along tortuous, jade-coloured corridors, and then took a lift to the second floor. Ward five was a great dormitory of a room with windows overlooking south London.

A staff sister at the desk informed them that Mr Elder was in an isolation room and receiving round-the-clock attention, and under no circumstances was he to receive visitors. As she was speaking, a tall, white-coated doctor swept past and the sister called after him, 'Oh, Doctor Robinson ... I have friends here of Mr Charles Elder.'

Dr Robinson halted and looked Langham and Maria up and down. He was a lithe ex-RAF type with a bristling moustache and a brusque manner. In his gaze Maria discerned curiosity about the acquaintances of the gunshot victim.

'Right,' he snapped. 'Suppose you want the gen on the old man, hm? This way,' and without waiting he set off along the corridor. Maria exchanged a glance with Langham and followed.

Dr Robinson ushered them into a tiny room, where he sat behind a desk and said without preamble, 'First gunshot wound I've operated on since the war. Your friend was lucky he didn't succumb within the first hour. Lost a lot of blood.'

Maria began, 'Will he...?'

'Pull through?' Robinson pulled a face. 'Hard to tell. I've seen them peg out as a result of much less serious wounds. Then again I've seen men survive much worse.'

'Is he conscious now?' Langham asked.

'He's still unconscious, and that's giving us cause for concern. We usually like 'em to come round after the op, y'know. That said, it's not all sackcloth and ashes. Your friend's as tough as old boots, and lucky too, which helps.'

Maria took heart. 'Lucky?'

'I'll say. Bullet missed his heart and lungs by a whisker. Now in my experience if the lead misses the old pump'n'bellows it takes a nick out of the spine. Not in this case, though. Don't take this the wrong way, but your friend's on the big side and some of the lard stopped the bullet. I fished it out last night. Oh, it caused a bit of damage in there – lots of blood loss and trauma, but mark my word it could've been a damn sight worse.'

Maria shook her head. 'When might you know

if Charles will pull through?' she asked in a timorous voice.

'I'll be frank. Impossible to tell. Your friend has jumped a few hurdles, but there's the rest of the race to see out yet. And obstacles ahead: risk of infection, blood loss. You name it. Look here, ask at the desk for a direct line through to sister and she'll give you the gen a couple of times a day. Fair enough?'

Maria smiled. 'That's wonderful, Doctor.'

'If he survives a couple of days, then I'd say that the signs are good. If so, then you'll be able to visit, once the bobbies have vetted you, that is.'

'The "bobbies"?' she repeated.

'Stationed at his door. They don't want a repeat of the incident that brought him in here.'

'That is good to know,' she said.

Robinson glanced at his watch. 'Crikey, is that the time? And I'm supposed to be sawing off a leg at noon. If you'll excuse me...'

He hurried from the room, leaving Maria and Langham staring at each other in bemusement. They returned to reception and, after asking at the desk for the sister's number, made their way from the hospital. Maria glanced at Langham, who was shaking his head wryly.

'What?' she asked.

'Doctor Robinson,' he told her. 'He'll be appearing in my next novel.'

'He was something of a character, wasn't he? Oh, I just hope Charles will get better, Donald!'

He squeezed her hand. 'If anyone can save him, it'll be an oddball like Robinson.'

They arrived back at the car and Langham said, 'Well, if you've nothing planned for the rest of the day, how about a stroll across Hampstead Heath and afternoon tea somewhere?'

She smiled. 'Capital idea, Mr Langham. Oh ... It's my father's birthday today and he's having a little do at his place this evening.' A thought occurred to her. 'Would you like to come along as my guest? Papa would be delighted.'

He frowned. 'Would you mind awfully if I didn't? I'm not sure I'm up to being cheerful in public at the moment.'

'Of course. I understand.' She smiled, despite the disappointment. She really wanted her father to meet Donald, but she reflected that there would be plenty of time for that in the weeks to come.

They drove to Hampstead and strolled hand in hand across the Heath. As if by some tacit agreement they refrained from speaking about what had happened yesterday. She watched Langham light his pipe and puff prodigious billows of smoke, and she hung on his arm and insisted that he tell her all about his next novel.

He squinted at her. 'Thought you didn't like my books?'

'I never said anything of the kind! I might have asked why you didn't write something other than mysteries, perhaps.'

He puffed on his pipe. 'Very well ... The next one will be about the theft of a priceless work of art. I've had quite enough of murder and skulduggery for a while, thank you.'

They entered the café in the park and he

210

steered her towards an empty table. For the next ten minutes he outlined a convoluted plot about a gang of art thieves who fake the theft of an old master by placing a false wall before the painting. 'You see, on this *false* wall is a reproduction of the painting.'

'Hiding the original?' she asked. 'But how do they steal the original?'

'Simple. The wall on which the old master hangs is the shared wall of an empty workroom. They simply make a hole in the wall from the workroom, one night, and take the painting. Hey presto! What do you think?'

'Mmm...' she temporized. 'I think it needs work.'

He laughed. 'Perhaps you're right. But ideas always sound half-baked in précis.'

They ate cucumber sandwiches and drank tea and talked of nothing at all and, before she knew it, it was four o'clock.

'It's been a lovely afternoon, Donald,' she said as they left the café.

'I'll drive you home. We could...' he began. Then, 'Are you doing anything tomorrow evening?'

'Nothing at all.'

'Then would you like to go out for dinner?'

She reached up and kissed him. 'That would be wonderful.'

He dropped her off at her apartment and drove off slowly, waving from the window of his little car.

She bathed and changed into something suitable

for the party, staring at herself in the bathroom mirror as she dried her hair. She could not wait to tell her father about Donald, and she laughed at the thought like a lovesick schoolgirl.

Then she remembered Charles and felt a twinge of guilt at her levity.

Before she left the house she rang the hospital and was informed that there was no change in his condition. He was still unconscious, but stable. Maria thanked the nurse and replaced the receiver with a sigh.

At six, heavy of heart, she took a taxi to her father's house in Hampstead.

The party was already under way, with perhaps thirty guests occupying the drawing room in small clusters and constellations, the bright stars of French émigré society attended by the transitory comets of waiters with trays of drinks and canapés.

She accepted a white wine and crossed to where her father was entertaining a knot of dignitaries. She kissed his cheeks.

'Happy birthday, Papa.' She proffered him the present she had bought last week, an early edition of Voltaire's *Candide* to add to his collection.

'Maria, how kind! You certainly know how to spoil your father.' He took her arm.

'But come. The statuette arrived a few days ago. I've had it wrapped. Let us surprise Monsieur Savagne. He is in need of consolation. He attempted to locate the buyer, but of course failed. He knew you were coming and said you would brighten his flagging spirits. Little did he

212

know...'

She smiled as her father led her across to a bureau and unlocked it. He withdrew the wrapped statuette and presented it to her. 'Now, let us accost old Savagne and watch his face when he opens it.'

He led her across to the guests before the window. Maria held the statuette behind her back.

'Maria!' Savagne exclaimed. 'How wonderful to see you! I have been regaling my friends here with my many woes!'

'Papa told me that you could not find the buyer.'

'Try as I might, the gentleman remained elusive.'

She tried not to smile. 'Gentleman? What makes you so sure that the buyer was a gentleman?'

Savagne laughed. 'Correct. My *bête noir* might have been a member of the fairer sex. Try as I might, I did not see who was bidding against that awful little man Gideon Martin – the very same who once had his beady eyes on you, my dear. The successful bidder was situated at the back of the hall, and for a man of my size...'

A tall, grey-haired woman to M Savagne's right regarded them through a lorgnette and said, 'That Martin should bid for the statuette, when he knew how you so desired the piece, speaks volumes for the man's duplicity and greed. Most disgraceful conduct!'

Her father cleared his throat. 'Monsieur Savagne ... I think Maria has something to tell you.'

213

Savagne turned his watery eyes on Maria and smiled. 'Your words, my dear, are always a consolation.'

'This time, Monsieur Savagne, I think you will be consoled by more than just my words.' And so saying she withdrew the parcel from behind her back and presented it to Monsieur Savagne.

He blinked. 'A present? My dear, but how thoughtful.'

A small crowd had gathered, individuals smiling with complicity as they watched Savagne unwrap the parcel.

The paper fell to the floor and the statuette, an exquisitely-wrought Madonna and child, perhaps six inches tall, stood on the little man's palm. Tears filled his eyes as he looked from the figure to Maria. 'But ... but ... my dear Maria – I am overwhelmed.' He clutched the statuette to his chest. 'But how ... why...?'

Her father said, 'It was Maria's idea. When she heard that Martin had designs on the piece, she thought that something must be done. I have contacts in Paris who will be more than happy to show the statuette.'

M Savagne planted kisses on Maria's cheeks, weeping freely now as he reiterated his gratitude and amazement.

Maria felt herself choke at his response, and beamed at her father.

The grey-haired lady – Maria recognized her as a French fellow from one of the Oxford colleges – chipped in with, 'I always thought Martin a disreputable specimen. I don't suppose you've heard the latest?'

'The latest?' Maria echoed.

'Well,' said the woman in lowered tones, 'Martin was seen at the Garrick the other evening, accosting a senior editor at Faber and threatening to shoot the poor man. The police were called in, but apparently no arrests were made. Martin was blind drunk, by all accounts.'

Savagne sighed. 'Ah, but I should not revel in his crazy troubles!' he said, eyes twinkling.

Maria smiled and sipped her wine. She only hoped that Martin's crazy behaviour had not been occasioned by the scene at her flat the other evening.

She recalled the slap she had landed on his shocked face.

Men! she thought.

Then she considered Donald and amended her stricture: *some* men...

The conversation at dinner was polite and inconsequential – her father was linguistically brilliant, as ever, on a variety of subjects – and Maria found herself musing that perhaps it was just as well Donald had not accompanied her tonight. He would have hated so formal and privileged a gathering. She wondered what he was doing now. It was eight thirty. Seated solidly in his armchair beneath his standard lamp, perhaps, reading a crime novel?

The thought warmed her.

She ate without really tasting the food (later, when describing the evening to Donald, she would be unable to say exactly what was on the menu) and listened politely to Savagne and Celia Legrande, a soprano taking the London opera

215

world by storm. She stared at the diva's large face; something about the woman's silver hair and pendulous jowls reminded her of Charles, and she felt a sudden wave of sorrow sweep over her.

After port and coffee the guests left the dining room and circulated around the house. Maria found herself discussing the contemporary novel with an earnest young man on a scholarship at Cambridge; her attention wandered, and she wished she was discussing mystery novels with Donald instead.

It was almost eleven when she decided that she'd had enough. She had a daunting day ahead of her at the office tomorrow, contacting clients with the news of Charles's hospitalization, and attempting to run the business single-handedly without Charles around to guide her. The very idea made her want to weep.

She went in search of her father, to say good-bye, and found him in the library. He took her arm and steered her towards the window; a million stars were out above the heath, and the window was open to admit the scent of honey-suckle.

He said, 'I was watching you earlier, Maria. Are you quite yourself?'

She smiled at the question. She had decided that she would not tell her father, on his birthday, of the attack on Charles; that news could wait. Instead, she had far better tidings.

'Out with it, Maria! You have something to tell me?'

She could feel a smile spreading across her

face, and she thought that she must have looked inane.

Her father's wise blue eyes twinkled. 'His name?'

'Is it *that* obvious?'

'Either you have fallen in love, Maria, or ... but there is no "or". It must be love, no?'

She nodded. 'His name is Donald Langham and he's a writer and he's tall and quiet and handsome and...' She gestured at the inadequacy of words to express the magic of how she felt.

'And his feelings towards you?'

'I think the same,' she murmured.

Her father stooped and kissed her cheek. 'I'm happy, Maria. You must bring him to meet me. What does he write?'

She described his books, saying they were honest and solid and dependable ... and realized that she was describing the writer as much as his work.

'Mysteries? Well, I'd like to read one. Bring the best, before you bring the man, hm?'

She promised that she would, kissed her father goodbye and took a taxi home.

EIGHTEEN

On Monday morning Langham woke late and breakfasted alone, contrasting the meal with the one he'd shared with Maria yesterday. He contemplated the weekend, the attempt on Charles's life and his time with Maria, and he experienced despair at Charles's condition and elation when he thought about Maria Dupré.

At ten he rang the hospital, spoke briefly to the duty sister and learned that there had been no change: Charles was alive but unconscious. He thanked her and said he'd ring again later. He got through to Maria at the agency and told her the news, then chatted about nothing in particular for ten minutes before ringing off with the excuse that he must get some work done.

He tried to settle down at his desk and read some notes, but found it impossible. He had the outline of a novel half completed – the heist story he'd told Maria about yesterday – and he wanted to finish it so that he could submit a chapter and outline to his editor at Harrington. When he started to read what he'd written, however, the plot seemed contrived, the characters flat and lifeless. And, superimposed on the scenes he'd dreamed up so far, he saw alternate images of Charles and Maria. He decided to set the work aside and come back to it when he was feeling more able to concentrate.

He was making himself a pot of Earl Grey when the phone rang.

'I've just heard about your agent,' Jeff Mallory said. 'Detective Inspector Bryce up at Bury St Edmunds gave me the details of the incident. He said you'd been doing some investigative work of your own concerning the blackmailer.'

'That's right.'

'I thought you said you left the detective work to Sam Brooke?'

'Guilty as charged.'

'Bryce mentioned some photos of tyre tracks you'd taken.'

'Along with the blackmailer's boot print.'

'Right ... Look, are you terribly busy right now? Could you possibly pop up to the Yard and see me?'

'I'm doing nothing, and I'd welcome the diversion.'

'Excellent. Tell you what, how about lunch at Antonio's café around the corner? Cheap but cheerful. Say twelve thirty?'

'I'll see you there.'

Thirty minutes later he drove into the city and found a parking place on the Embankment.

Antonio's was, as Mallory had said, cheap but cheerful, a small café packed with rickety tables and decorated with posters advertising Italian holiday destinations. Their speciality, according to a chalked-up menu board hanging over the counter, was spaghetti on toast, a combination Langham thought revolting. Charles would have

railed eloquently at the concatenation of carbo-
hydrates.

Mallory hurried in just as Langham was
seating himself at a window table. The big man
joined him, discarded his overcoat, loosened his
tie and dumped a heavy cardboard folder on the
table.

Antonio himself approached, smiling at Mallory. 'The usual, Inspector?'

'With coffee today. Don?'

Langham said, 'I'll just have tea ... and a
toasted teacake.'

'Un momento.'

Langham indicated Mallory's folder, full to
bursting. 'I'm afraid I can't match that.' He laid
the envelope containing the photographs of the
foot- and tyre-prints on the table.

Mallory looked across at Langham, his expression stony. 'I've been landed four cases, Don, on
account of the possibility that they *might* be
linked – and because the illiterates at the Yard
still think of me as a scribbler.'

A cold sensation lodged itself in Langham's
gut. 'Linked?'

'The Elder case, the Gervaise Cartwright murder, then there's the apparent suicide of Max
Sidley, and I don't know if you heard about it a
couple of weeks ago: a writer chappie threw
himself under a train in Kent.'

'Frankie Pearson. I was at his memorial service last Friday.'

'That's the chap.'

'And you say they might be linked? But I
thought Sidley and Pearson were suicides?'

220

'I'm looking into the possibility that they weren't.' Mallory leaned back as Antonio arrived with his order – spaghetti on toast. The spaghetti looked watery and the toast underdone. Langham accepted his teacake with gratitude, thankful he'd foregone the speciality of the house.

Mallory tucked in. 'Anyway,' he said through a mouthful, 'we haven't concluded yet that there is a link, or that Sidley and Pearson weren't suicides. We're keeping an open mind, though it does look a bit odd – three deaths and an attempted murder in the scribbling business all in the space of a couple of weeks.' He pointed his fork at Langham's envelope. 'Those the pictures?'

Langham slipped the six prints on to the tabletop, recalling the bemusement of the farmer when he'd taken the photographs, and Maria's subsequent amusement.

From his folder, Mallory extracted a couple of glossy photographs showing the motorcycle tracks in the lane behind Charles's mansion. He arranged them side by side and Langham nodded. 'They're identical.'

'That's what I wanted, Don. Good work.' He indicated Langham with his fork. 'And if you and that filly of yours hadn't interrupted the gunman on Saturday, Elder might be stone cold dead now.'

Langham regarded his under-toasted teacake. 'It's still touch and go as to whether he'll pull through.'

Mallory chewed pensively. 'All four men were

221

known to each other, all were in the trade, and all were members of the London Crime Club.' He laughed with little humour. 'The press'll have a field day when this one breaks.'

Langham bit into his teacake, which was stale and tasteless. The tea, at least, was passable.

Mallory went on: 'All we have so far is what you've found out – the fact that the blackmailer rides a Triumph Thunderbird, wears size ten boots and smokes Camel cigarettes.'

'I take it you've questioned Kenny Wilson, the rent-boy who Charles—'

He was halted by the expression on Mallory's face. 'I wanted to haul him in, of course, but the little bugger's done a runner. Broken the terms of his bail and scarpered. He's the only person who's seen the blackmailer – I wanted to get an artist's impression from him.'

Langham sipped his tea, recalling the fear on the boy's face at their only meeting. He felt sorry for Kenny Wilson.

Mallory finished his spaghetti on toast.

Langham said, 'Do you think the killer is someone in the scribbling business?'

'Early days yet,' Mallory replied. 'If there's one thing I've learned in this job, it's don't jump to conclusions. The "suicides" might turn out to be just that. I'll keep you posted. Oh, can I take one of the snaps?'

'Help yourself.'

Mallory slid the photo into his folder. 'How's it going with the little French number?'

'Early days, to borrow your phrase.'

'Good luck with that, Don.' He left a half

222

crown on the table. 'Right, back to the bloody grindstone. Some of us have to work for a living.' He winked at Langham as he stood and struggled into his overcoat. 'I'll be in touch.'

Langham watched the detective ease his bulk through the door and stride along the street, then sat back and finished his tea.

He watched the other patrons of the café: workmen bolting down beans on toast, old dears chatting over tea and biscuits, office workers abstractedly eating sandwiches while browsing the daily papers. He considered Mallory's 'Some of us have to work for a living' and thought that, on the whole, he was fortunate to be relatively successful at his profession.

He left the café and drove back to Notting Hill, promising himself that when he returned he'd phone Maria at the agency to see how she was getting on.

In the event, the phone was ringing when he let himself into the flat. He hurried to the study, hoping to hear Maria on the other end but fearing a call from the hospital.

'Donald Langham?' a woman's voice enquired, high-pitched and anxious.

He sat down. 'Yes?'

'I'm sorry to bother you. We have met. I'm Caroline Lassiter. You know my husband, Nigel.'

'Caroline. Of course. I saw Nigel just last week.'

'I'm sorry to bother you – I know you must be busy, if you're anything like Nigel...'

She paused, and Langham said, 'That's perfectly all right. How can I help?'

'Well...' Caroline Lassiter sounded not only hesitant but unsure. 'I know this might sound unusual ... I think Nigel told you something about going down to Kent on Saturday to see a solicitor about a cottage he'd been left in a will?'

'That's right.' Langham stared at the flower-patterned wallpaper, wondering where this might be leading.

'Well, he took the car early on Saturday morning, saying he'd be back in time for lunch.'

Langham waited for her to continue, his apprehension mounting.

'The thing is ... Nigel hasn't returned. He's been away over two days now and I must say I'm getting worried.' Another pause, then: 'I don't know quite how to say this, but ... Nigel has from time to time spent a night away from home, but never like this, without telling me beforehand.'

Langham told himself that there was no reason to fear that anything had happened to Lassiter, but at the same time a nasty, pernicious voice in the back of his head was saying that there was every reason.

'OK.' He tried to sound businesslike. 'Nigel said he'd had a letter from the solicitor. Do you know if he took it with him?'

'I checked. I found it on his desk. The thing is ... I rang the phone number, but there was no reply. The line seems to be disconnected.'

'I'm sure there's a simple explanation.' He

224

paused. 'Would you mind if I came over and took a look at the letter?'

She sounded relieved. 'Would you? That would be wonderful. I don't mind admitting that I'm a little worried.'

'Don't be,' he said, while feeling more than worried himself. 'I'll be round in five minutes. Islington, isn't it? Belgrave Square?'

'Number twenty-two, yes. Thank you so much.'

He cut the connection and hurried out, slipped into the Austin and motored to Islington.

As he drove he asked himself why Nigel Lassiter might stay away from home for more than two nights, especially as he was, in his own words, 'under Caroline's thumb', and was usually scrupulous about keeping her informed as to his whereabouts.

He recalled his meeting with Jeff Mallory earlier and tried to dismiss his fears.

The three-storey Georgian town house stood in one of the most fashionable Islington squares, a grand white-fronted building that befitted a popular, best-selling author like Nigel Lassiter. As he climbed the steps and rang the doorbell, Langham thought back to the last time he'd been here – a launch party just after the war. He recalled Caroline Lassiter as a slim, vivacious host in her mid-thirties, just married to the older writer and delighted by her catch.

The woman who opened the door seemed much older than someone in her mid-forties, and Langham wondered if this was the result of a decade of marriage to a cynical scribbler with a drink problem. Caroline's piled hair was dishevelled and greying, and wrinkles around her eyes and mouth had been plastered over with a thick application of foundation.

'Donald, I'm so grateful you could come. Please, this way...'

She led Langham along a thickly-carpeted corridor and up a short flight of stairs to a big room overlooking the square.

'Nigel's study. Can I get you a drink?'

'No, I'm fine. I've just had lunch.'

He looked around the room. Hundreds of books lined the walls, and next to a writing desk stood a bookcase containing what appeared to be all of Nigel's first editions, along with paperback editions and translations.

Caroline was worrying a strand of pearls around her neck. 'Well, this is where the great man churns them out,' she said with more than a touch of sarcasm. Something about her uneven diction, and her flighty glances at him and away, suggested she'd calmed her nerves with a drink or two.

'Is this the letter...?' He pointed to an envelope beside the typewriter. 'May I?'

'Please.'

She watched him closely, fingers to her rouged lips, as he slipped a single sheet of expensive writing paper from the envelope and unfolded it.

Below the letter-heading bearing the name of Cobley and Cotton, solicitors, and their address in Regent Street, the body of the letter informed Nigel about the cottage in Kent and suggested he meet a representative of the firm there on the

Saturday morning.

'Nigel has never, ever gone off like this before. He always calls if he's going to be late. I can only assume he's had an accident.'

'And you say you've tried ringing...?' He held up the letter.

'The line is completely dead.'

'May I try?'

'By all means.' She gestured towards a phone on the desk. Langham picked it up and rang the number. The line was silent.

He replaced the receiver. 'Odd. Have you tried the directory?'

She nodded. 'They were not listed, but then not every company is.'

'Right.' He considered the options. 'Do you mind if I take the letter? I'll drive over to Regent Street and see if I can learn anything there. I might even motor down to the cottage.' He glanced at the solicitor's letter and read the address: Ivy Cottage, Greenleaf Lane, Little Hadleigh.

Caroline smiled. 'It was where he and Frankie Pearson worked, in the early days. I never met him, and from what Nigel says about him I think that was just as well – but what happened to the poor man was terrible. Nigel was awfully cut up about it. He felt guilty. I know he told you about it.'

Langham nodded. 'But as I told Nigel, he had no reason to feel guilty. I would have done the same thing back then, had I been in Nigel's shoes.'

She smiled. 'Nigel said you were a good man.'

227

Langham found himself colouring. 'I'll be in touch when I've checked this,' he said, tapping the letter against his thigh.

She thanked him again as she showed him to the front door.

Langham returned to his Austin and drove from the square, trying to fathom what might account for Nigel's non-appearance. The obvious explanation was that Caroline was being economical with the facts: they'd had a spat and Nigel had used the trip to Kent as an excuse to cool off for a night or so ... But that scenario did nothing to explain Caroline's apprehension.

Regent Street was busy with traffic which seemed to consist mainly of black cabs and omnibuses. He parked in a side street and walked south, counting off the buildings until he reached the twenties. A jeweller's shop occupied number twenty, and next door to that was a furrier. He looked for a door between the premises which might give access to stairs and the rooms where Cobley and Cotton had their offices.

He stood in the street, buffeted by pedestrians, holding the letter before him and staring blankly at the wall where the door should have been. There was no door. Number twenty-two Regent Street was the high-class furrier.

He wondered if the address in the letter was mistaken, and should be either thirty-two or twelve. Unlikely as this seemed, he nevertheless walked five buildings along in both directions to confirm his doubt: number twelve was a French restaurant and number thirty-two a tobacconist's shop.

He returned to number twenty-two and entered the furriers. An elderly gentleman behind the counter smiled benignly and asked if he might be of assistance. Feeling not a little silly, Langham proffered the letter and explained, 'I'm trying to locate a company of solicitors by the name of Cobley and Cotton. As you can see, the address given here seems to be mistaken.'

The old man squinted at the letter, shaking his head. 'I'm sorry, I can't be of any help. We've occupied this site for almost forty years, and I've never heard of Cobley and Cotton. You might try number thirty-two?'

Langham said he'd do that and left the building. He stood on the busy sunlit pavement and considered what to do next. He set off down the street, found a phone box, and got through to Maria at the agency.

'Donald, where are you? It sounds busy!'

He smiled at the wonderful sound of her voice. 'I'm in Regent Street, looking for a lost writer,' he said with a levity he did not feel.

'What?'

He explained the situation and she interrupted, 'I don't like the sound of this, Donald.'

'I've got to go down to Kent. Nigel was due to meet a solicitor down there on Saturday. If I set off now, I should be back by around six.'

'Donald ... Please be careful, OK? For me?'

He smiled. 'I'll be fine, Maria,' he said, and hung up.

He returned to the car and consulted his road map. The village of Little Hadleigh was situated five miles south of Hawkhurst, perhaps a little over an hour away from central London.

He decided not to consider the possibility that he might find something down there which would delay his return. In all likelihood he would come across nothing untoward, and Nigel would turn up of his own accord, drunkenly lachrymose and regretful after a two-day bender.

He left the capital in his wake and hit the open road. The traffic was light and the sun dazzling. He wound down the window and lodged his right arm on the sill. He was thinking of Maria, her big eyes and wonderful smile, but these pleasant thoughts were short-lived. He entered Tonbridge and passed the exclusive French restaurant on the main street to which Charles, in one of his expansive, generous moods, had insisted he take Langham in order to celebrate the publication of his twentieth novel. The evening, in the company of a select group of friends, was a memory he cherished.

He was sunk in melancholy for the remainder of the journey.

The village of Little Hadleigh proved to be another example of chocolate-box England, a rural backwater seemingly bypassed by the twentieth century. The obligatory village green boasted a duck pond overlooked by the twin custodians of a Norman church and a half-timbered public house, The Duck and Drake.

His was the only car abroad in the village that day, and the grumble of the engine, when he left it idling while he popped into the post office to ask for directions to Greenleaf Lane, seemed

230

raucous on his return.

He passed the pub, turned right and motored on for half a mile before he came to a tiny redstone cottage set back in an overgrown rose garden. He looked up and down the lane, but there was no sign of Nigel Lassiter's car. He pulled up and examined the property.

The downstairs window frames were rotten, the glass grey and cracked. The front door, likewise, was in need of attention, and the roof tiles had suffered slippage in many places.

He climbed from the car, walked up the garden path and knocked on the front door, the timber spongy beneath his knuckles. There was no reply, as he'd expected, and he stepped across the unkempt lawn and peered in through the tiny front window.

The sitting room was bare of furniture, the plasterwork of the far wall exposed to the laths in great patches. He knocked again, then moved around the side of the house and came to the back garden.

It must have been beautiful once, with a lawn and climbing roses and a couple of apple trees, but like the rest of the property the garden had been left to its own devices and nature had run rampant. He pushed at the back door, expecting it to be locked, but to his surprise it swung open at his touch.

He opened it further and stepped inside.

The entrance gave on to a poky tiled kitchen, which he crossed and entered a small hallway. To the right was a living room, and to the left a room which once, he guessed, had passed as a study. Bookshelves lined the walls, and a couple of them still held half-a-dozen mouldering paperbacks. He crossed the room and took down one of the books, an imported American thriller bearing the lurid illustration of a half-naked woman and an even more lurid title, *She Killed for Love*. Beside the window was an old desk, and Langham wondered if this was where, before the war, Lassiter and Pearson had bashed out their collaborative potboilers.

The house stank of damp and mice. He hurried back into the sunlight and fresh air, stood outside the back door and stared down the long garden.

He was wondering if the journey down here had been a waste of time when he glimpsed, in the grass beside the crumbled path, the tab end of a cigarette. He knelt and peered at the filter; it appeared fresh, and the brand-name printed above the speckled beige paper was Pall Mall.

The brand Nigel Lassiter chain-smoked.

He saw another filter a couple of yards away and moved to it. Pall Mall, again. And again, like the first, it appeared to have been recently smoked.

So Nigel had been here, standing in the garden, perhaps enjoying a cigarette in the sunlight while awaiting the arrival of the solicitor's representative.

Then he saw the third discarded butt, and something about this one – the distinctive, darker colouration of its filter paper – caused his heart to beat a little faster.

Rather than pick it up and destroy any fingerprint evidence, he knelt to examine it. The cigarette had been smoked right down to the filter, obliterating any identifying trade-name. He lowered his face to the ground and sniffed. The odour was distinctive: Camel.

He stood and looked around the garden as if suddenly fearing he might be under surveillance, despite knowing how irrational that fear was.

He was staring down the length of the garden when he saw the vegetable patch, or what he took at first to be a vegetable patch, concealed behind a tangle of overgrown raspberry canes.

But what was a freshly dug vegetable patch doing in the middle of a garden that had been neglected for years?

Heart thudding, he walked down the garden until he came to the dark rectangle of recently turned earth.

He knelt beside the soil and crumbled its loam between his fingertips. The patch was perhaps six feet long, three wide, and its resemblance to a grave was unmistakable. He closed his eyes, feeling dizzy.

To his right was a dilapidated timber hut, leaning so much that it had assumed a parallelogram shape. He stood and yanked open the door. A spade was propped up inside, with soil on its blade. He reached out to take the spade, then stopped himself.

Another spade stood against the far wall. He took this one and paused before the rectangle of recently dug earth. He knew that he should leave this for the police, but he wanted to have his suspicion, his fear, proved either right or wrong.

He began digging tentatively, not wanting to

233

drive the blade too deep for fear of cutting into whatever might be down there. He piled the discarded soil further down the dug patch, expecting to feel the solidity of something buried every time he carefully stamped the spade into the ground. He was sweating within minutes, the sunlight burning his neck.

He had reached the depth of twelve inches when the blade struck something – not a stone or some similar obstruction, but an object solid yet yielding.

He squatted, peering into the shadow of the conical hole, and his throat constricted as he made out the leather upper of a shoe. With the corner of the spade he scraped away the soil, enough to confirm that a trousered leg emerged from the brogue. He stood quickly, swaying, and stared down at the shoe and the soiled trouser cuff. The body was evidently face-up, stretched out in the makeshift grave.

He thought of Caroline Lassiter, worried sick back in Islington, and a hot wave of despair passed through him.

He threw the spade down and retraced his steps around the cottage and back to the car. He found a turning place in the lane a little further along and motored back into the village. A phone box stood beside the lychgate of the church. He parked the Austin and jumped out.

He had Jeff Mallory's number in his address book, and he prayed the inspector would still be at his desk. The dial tone rang for what seemed like five minutes, only to be answered by someone who wasn't Mallory.

234

'I'd like to speak to Detective Inspector Jeff Mallory,' Langham said, aware of the breathless flutter in his voice.

'Who's speaking, please?'

Calmly Langham gave his name. 'One moment,' the voice said.

He heard muffled voices, imagined a palm cupped over the receiver while a hurried consultation took place.

Seconds later Mallory said, 'Donald?'

'Jeff, I'm in Kent. I've ... I've found a body. Nigel Lassiter. In a shallow grave. I...'

'What? Slow down, Donald. Slow down. Now, where did you say you are?'

Langham took a breath and began a detailed explanation, starting with Caroline Lassiter's summons earlier that afternoon and finishing with his grisly discovery in the cottage garden.

'Right, I'm on my way. Don't dig any further and don't touch anything else. I'll be down in about an hour.'

Langham replaced the receiver with a shaking hand, feeling sick. He wondered if he would ever again write about murder, or the discovery of a corpse, with the same cavalier attitude of 'all in a day's work'.

He drove back to the cottage and sat in the car for about fifteen minutes, unable to bring himself to revisit the location where Nigel Lassiter, a friend and colleague, had met his death.

He climbed from the car and walked up and down the lane, hands thrust deep into his trouser pockets. He imagined Nigel Lassiter driving down here, parking up and approaching the

235

cottage, imagining his imminent meeting with the solicitor but little realizing what was in store.

Langham stopped in his tracks. If Nigel had parked here, then where was his car now? Driven away by the killer, presumably.

He thought of the other victims: an editor, an agent and two writers, all active in the publishing of crime novels, and now Nigel Lassiter, undoubtedly the most famous of them all.

Fifty minutes after he'd phoned Mallory, a bulky black police van drew up outside the cottage, followed by the detective inspector's racing green Humber. Mallory jumped out and approached Langham, who gestured to the path around the cottage.

As they went, a forensic team debouched from the van, carrying spades, rolls of scene-of-crime tape and a camera on a tripod.

'You say the cottage belonged to Frank Pearson, the writer found on a railway line a couple of weeks ago?'

'I saw Nigel Lassiter on Friday, at Frankie Pearson's memorial service. He told me he was coming down here on Saturday to meet a solicitor. Pearson left him the cottage in his will.'

They rounded the end of the cottage. Langham indicated the discarded cigarette ends, then led Mallory down the garden towards the grave.

'You think it was a set up?' Mallory asked. 'He was lured down here?'

'It certainly looks that way.' He showed Mallory the letter from the spurious solicitor.

'Mind if I keep this?'

'It's all yours.'

236

They came to the patch of the turned earth and Mallory squatted to examine the revealed foot.

A minute later the grave was surrounded by officers, uniformed and plainclothes, as well as several men in navy-blue boiler suits. Langham indicated the tool shed. 'There's a soiled spade in there – the one the killer used, presumably. I used that one.' He pointed to the spade lying in the grass.

A police officer in blue overalls pulled on a pair of rubber gloves and carefully picked up the first spade, labelling it and taking it back to the van for later inspection.

A forensics officer began digging alongside a second colleague.

Langham stood beside Mallory and watched as the pair removed the topsoil with exaggerated care, taking off the first six inches along the length of the grave.

'You knew Nigel Lassiter well?' Mallory asked.

'He was a friend. His wife was worried sick ... Christ, poor Caroline.'

The bulky South African looked at him. 'What the hell's going on, Donald?'

'I've been trying to work that out myself. An editor, an agent, three writers...'

'It's someone in the trade,' Mallory said. 'It has to be. Someone who bears a hell of a grudge.' He paused. 'You know what they're calling the case, back at the Yard?'

'Go on.'

'The Grub Street Murders.'

'You coppers are a bloody cynical bunch,'

Langham said.

The diggers had removed the soil to the depth of twelve inches, and here and there along the length of the grave Langham made out patches of material, dark trousers and a casual jacket. The very same tweed jacket Nigel Lassiter had been wearing when they'd gone for a drink at Tolly's last week.

The forensics pair knelt and scraped away the last of the soil from Lassiter's corpse. The body lay on its back, hands by its sides. Langham glanced down, not wanting to see Nigel's face.

Mallory said, 'What the hell's that?'

He pointed, and Langham made out what looked like the shaft of an arrow protruding from Lassiter's sternum.

A police photographer circled the scene, snapping the grave and the corpse from every angle and elevation. Other officers moved around it, combing through the grass and bagging any items of potential evidence they came across.

A stretcher was brought from the van and set down beside the grave. When the body was totally uncovered, four officers eased themselves into the grave, slipped their hands beneath the corpse, and after a count of three lifted it gently on to the stretcher, laying it on its side so as not to disturb the arrow.

Mallory said, 'Christ, it's a crossbow bolt.'

Langham's vision swam and he knew he was in danger of passing out. He moved to a rickety garden bench beside the tool shed and sat down quickly.

Mallory glanced across at him. 'You OK, Donald?'

Langham waved. 'I'll be fine.'

A crossbow bolt, a shallow grave in a cottage garden...

Mallory joined him on the bench. 'We'll take the body back to the lab, let forensics get to work. The killer obligingly left the bolt *in situ*, which might prove helpful.'

At last Langham found his voice. 'Jeff ... the crossbow, the grave...'

Mallory looked at him.

'It's ... it's so bloody familiar, Jeff. It's as if I've been here before. Déjà vu. I'm sure I've read of a killing just like this.'

Mallory smiled. 'How many detective yarns have you read for review? Hundreds?'

'Thousands over the years, for review and for pleasure.' There was something horribly familiar about this particular scene, though. It stuck in his mind. Then he recalled something that Mallory had told him the other day. 'Jesus, Jeff.'

'What is it?'

'The murder you mentioned, the stabbing of Gervaise Cartwright with a stiletto, the hood...'

'Yes?'

'I thought at the time it was familiar, and I wondered then if I'd read something similar somewhere.'

'Don't you think it's just coincidence? As you said, you've read thousands of mysteries, or are you trying to say ... what? That some killer's perpetrating copycat killings, based on murders he's read in crime novels?'

239

Langham shook his head. 'I don't know. I feel as if I'm locked in a dream, a dream where the images are falling away the more I try to concentrate on them.'

Two officers passed by, bearing Nigel Lassiter's body on the stretcher. Langham closed his eyes.

They left the decrepit cottage, which was being cordoned off with red and white tape. Langham climbed into his Austin, took one last look at the cottage, and set off back to London.

An hour later he rapped on the door of Maria's apartment, and after a minute she appeared and almost fell into his arms. 'Donald.'

He held her to him, inhaling her scent.

'I've cooked something, rather than go out. Donald, I was so worried.'

They climbed the stairs to her apartment. Langham marvelled at the luxury of the furnishings, the Queen Anne chairs and mahogany bureau. 'Makes my place look very drab,' he said.

She poured him a beer and herself a red wine. 'What happened, Donald? Did you find...?' She stopped when she saw his expression.

'Nigel Lassiter is dead.'

She slumped on to the settee and Langham sat beside her. The beer tasted like nectar. 'What happened?'

He told her everything, omitting no detail, and continued the description of his day and the grisly find over dinner. He finished his beer and she poured him another, replenishing her wine at

240

the same time.

She sat in silence for seconds when he brought the events of the day to a close. Then she said, 'Donald, stay here tonight, please.'

'Would that be all right?'

She smiled, gripping his hand. 'I want you here.'

They moved back to the settee and Maria leaned against him. 'I've been answering the phone all day at the office,' she went on. 'Calls from publishers and writers. They were all so shocked at what happened.' She smiled bravely. 'I rang the hospital this evening, Donald. But there is no change. Charles is still unconscious.'

He held her as she wept.

NINETEEN

Langham was in his study the following morning, looking over the first draft of a short story, when the phone bell rang.

'Donald?' It was Maria, and she sounded breathless.

'Maria, are you all right?'

'Good news!'

His heart kicked. 'Charles?'

'Yes, I've just called the hospital and talked to the ward sister. Charles regained consciousness earlier this morning. She stressed that he wasn't yet "out of the woods", and has a long way to go, but she said that this was an encouraging sign.'

Langham felt himself grinning inanely. 'That's wonderful. I don't suppose he recalls anything...?'

Maria interrupted. 'No. The sister said that he has no memory at all of the incident.'

'Well, I'm just delighted that he's back in the land of the living.'

'And Donald, the sister said that we might – just *might* – be able to visit him this evening, depending on how he is then.'

'Capital! Shall we do that, then?'

'Visiting hours from six till seven. Could you pick me up?'

'I'll do that,' he said. 'What are you doing now?'

She groaned. 'Working. Everything has piled up here over the past few days. And just when I am getting down to work, some well-meaning writer or editor phones up about Charles. Anyway, what are you doing?'

He told her about the short story and added, 'But to be honest I can't concentrate on the thing.'

'Take my advice and go for a long walk, Donald.'

He smiled. 'Might just do that.'

They chatted for a few minutes, then Maria said that she really *must* get a manuscript read and said goodbye.

Langham was wondering whether to persevere with the story or take Maria's advice and go for a walk, when the phone bell rang again.

'Donald Langham here.'

'Don.' Ralph Ryland's piercing Cockney tones sounded down the line. 'I said I'd get back to you if I came up with anything.'

'Good man,' Langham said. 'What have you got?'

'Not that much, to be honest. A name and address—'

'Excellent.'

'Before you get excited, I'd better tell you that I think the name's a *nom-de-plume*, as they say in France, and as for the address...'

Langham's spirits sank. 'What about it?'

'Well, come over and take a look. You busy at the moment?'

'I'm not doing anything that can't wait. Where are you?'

'Streatham. I'll meet you on the corner of Wavertree Road, near the bus station.'

'I'm on my way.'

He drove across the river to Streatham, recalling the same journey he'd made last week to drop off the money at the bombed-out mill. He hoped this trip would prove more fruitful.

Ryland had had little to go on, and he supposed it was a miracle he'd come up with anything at all, even if it were just a fictitious name and an address. Langham wondered why the private investigator had sounded so negative about the address he'd discovered. Any lead at this stage, no matter how seemingly insignificant, might prove valuable.

He parked on the corner and crossed the busy road. Ryland was standing next to his battered Morris Minor, stoat-thin in his grey raincoat, a tab end stuck to his bottom lip and his collar turned up, even though the sun was out.

Ryland nodded across the road to Langham's Austin Healey. 'Nice machine. The books must be selling like hot cakes.'

Langham laughed. 'An extravagance I can barely afford. I see you're still driving the Camel.'

Ryland kicked the Morris Minor's front tyre. 'The old girl'll see me out,' he said. 'Anyway, talking about Camels...'

He indicated along the street. Beyond the bus station a long row of red-brick terrace houses receded into the distance. They began walking.

'You've done well, Ralph. How did you find the address?'

'Hard slog,' Ryland grunted. 'Hours and hours of bloody footwork. All I had to go on were the Camels, the bullets, and the fact our friend rode a Triumph.'

'A needle in a haystack comes to mind.'

'Yeah, well, I don't like blowin' me own trumpet. But I'm like a bleedin' terrier when I get the bit between me teeth, to mix metaphysics as you writer chappies say.'

Ryland nipped the fag end from his thin lips, flicked it into the gutter and lit another cigarette, all without slowing his pace. 'I know this geezer down Bermondsey. What he doesn't know about stolen shooters isn't worth knowing. He owes me a trick or two, so I ask him if anyone's been asking around for a .38 recent like. A day later he comes back to me with a couple of likely suspects: a toff – who I discounted straight away

244

– and a small ginger bloke riding a Triumph. Ginger bought a pistol off a mate of his, and this mate is canny, right? Didn't want to do the swap on his own territory, so he said to Ginger that he'd deliver. Ginger agreed and said meet him in the Crown and Sceptre, Streatham.'

'So that narrowed it down a bit,' Langham laughed.

'Just a bit,' Ryland agreed. 'All I had to do then was a bit of door to door calling in the Streatham area.'

'And?'

'I asked if the householders knew anyone with a motorbike, specifically a Triumph. Took me two bleedin' days, it did. Talk about shoe leather. Anyway, this old biddy in her nineties bent me ear about the noise this bloke made with his motorbike – said he lived just across the road. A short, fat, ginger bloke, never without a cig in his cake 'ole...'

Ryland stopped dramatically and, with a flourish of his right hand, indicated the terrace house they were standing outside.

Langham stared at the house. 'Right ... now I see what you were driving at.'

The house was burned-out, its windows missing and half of its roof collapsed. Langham thought that there was nothing as sad as a fire-damaged house with its pathetic reminders – in this case singed lace curtains and a hat stand just inside the door – of the former home it had been.

'Any idea when this happened?'

'The old biddy said about a month ago. One night she was woken up in the early hours by a

245

right commotion across the street.'

Langham glanced at Ryland. 'Been inside?'

The investigator shook his head. 'There was a fire officer inspecting the place when I came round yesterday. I thought I'd leave off till I contacted you.'

Langham nodded and looked up and down the street. The place was deserted. He nipped up the short garden path and slipped in past the remains of the incinerated door, askew on its hinges. Ryland followed.

He looked up a flight of stairs, abbreviated halfway by the fire. To the left was a gutted kitchen and to the right a front room occupied by blackened chunks of furniture, a three-piece suite and what might have been a Welsh dresser.

Langham crunched over debris and stood in the middle of the room. The charcoal reek was matched only by the fuggy aroma of water-logged plasterboard.

Ryland was saying, 'I looked into who owned the place, of course. Some slumlord down Greenwich way, he says he rented it for a couple of months to a geezer called Smith, who match-ed my description in every department – viz, short, fat and ginger. Smith paid on time and the landlord never had any complaints. The rent was paid right up to last month.'

Langham turned, taking in the blackened bricks, charred carpet and sagging ceiling. 'What do you think happened?'

'You want my opinion? I think Mr Effing Smith, before he starts killing, he decides to cover his trail. Just to be on the safe side, he thinks he'll torch the place so no one sniffing around can find any incriminatory evidence.' He shrugged. 'Makes sense, if you ask me.'

Langham nodded in agreement. 'Burns the place down, covering all traces of who lived here, takes off and goes to earth. He might be anywhere now.'

'I asked the biddy if she ever talked to this geezer, Mr Smith. Said she complained about him revving his bike at midnight a few weeks back, and all she got for her trouble was a mouthful. The other neighbours didn't have anything to do with him. Said he kept himself to himself, never had anyone round. I tried the Crown and Sceptre and a few other boozers in the area, but if anyone recognized Smith's description they weren't saying nothing.'

Langham said, 'You did well, Ralph.'

Ryland grunted. 'Not as well as I wanted to, mind.'

Langham noticed the crocodile-skin remains of a small bookcase in the corner of the room. He crossed to it, stepping over a hole in the floorboards, and squatted beside the case.

A row of a dozen damp-fattened paperbacks occupied the top shelf. There was something about the arrangement of the titles that struck Langham as odd, as if the books had been placed there *after* the immolation of the house. Surely, if in situ at the time of the fire, they would have been incinerated beyond recognition?

He pulled out the books and stacked them on the floor, his stomach turning.

There were seven titles in all, by Nigel Lassiter, Gerry Carter, Frank L. Pearson, Justin Fellowes, Dan Greeley and Amelia Hampstead, and the last one – *Murder in Malapur* – by none other than Donald Langham.

'Found something?' Ryland asked.

'What do you make of these?'

Ryland squatted beside him. 'Mr Smith was a reader with good taste?'

Langham grunted a laugh without humour. 'These weren't here when the fire was started, Ralph. They're not fire-damaged, just damp. My guess is they were left here afterwards.'

The weaselly investigator gave him a sceptical look. 'OK – but why?'

Langham went through the books one by one. 'Nigel Lassiter – dead. Gervaise Cartwright – writing here as Gerry Carter – dead. Frank Pearson – dead. That leaves Fellowes, Greeley, Hampstead and ... myself.'

Ryland squinted at him. 'Coincidence?'

'Bloody strange coincidence, I'd say. I think Mr Smith is having a little fun at our expense.'

Ryland nodded, slowly. 'OK, so ... Look, you don't need me to tell you this, but you take care, Don. Lie low. Want my opinion, you get yourself out of London.'

Langham nodded. 'I intend to do just that.' He decided to take the books with him as evidence.

Ryland took Langham's elbow and helped him to his feet. 'Seen enough? Let's get out of here.'

As they left the house and made their way back down the long street, Ryland said, 'What now?'

'I think I'll contact the writers.' Langham held up the books. 'Tell them about what's happened and suggest they take precautions.'

'Good idea. You want me to keep looking for the bastard?'

Langham stopped by Ryland's Morris Minor. 'It can't do any harm to have an independent on the case.'

They shook hands. Langham thanked him again and crossed the road to his car.

He drove on automatic pilot, the damp paper-backs on the passenger seat beside him. Why did he have the distinct impression that, to the mur-derer, this was little more than a macabre game?

Once back at his flat he sat at his desk and rang Jeff Mallory at Scotland Yard. He'd tell Jeff what he'd found at the burned-out house and say that he intended to contact the writers in person to explain the situation.

The phone was answered after a minute by a receptionist who informed him that Detective Inspector Mallory was not available. Langham said he'd ring back later.

He stared at the pile of sad-looking paperbacks on his desk. He picked up the Nigel Lassiter, the Frank Pearson and the Gerry Carter and set them aside. The next on the pile was the title by Dan Greeley, which he was pretty sure was a pseudo-nym. The publisher was Digit Books, and he knew an editor there. He got through to the editorial office and asked to speak to Bill Riley.

A minute later Riley's County Clare brogue boomed down the line. 'Donald! It's been a long time. How's life treating you?'

Langham said he was fine, then went on: 'I'm

249

actually trying to get in touch with "Dan Greeley", but I'm right in thinking it's a pseudonym, aren't I?'

A silence, then, 'That's right. Greeley was the pen name of Alexander Southern. But you obviously haven't heard.'

Something turned to ice in his stomach. 'Heard?'

'Poor Alex died last week in a road traffic accident in Canterbury. Knocked down by a hit-and-run driver. Didn't stand a chance. Killed instantly. He was such a gentleman. We're all devastated here.'

Langham murmured his shock and commiserations, and said something about having wanted to do an interview with 'Greeley'. He chatted with Riley for another minute, said they'd have to meet up again for old time's sake, then rang off.

He sat back in his seat and picked up the Greeley title. He'd never heard of the writer Alexander Southern – but clearly he was another scribbler who had in some way earned the ire of the killer. 'Dan Greeley,' he pronounced, 'aka Alexander Southern – dead.' He placed the book in the discard pile.

He picked up the next book – *Murder in Confidence* by Justin Fellowes – and riffled through his address book until he found Fellowes's number.

The call was answered by a housekeeper, who informed Langham that Fellowes had just gone into town and wouldn't be back until at least six that evening. Langham thanked her and said he'd call back later.

That left one writer to contact – Amelia Hampstead.

If Justin Fellowes was the Grand Old Man of British crime fiction, then Dame Amelia Hampstead was the Grand Old Lady. In her seventies now, she had fifty titles behind her, a trophy cupboard full of awards and sales in their tens of millions. Despite all that, she was as personable now as she had been twenty years ago when Langham had first met her. The youngest of Lord Pastonbury's three daughters, Dame Amelia wrote whodunits in the Agatha Christie mould which, while not to Langham's taste, of their kind were excellent.

She had a townhouse in Chelsea and kept a country retreat in Berkshire. Langham tried her London number and got through to her secretary, who informed him that Dame Amelia had left that very morning for Castle Melacorum – the rather highfalutin' name she gave her country pile.

Langham thanked her and rang off. He dialled the castle and a minute later Amelia Hampstead herself answered the phone. 'Why, Donald Langham,' she declared in her rather plummy contralto. 'I was thinking about you just the other day.'

'You were?'

'Indeed. I was reading your column in the *Herald*, and it occurred to me that you hadn't covered one of my titles for a positive aeon. Remiss of you, my dear boy. Most remiss.'

'My apologies, Amelia. I promise I'll rectify

that at the earliest opportunity.'

'I should jolly well think so, Donald. Now, you're interrupting the first day of my holiday. How can I help you? Out with it, boy.'

Langham smiled to himself and said, 'This is a rather delicate matter, Amelia. You've no doubt heard about the recent deaths of Nigel Lassiter, Gervaise Cartwright and—'

She interrupted. 'If you think for a minute I'm going to write their obituaries...'

Taking a deep breath, Langham assured her that this was the last thing he was ringing about and went on to explain the situation. Four dead writers, a dead editor and an agent shot and left for dead... 'And far be it for me to be sensationalist, but I think you and I are on the hit list, too.'

'What is this?' Amelia exclaimed. 'Are you running the plot of your latest thriller past me, young man?'

'I wish I were, Dame Amelia. No, this is serious.' He explained the other deaths and what he'd found in the shell of the house in Streatham.

A lengthy silence was followed by, 'And just what do you expect me to do about it, Donald? Hire a bodyguard?'

'Dame Amelia, don't think this melodramatic, but I advise getting away for a while. That's what I intend to do – leave London and lie low.'

Amelia harrumphed. 'But Donald, that is exactly what I have just done. I *am* – I was, until you called – enjoying my first country break in months.'

Langham pulled a pained face. 'If I may say

252

so, the killer probably knows about Castle Melacorum.' He stopped, then said, 'You haven't
noticed anyone strange lurking in the vicinity of
the castle since your arrival, have you? He rides
a motorbike—'

A silence greeted his words.

'Dame Amelia?'

'A motorbike, you say? Why, Harker — my
driver — mentioned on the way up that a motorcyclist had been following us all the way from
Ealing.'

Oh, Christ ... Langham thought. 'Right,' he
said, suddenly businesslike. 'Get Harker to drive
you to a hotel somewhere well away from where
you are now. And stay there until I say so. I'll
give you my number.'

'But I've dismissed Harker an hour ago,' Amelia said. 'I told him to have a few days off.'

'Very well. Ring for a taxi.'

'A taxi. Do you realize how isolated I am out
here, Donald?' To give the old girl her due, she
sounded to be taking the situation in her stride.

'Very well, I'm on my way.'

'What? Donald, don't you think you're being a
trifle sensationalist about all this? The motorcyclist was probably just a coincidence.'

'I'm not taking any chances. Lock the doors to
the castle and don't let anyone in. I'm on my
way. And Dame Amelia, ring the local police
and explain the situation, understood?'

'Well, if you say so,' Amelia said dubiously.

Langham thanked her and rang off.

He tried to get through to Mallory again, but
the receptionist said he was still out on a case.

253

Langham swore to himself and said he'd be in touch.

Next he rang Ralph Ryland.

'Don,' Ryland quipped, 'twice in one day. You must really like me...'

'Fancy a spin in the country?' Langham asked.

'If it's business and I can put it on expenses...' Ryland said.

Langham explained the situation and Ryland said, 'I'll bring the shooter. Be faster if I pick you up. Be there in ... say twenty minutes, tops.'

'Good man,' Langham said, and put the phone down.

He paced up and down in considerable agitation for fifteen minutes, tried phoning Mallory twice – each time to no avail – then hurried from his flat and spent an anxious few minutes looking up and down the street for Ryland's decrepit Morris Minor.

Eighteen minutes after their telephone conversation Ryland – as good as his word – braked before the kerb and Langham jumped into the passenger seat. Ryland took off, burning rubber and exceeding the speed limit. They headed west through light traffic. Langham looked at his watch. It had just turned two.

Ryland said, 'I reckon we'll be in Berkshire by three. Where's the old bird live?'

Langham gave the name of the village. 'About five miles north of Bracknell.'

Ryland glanced at him. 'You say a motorbike trailed her all the way from Ealing?'

'Apparently. But, God willing, it might have been a coincidence, as Amelia said.'

'Never had you down as a believer, Don.'

Langham grinned. 'Slip of the tongue due to stress,' he said. 'I like Amelia, and I hate to think...' He trailed off, telling himself that everything would be fine; they'd get to Castle Melacorum, find Amelia in high dudgeon and willing to be moved *only* if they promised to chauffeur her to the very finest hotel in Cheltenham...

They were bowling through Ealing twenty minutes later. Ryland put his foot down and they left London behind them and sped into the country.

'Just like being on ops again, Cap'n.'

Langham glanced across at his driver. 'Do you miss Madagascar?'

Ryland pursed his lips. 'Madagascar? No. I miss the ... what d'you call it...? The camaraderie, the adrenaline rush. Tailing suspected philandering husbands isn't quite the same. You?'

Langham stared out at the passing countryside. 'The same. The intensity of the experience out there cemented relationships. Looking back, I realize I had a good war. Thing is, I feel guilty for admitting that.'

Ryland nodded. 'I know what you mean.' He glanced across at Langham, then said, 'You're doing it again, Don.'

'Doing what?' he asked, mystified.

'This,' Ryland said, and with his left hand he mimed fingering an imaginary scar on his forehead.

Langham quickly lowered his hand and smiled.

'Oh ... apparently it's something I do without realizing.'

'You recall the night that happened?'

'Vaguely, but to be honest all the ops have merged into one, in retrospect.' He thought about it. 'It was the first push into Antananarivo, wasn't it? Midnight. A recce on a coastal Vichy post.'

Ryland said, 'I was pinned down. I'd been bloody stupid and gone ahead against orders. You found me, dragged me back, and somewhere in there we came under fire. Saved my life, Don.'

'Rubbish. You'd have lain low until we reached you anyway.'

Ryland shook his head. 'With that sniper picking us off? You did for him like a bleedin' commando.'

It was not a memory Langham was comfortable with, and now he just said, 'Water under the bridge, Ralph. Lived to fight another day. And look at us now.'

Ryland laughed. 'Riding to the rescue of some damsel in distress.'

'Well, I'd hardly describe Dame Amelia as a damsel.'

They bypassed Bracknell and headed north into the countryside towards the village of Bradley Hinton. Amelia Hampstead's country pile was on the outskirts of the village. Langham had been there once, many years ago, when Amelia had thrown a fête to celebrate winning the Silver Dagger award.

Five minutes later, a little over an hour after

256

setting off from London, they passed through Bradley Hinton and motored down the lane towards Castle Melacorum.

Ryland gave vent to a prolonged whistle when the tower rose into view over a line of ash trees to their right. 'How the other half live, eh, Don?'

'Certainly is impressive,' Langham said.

All that remained of the thirteenth-century castle was a round corner tower, to which thirty years ago Amelia had added a rambling thatched cottage built from the original honey-coloured stones. The courtyard of the old castle, retained by three tumbledown walls, she had transformed into a riotous cottage garden.

Langham scanned the lane and the surrounding fields for any sign of a motorcyclist. Ryland slowed to a crawl and turned down a gravelled driveway. The countryside was still, almost silent, stunned by the heat of the day.

Ryland braked suddenly before a timber bridge that approached the castle's tower. He leapt from the car and bent to examine the gravel. Langham joined him, his heart in his mouth. 'What is it?'

Ryland pointed to a narrow trench in the gravel. 'I'm no expert, Don, but I'd say that was made by a motorbike.'

Langham swore and hurried over the bridge that crossed the moat, its waters green with algae. He came to the tower's arched doorway and stopped. The door stood ajar, the timbers around the lock shattered.

'It's been shot open,' Ryland said. 'What's that?'

He pointed to a stone positioned to one side of

257

the door. It was a huge sandstone block bound securely by a thick rope; a thick cord extended from the stone and ended in a noose.

'Oh, Christ,' Langham said.

Ryland slipped his pistol from inside his jacket and stepped forward. He eased the door open, paused on the threshold and listened. He stepped inside cautiously and Langham followed, wishing that he too was armed.

They crossed a large timbered hallway. To their right was a staircase rising up the tower, and to the left an open doorway giving on to a long sitting room that occupied the length of the cottage. At the far end of the room, French windows were flung open on to the abundant garden.

Stepping carefully and looking right and left as he went, Ryland led the way into the room. A small bookcase and a coffee table had been overturned, and Langham stared with mounting dread at the books spilled across the parquet flooring.

Ryland hurried to the open French windows just as Langham heard a faint cry. 'Donald? Donald, is that you?'

Langham felt a surge of relief. 'Amelia has her study in the tower,' he said, turning back into the hall.

'I'll check out here,' Ryland said, stepping tentatively into the garden.

'Dame Amelia?' Langham called up the stairs.

'Donald! I'm in the tower. The wretch tried to abduct me!'

Langham took the stairs two at a time, more

258

than a little amazed that Amelia had survived the encounter. He rapped on the massive timber door to the study, which Amelia unlocked. He slipped inside.

Dame Amelia was almost six feet tall, but looked all the more imposing for having a silver-grey bouffant beehive hairdo that added another twelve inches to her height. She grasped his hand and said, 'Never in my life have I been as grateful to see a friendly face.'

'What happened?' He hurried across to a mullioned window and peered out at the garden.

'The miscreant shot his way into my castle!' Amelia cried. 'I was downstairs, in the process of calling the police when I heard the shots. I nearly succumbed on the spot, Donald!'

In the garden Langham caught sight of Ryland, pistol poised, as he moved around a stand of topiary in the shape of a cockerel.

He turned and stared at Amelia. She had scooped a small dog from the floor and was hugging it to her considerable chest.

'I was frozen to the spot, Donald. Frozen! A man entered the hallway, saw me and raised a pistol! I don't know what came over me but I let out a bellow and threw the first thing that came to hand. Luckily it was a marble statuette – and with beginner's luck I hit the devil in the chest. By this time Poirot joined in the attack.'

Langham blinked. 'Poirot?'

Amelia held up the dog, a jet black ball of fur with a pointed muzzle. 'My little Belgian Schipperke, Poirot.'

On cue, the dog yapped at him.

259

He laughed. 'Does Agatha know that you've named him after her detective?'

'Of course she does, and she thinks it a positive *hoot*. Anyway, Poirot launched himself at the intruder, latched on to his hand and wouldn't let go. Drew blood, I'm proud to report. And I took the opportunity to attack him with my walking stick!'

'He met his match when he tried to mess with you, Amelia.'

'While he was on the floor, Poirot and I made a beeline for the study and locked ourselves in here.' She drew a deep breath and smiled at him. 'And minutes later I heard the sound of your car in the drive. Oh, the relief, Donald, the relief!'

'I think you've done jolly well on your own,' he said.

'But what I don't understand is why, if this awful little man is so intent on bumping off us scribblers, he didn't take the opportunity to shoot me when he had the chance.'

Langham shook his head. 'I don't know, Amelia.' He recalled the bound stone on the threshold of the castle, obviously pre-prepared and brought here for a reason...

'Can you describe him?' he asked.

Amelia's vast, powdered visage pulled a pained expression. 'The appalling little man wore a balaclava, goggles, and a scarf concealing the lower half of his face. All I can say about him was that he was short and rather dumpy.'

He heard the dull report of a gunshot, followed closely by another. He whirled towards the window and stared out. He saw Ryland and his heart

260

leapt. His friend was flat on his belly, and at first Langham thought he'd taken a hit. Then, as quick as lightning, the detective sprang to his feet and ran into the insubstantial cover of a rose-covered pergola. He took aim and fired.

At the far end of the garden Langham made out the small figure of the interloper. He ducked as Ryland fired, climbed a tumbledown section of wall and vanished from sight. Seconds later he heard the catarrhal cough of a motorcycle engine being kicked into life.

Down below, Ryland lost no time in giving chase. He sprinted back into the house and seconds later Langham heard the detective clatter across the wooden bridge. The car engine sounded, gravel crunched, and Ryland's ancient Morris Minor sped off in pursuit of the motor-cyclist.

Dame Amelia flopped into an armchair still clutching her dog. 'If it were not for you and your brave friend...' she began.

'Don't underestimate your own contribution,' Langham said, 'or Poirot's.'

'But why,' she pleaded, 'is the evil little man doing this? Why target us, Donald?'

Psychological motivation had never been the strong point of Amelia's whodunits. He shook his head. 'Someone with a grudge, a deep-seated pathological envy of those he considers more successful than himself? I don't really know, Amelia. But I hope we find out soon.'

She stared at him. 'Do you think it's one of our colleagues?'

'It's a possibility. Or someone within the

trade...' He stopped when he heard the sound of a car's engine approaching, and moved to the window overlooking the drive.

Seconds later Ryland's Morris hove into view. The detective leapt out and hurried to the tower. Langham opened the door and called out, 'Up here, Ralph.'

Ryland appeared seconds later, out of breath. 'Bastard gave me the slip at a crossroads!' He saw Dame Amelia and bobbed his head. ''Scuse me French, m'am.'

'I have been employing the vernacular to describe the man, so no apologies needed on that score.'

'You all right, Ralph?' Langham asked.

'Right as rain. The bloke's no marksman, Don. But I'm getting rusty. He surprised me. I was a sitting duck at one point down there, but he didn't take his chance. If that'd been the Vichy in Madagascar...' He shrugged. 'For my part, I could only get off a couple of shots, but he was a moving target.'

'You did exceptionally well in chasing the blackguard away,' Dame Amelia opined. 'And for that you have my eternal gratitude.'

'Right,' Langham said. 'There's little we can do around here. My advice, Dame Amelia, would be come with us to London and book into an out-of-the-way hotel for a week or so.'

'That sounds like an eminently sensible suggestion, Donald. Would you give me a minute to pack a few essentials?'

'Quite a character,' Ryland said as she swept from the room, Poirot lodged under her arm.

'Wait till you hear how she beat off the gunman,' Langham said, and recounted Dame Amelia and Poirot's concerted attack.

Ralph looked puzzled. 'But why didn't the geezer just shoot her dead?'

'Recall the stone down there? I think he brought it with him with the express purpose of drowning Dame Amelia in her own moat.'

Ten minutes later they departed Castle Melacorum. Amelia fussed about leaving the castle unlocked, but Langham said he'd call a locksmith just as soon as they reached London. Their first priority was to see Dame Amelia lodged in a hotel off the beaten track.

'And I know just the place,' she said. 'A *chichi* little establishment in Belgravia I've used many times in the past.'

'Which,' Langham said, 'is exactly why I don't want you going there now. There's a decent place in Highgate.'

He gave the address to Ryland, who nodded and glanced at Dame Amelia in the passenger seat. 'Don told me all about you attacking the gunman, Dame Amelia.'

She trilled a laugh and, as they approached the capital, gave an exaggerated account of the mêlée at the castle. Langham smiled to himself and had no doubt that the episode would find its way into her next best-seller.

Langham ensured that Dame Amelia was ensconced in the Royal at Highgate. He accepted her fulsome thanks for, as she said, 'saving her bacon', but refused the offer of a drink.

He returned to Ryland in the hotel car park. 'Home, Don?' the detective enquired.

'Could you drop me round the corner, Ralph? There's a scribbler in the area I must see pretty sharpish.'

'Will do.'

As they pulled out into the street, Langham said, 'And would you mind contacting a locksmith and carpenter about the door at Castle Melacorum? Charge it to expenses. And if you could inform the boys in blue...'

'Leave it to me, Don. Here do?'

'This'll be fine.' He turned to Ryland. 'And thanks awfully for your help, Ralph. I couldn't have done it alone.'

Ryland grinned. 'Don't mention it, Don. Just like old times, eh?'

Langham laughed, thanked him again and climbed from the car. He watched the battered Morris drive off, then found a phone box and consulted his address book. A minute later he got through to Justin Fellowes.

'Donald, Donald...' the old man replied in fruity tones. 'I was hoping for a longer chat at the service last week.'

'Justin, I hope this doesn't sound too melo-dramatic, but I need to see you pretty urgently.'

'Urgently? My word, you sound like one of your novels. How urgent is urgent?'

'Now, perhaps?'

'Now? But my dear man, I was just about to dine—'

'Justin, I assure you this is a matter of life or death.'

A silence from the other end of the line. 'Life or death? Then you'd better come over directly. You know where I am?'

'Still at Stable Row, Highgate?'

'The same.'

'I'll be right over.'

He slipped from the phone box and hurried down the street.

Justin Fellowes, the Grand Old Man of the crime scene, the purveyor of over two dozen novels at the literary end of the mystery spectrum, owned a big three-storey Regency townhouse overlooking Hampstead Heath. Langham took the steps to the front door two at a time.

An elderly woman opened the door to his summons. 'Ah, you must be Mr Langham. Mr Fellowes said you'd be calling. Please, come in.'

Langham stepped inside as the woman took up a basket from a side table and called out, 'Mr Langham is here, sir! I'll be off now.' To Langham she said, 'Just along the corridor to the left. You'll find Mr Fellowes in his study.'

She slipped through the front door and shut it behind her. Langham moved along the hallway and knocked on the study door.

'Langham, come in and explain yourself. What's all this about? A matter of life and death?'

Fellowes was an abnormally tall, balding man, stooped and benign, with the comfortable tweedy gravitas Langham associated with Hampstead literary types. He waved Langham to an armchair in the bow window and resumed his own swivel chair before a desk bearing an ancient

265

upright typewriter.

Utilized as paperweights on the desk, and as bookends, were the various awards he'd won in a long and distinguished career: the Golden Revolver for the Perfect Murder short story, the Blunt Instrument Lifetime Achievement Award and, taking pride of place on the wall above the desk, the Silver Stiletto for the best crime novel of 1950.

'Now, out with it, man. What's all this about?'

Langham leaned forward in the chair. 'I know this might sound fantastic, Justin, but I have good reason to think that your life is in danger.'

Fellowes regarded him evenly over his half-moon reading glasses. He seemed not in the slightest put out. 'You do?'

For the next ten minutes he told Fellowes about the deaths of Max Sidley, Nigel Lassiter, Gervaise Cartwright, Dan Greeley and Frankie Pearson, and the attempts on the lives of Charles Elder and Amelia Hampstead. He finished by describing his finding the paperbacks in the burned-out Streatham terrace house.

Fellowes listened without the slightest expression crossing his liver-spotted visage.

'This sounds like a plot from a pre-war pulp yarn,' he drawled. 'Poor Nigel ... and Max! I didn't know Greeley, and hardly knew Frankie Pearson. As for Gervaise, well, the cad had it coming to him. But I'd rather I avoided the same fate.'

'I advise you take a week or two away, until the police track the killer down.'

Fellowes looked sceptical. 'And they're confident of doing so?'

'Well, they're on the case,' Langham said inadequately.

Fellowes nodded. 'Thank you, Donald. I have the latest chapter to finish, but as soon as I do so I'll take a vacation. I have a sister in Dorset...'

'If I were you I'd get out sooner rather than later,' he said. 'I'll be leaving the capital just as soon as I can.'

Fellowes nodded. 'Point taken, Donald.' He glanced at his watch. 'Now, if you don't mind...?'

Langham smiled, bid the old man *bon appetit*, and took his leave.

He considered ringing Maria to ensure it would be all right if he called round, but as he turned the corner into the High Street he saw a passing taxi and hailed it. On the way to Kensington he realized how tired he was. The events of the day had taken their toll, along with the stress of knowing he was on the killer's list of victims.

He paid the driver, hurried up the steps to Maria's flat and rang the bell. She seemed to take an age to answer, but when she pulled open the door he decided that the vision before him had been well worth the wait.

She gasped. 'But Donald, you look absolutely done for!'

He almost staggered into her embrace. 'I was wondering if I might stay here tonight, Maria? The settee will be fine.'

She ushered him up the steps to her apartment. 'Of course. But Donald, what has happened?'

He found himself recounting, for the third time that day, his discovery of the paperbacks at Streatham, and went on to tell her about the incident at Castle Melacorum.

She listened, wide-eyed, but interrupted him with a graceful hand on his knee. 'But I am a *terrible* host, Donald, and you must need a drink, *oui*?'

He smiled as he watched her hurry into the kitchen, and for the first time that day he began to relax.

TWENTY

The following morning Maria sat behind Charles's desk and fielded the twentieth phone call that day. 'The latest news is that Charles is in a serious but stable condition. No, he isn't up to seeing visitors at the moment, but I will be in touch with all his clients just as soon as the situation changes. Thank you. Yes, I will. Certainly. Goodbye.'

She replaced the receiver and sighed. She had repeated the same tired words on at least a dozen occasions that morning, and with each rendition of his condition she grew ever more depressed. More than anything she wanted to visit Charles, sit by his bedside and simply hold his hand. The medical staff at the hospital had been adamant, however: absolutely no visitors were to be allowed until Mr Elder's condition had changed for the better.

She glanced at the wall clock and was surprised to find that it was almost one. She had been working continually since nine that morning and now she was famished.

She was considering taking a break for lunch when the phone rang again. She took a deep breath, fixed a smile on her face – which she found always made her sound a little more cheerful, even if she were feeling dreadful – and said, 'Hello, this is the Charles Elder Agency. Maria speaking...'

'Maria, my dear.'

'Amelia, how nice you called.'

'I said I'd be in touch about meeting up. I suppose you've already eaten – but we could always meet for a drink, if you can tear yourself away from the office, that is.'

'Actually I've been so busy I haven't had time for lunch. I was just thinking of taking a break.'

'Wonderful! I'm in Highgate, and there's a wonderful little French place around the corner. Le Moulin Bleu.'

'I know it. I'll drive over and meet you there at ... say one thirty?'

'Delightful. And I have *so* much to tell you, Maria.'

'Well, I heard from Donald about what happened at the castle.'

'Oh, "Donald" is it, now? Are you two by any chance...?' Amelia paused suggestively.

Maria laughed. 'And I have a few things to tell you, too, Amelia,' she said.

269

'Oh,' trilled Amelia, 'how talk of romance cheers a dull day!'

Maria replaced the receiver and attended to her make-up, applied a little lipstick and was just about to step from the office when she saw, through the window overlooking the street, the unmistakable form of Gideon Martin striding across the road towards the agency. What a ridiculous little man he was, she thought with annoyance, with his thick, barrel-shaped chest thrust forward, his disproportionately short legs – and his big, lantern-jawed face and tiny eyes!

She swore to herself and ran, as fast as her high heels would allow, through the outer office to the door. She dropped the catch and sagged against the door with relief. Seconds later she heard the handle turn, followed by a sharp knocking.

'Hello! Hello, Maria!' His presumptuous summons filled the room.

Maria crept away from the door on tiptoe, cringing. She cursed the man and hoped he'd desist and leave sooner rather than later.

He knocked again, then rapped on the door with something more substantial than his knuckles – his pretentious swordstick, no doubt. He sounded as if he were intent on battering the door down.

'Maria!' The tattoo sounded again. 'Maria, will you please open up!' Was it her imagination, or did he sound a little drunk? 'I have ... have an important matter to discuss.'

And she could guess what that might be – his farcical infatuation with her, his 'undying love' ... She felt a welling anger, and she almost ran to

270

the door, snatched it open and told him to go to hell.

Seconds later, however, she heard the sound of his rapid footsteps beating a retreat down the steps. She moved to the window and, peeping out, saw Martin stride off down the pavement, aggressively swinging his swordstick.

She took a deep breath and wondered how long it might be before the coast would be clear. She gave it a couple of minutes, gathered her handbag, then slipped through the door. Her Sunbeam was parked directly outside the agency. Martin might still be lurking in the area, but if she ran to the car, ducked in and made a quick getaway...

She tapped down the steps at speed, unlocked the car door in record time, jumped in and started the engine. A glance in the wing-mirror satisfied her that he was not racing along the pavement in pursuit. She put the car into gear and eased it out into the quiet street, and seconds later she was bowling through the leafy environs of Pimlico with a growing sense of accomplishment.

Five minutes later she arrived at Highgate and pulled up outside Le Moulin Bleu. She looked at her watch: one twenty. Despite Gideon Martin's importunate arrival, she was on time.

She swept into the restaurant, scanned the diners for Dame Amelia and, not seeing her, asked the maître d' for a table for two.

She was escorted to a table at the back of the restaurant. She ordered a sparkling mineral water and scanned the menu. She normally only

271

ever dined at expensive restaurants with her father, who always insisted on footing the bill, but she supposed that this was a special occasion as she only saw Dame Amelia once or twice a year.

A minute later she looked up as a shadow fell across the table, and expecting to see Dame Amelia she arranged her features in a smile.

Her smile froze, however, when she saw who was staring down at her, his face thunderous.

'Why, Gideon ... What are you doing—?'

'I saw you leave ... leave the agency,' he said, his barrel torso thrust forward, his teeth showing, 'after having ignored my summons.' He swayed, reached out and steadied himself by clutching the back of a chair. 'So I had my taxi follow you here!'

He pulled out the chair and sat down quickly – or rather slumped down. He was, she decided, very drunk. She looked around, nervously, to see if the other diners had noticed his inebriated arrival. To her relief they were absorbed in their meals.

He stared at her, resting one hand on his ridiculous swordstick.

She leaned forward and hissed, 'What do you want, Gideon!'

His face, reddened with drink, seemed even larger than usual. His little piggy eyes were lachrymose. She prayed he wasn't about to cause an even bigger scene.

'I want,' he said and hiccupped. 'I want you to return my pistol!'

She sat back, relieved. She had feared he might

272

pledge his undying devotion to her, and cause a ruckus when she spurned his entreaties.

'Well,' he said, swaying in his seat, 'are you going ... going to give it to me?'

She smiled sweetly. 'I am afraid, Gideon, that I am not in the habit of carrying a weapon around in my handbag. And even if I were, I would hardly hand it over to you while you're in your present condition.'

She sat back, pleased with her little peroration.

He blinked at her. 'My ... my *present* condition has little to do with it!' he said. 'I need the pistol!'

She could not resist the cruel taunt, 'Whatever for, Gideon? Are you finally going to do the honourable thing and shoot yourself?'

'Not myself, Maria. I intend to ... to perforate...' and he laughed at his fancy turn of phrase, 'a blaggard or two at the Crime Club dinner this evening.'

Maria concealed her alarm and said, 'Well, in that case I would certainly not give up the weapon, even if I *were* carrying it.'

He leaned forward, clutched the edge of the table, and slurred, 'Please, the pistol. Drive me back to your place, trot up those steps like a good little thing, and just give me the blasted pistol!'

Her anger rising, Maria hissed, 'Gideon, if you don't leave now I shall call the maître d' and request he summon the police. You're making a damnable scene, and you'll only be sorry when you sober up. Please, just muster whatever dignity you can summon and *go*.'

273

He regarded her with that glassy-eyed stare of the unfeasibly drunk, and she wondered if he'd comprehended a word of her request. At last he said, enunciating his words with exaggerated care, 'I don't think you quite understand, Maria. I've had enough. Enough! Do y'know ... do you know – even the Crime Club barred my entry last year! Me! I've published ... published enough in their grubby little genre to deserve membership ... but no! Not me! So...' He stared at her. 'So I intend to ventilate a liver or two tonight – if not with my trusty but elusive pistol, then with this!' And so saying he lofted his swordstick and swung it about his head.

This latest exhibition of his insobriety had alerted the attention of the diners. Heads turned and eyes goggled at Martin's feeble imitation of a gyrocopter.

'Gideon! For God's sake *just go*!'

The maître d' hurried to the table and said, 'Madam, if this gentleman is causing you...'

'He is just about to leave, *aren't* you?' she said.

To her surprise, Martin almost jumped to his feet. 'I know when I am not welcome, Maria – and despite your refusal to give me the pistol, be in no doubt that my love for you is eternal.' And, with this farcical avowal, and a ludicrous little bow, he turned on his heel and staggered from the restaurant.

She apologized to the maître d' and said, 'He was *not* my guest, I assure you. Ah...' She raised a hand and waved as Dame Amelia appeared on the threshold.

Amelia swept through the restaurant, clutching

Poirot to her bosom, her entry earning as many turned heads as had Martin's exit. 'My dear, but was that Gideon Martin I saw debouch with ill-grace from this establishment not seconds ago?'

'I'm afraid so, Amelia. He followed me here from the agency.'

'He did? But what did he want this time, my dear?'

The maître d' eased the chair beneath Dame Amelia's ample bottom and provided a cushion for the dog. Amelia settled Poirot on the third chair, then ordered a bottle of champagne. 'And Thierry, a plate of chicken livers for Poirot, if you please.'

Maria said, 'Would you believe, Amelia, that Martin wanted me to return his pistol?'

'His pistol? Why, this gets juicier by the second! Do tell.'

They ordered grilled sole with asparagus, and Poirot tucked into the chicken livers. Maria recounted the contretemps at her flat a few nights ago. 'The upshot was that I snatched the gun from his grip and tossed it across the room, and he left rather hastily. With his tail, I think the saying goes, firmly between his legs.'

'Good for you,' Amelia said. 'But what on earth did he want with the gun today?'

'Oh, nothing much. He just wanted to, and these are his own words, "perforate a few livers" at the Crime Club dinner this evening.'

'In that case I'm delighted I shan't be there,' said Dame Amelia. 'What a frightful little man. I take it you refused to give him what he wanted?'

275

'Of course – so he said he'd run a few members through with his swordstick instead.'

'Remarkable. The jackanape ought to be locked up. I say, this sole is rather exquisite, don't you agree?'

'Divine,' Maria said. 'But tell me about your encounter at the castle, Amelia. Donald said you and Poirot were a formidable double act.'

Amelia waved modestly. 'If not for Donald and his friend, Maria, I might not be here to tell the tale. They arrived in the veritable nick of time.'

And Dame Amelia proceeded to recount – with embellishments and many witty asides – what had obviously been a rather terrifying ordeal. 'And would you believe,' she said, 'that he had even brought a vast stone – he intended to tie it around my neck and pitch me into the moat! The cheek of it!'

Maria murmured her shock, but could not hide a smile at Amelia's *savoir faire*.

'But enough of that little escapade,' she said. 'Now, do tell me more about you and Donald. And before you start, I must say that he is a rather eligible catch, my dear.'

Maria tried not to blush. She shrugged. 'Where to begin? I have admired Donald for many years. But Donald, being English and therefore reserved, he would not screw up his courage to ask me to dinner.'

'Ah, the malaise of the English male,' Amelia sighed. 'But in that case how did you two...?'

Maria sipped her champagne. 'We were thrown together, as it were, by the events of the past week – the blackmail of Charles and his subsequent shooting. It has been a terrible business, Amelia.'

'Donald told me all about it. I rather think that someone in our dear little fraternity has it in for us. Donald told me that he, too, was on the "hit list" as he called it – though how I dislike that American term! He mentioned a clutch of soggy paperbacks ... Quite the detective, your Donald.'

Open-mouthed, Maria stared at Dame Amelia for a second or two in absolute silence.

'Maria? Maria, are you quite all right? You look as if you've seen a ghost.'

'I ... I think I have, Amelia,' she said. 'Oh, what a blind fool I've been,' she whispered.

'My girl, what's come over you?'

'The killer ... the gunman. He's short, portly, ginger – according to the description of the only person to have seen him.'

'I don't quite see...'

'And the killer, he has a grudge, Donald told me, a grudge against those writers more successful than himself in the crime genre, and against agents and editors who might have slighted him in the past.'

She stopped, feeling alternately hot and cold as the realization dawned. She whispered, 'Who do you think that description fits to a tee, Amelia?'

'Why,' Dame Amelia began, then fell silent and stared at Maria with a shocked expression. 'You don't think...?'

'He fits the bill,' Maria murmured, 'and tonight, on his own admission, he intends to go to the Crime Club dinner and...'

277

Amelia reached out and clutched her hand. 'You must contact Donald forthwith,' she said, 'and dessert can go to hell.'

'There's a phone box around the corner,' Maria said. 'I'll phone the flat and see if he's in. Do excuse me. I'll leave some money...' she went on, indicating her plate.

'Nonsense, child! This meal is my pleasure. Now, go and ring Donald, and do keep me informed.'

Maria kissed Dame Amelia on her soft, powdery cheek, gathered her bag and hurried from the restaurant.

She found the phone box and rang her flat. The call tone rang out for a minute without reply. 'Come on, come on ... Oh, Donald, do please pick up the phone!' She gave it another minute – which seemed like an hour – and was about to replace the receiver when the line clicked and Donald said, 'Hello? Hello...?'

'Donald. Oh, thank God you're there.'

'Maria? You sound terrible.'

She tried to order her thoughts. 'Donald, I think I know who the killer is.'

'What?'

'Stay there. I can't explain over the phone. I'm on my way!'

'But Maria—'

She slammed down the receiver and ran back to the Sunbeam.

On the way to Kensington she went through the logic of her deductions, alternatively thinking it absurd that someone she knew should turn out to be the culprit, then assessing the evidence

278

and realizing that in all likelihood Gideon Martin was indeed the guilty party.

She recalled the touch of his hand all those months ago, his kiss, and she felt physically sick.

She pulled up outside her flat and raced up the steps, unlocked the door and ran up the stairs to her apartment, almost tripping in her haste. Before she could fumble with the key, Donald pulled open the door and embraced her.

He led her into the lounge, sat her on the settee and knelt before her. 'Now, Maria, what's all this about the killer?'

She took a deep breath, her heart racing. She nodded, ordering her thoughts, and said, 'Do you recall me describing an encounter with someone I knew last year, a man called Gideon Martin? He came here with a gun last week, threatening to shoot himself. He's a failed writer and a little crazy...'

Donald looked incredulous. 'And you think *he's* the killer?'

She grasped his hands. '*Listen* to me, Donald. I saw him today. He followed me from the agency and confronted me in a restaurant. He demanded I return his pistol. He was drunk, a little mad. He said ... he said he was going to the Crime Club dinner this evening and wanted to shoot...'

'The dinner? My God, I'd forgotten all about it.'

'In the end he left, but he's threatening to attack diners with his swordstick.'

Donald nodded matter-of-factly. 'Very well,

but threatening to attack members of the club and actually killing...'

'Donald! Listen to me! He fits the description of the motorcyclist – the man in the public baths described by that boy. He's short, plump, ginger-complexioned and balding. And ... and I know he hates Charles and Dame Amelia.'

'But I thought...' Donald began. 'I mean, wasn't he chasing after you?'

Maria blinked. 'So...?'

'So, the killer is the other way inclined. He used Kenny Wilson in the baths, remember?'

'So,' she said impatiently, 'Martin must be bisexual – not that I ever suspected.' She clutched his hand. 'Donald, you've got to do something!'

He gave her hand a last squeeze, hurried across to the phone and dialled. He looked at her from the bureau and said, 'I'll contact Jeff Mallory.'

Maria nodded, sitting on the edge of the settee.

'Hello, could you put me through to Detective Inspector Mallory? If you could tell him it's Donald Langham.'

She sat with her fingers to her lips and watched him as he traced the scar on his forehead impatiently.

'Jeff,' Langham said, sitting up. 'Developments. Long story, but Maria just had an encounter with someone who fits the killer's description, and he's threatening to attend the Crime Club dinner tonight.'

Donald listened, staring down at the rug and still fingering his scar. He nodded. 'That's right. The Albemarle Club, Pall Mall. It's due to kick

280

off at seven thirty.'

He was silent for a second, then looked across at Maria. 'The man's name – and do you know his address?'

She stood and crossed the room to him. 'He is Gideon Martin. And his address ... Let me think, let me think! He lives in Belsize Park, Victoria Street, but I can't recall the number.'

Donald relayed the information to Mallory, then said, 'Right-ho. Excellent. I'll see you then.'

He replaced the receiver and looked up at her. 'Jeff says you deserve a medal. He's coming for me right away.'

They embraced. 'Donald, do be careful.'

'No heroics,' he promised her. 'Jeff said he'll station people in the club and flood the area with plain clothes officers. I'll be fine.'

TWENTY-ONE

At seven that evening Langham sat with Mallory in his Humber across the road from the Albemarle Club.

He wound the window halfway down and lit his pipe, then finished telling Mallory about the paperbacks left in the Streatham house and what had happened at Castle Melacorum yesterday. He recalled speaking to the editor at Digit Books, and mentioned the hit-and-run death of

Alexander Southern, aka Dan Greeley.

'So...' Mallory said, 'of the seven writers of the books you found, four are dead and three, yourself, Fellowes and Amelia Hampstead, are still alive. Perhaps, Don, the seven of you are all the *writers* the killer – this Gideon Martin chap – intends to target?'

Langham thought about it. 'Maybe, but that still leaves the editors, agents, and who knows who else in the trade that the bastard has a grudge against.'

Mallory stared across the road at the club. He said at last, 'Well, I hope what your girl said is right – and he is only armed with a swordstick.'

'I've been thinking about that,' Langham said. 'Something doesn't add up. Yesterday at Castle Melacorum he was armed with a pistol. He used it to destroy the lock on the door, and fire at Ralph Ryland later.'

Mallory shook his head. 'So why, if he had a pistol yesterday, did he want another one back from Maria?'

'Exactly.' Langham thought about it, then said, 'How about this: in getting away from Ryland the other day, he dropped the pistol and didn't have time to search for it. That'd explain his demand for Maria to return the other one.'

'It's possible,' Mallory grunted. 'I just hope he hasn't been able to get his hands on one in the meantime. But according to Maria, he's not the sort who consorts with underworld types. Not that I'm taking any chances,' he went on. 'I have men stationed at all the tube stations in the vicinity, and the four nearby taxi ranks.'

'What about in the Albemarle itself?'

Mallory nodded. 'Two men in the foyer, two manning the staircases on every floor and a couple of men outside the meeting room. All plainclothes, needless to say. Oh, and I've had a word with the secretary and ordered the meeting and dinner to be held in rooms other than those originally scheduled. It was too late when all this blew up to contact everyone and cancel the do, so I reckoned the next best thing was to move it up a floor.'

'Good thinking.'

'It'll be a miracle if he gets past the front door, but I'm not taking any chances. Good work on Maria's part, Don.'

'It came to her while she was dining with Dame Amelia. Martin had just accosted her, asking her for the gun, and when he'd gone she and Amelia were discussing the deaths when the penny dropped. She was pretty shaken up by the time I saw her.'

'I can't wait to meet this little number. Looks, intelligence and a fine deductive capability.'

Langham smiled. 'When all this is over, let's go out to dinner.'

'I'll keep you to that, Don.' He glanced at his watch. 'Seven fifteen, and here they come.'

Langham puffed on his pipe and stared through the window. Cars were beginning to draw up outside the Albemarle, and the great and the good of the crime-writing fraternity were alighting and moving sedately up the steps between the club's marble pillars. Langham recognized many writers and editors, men and women

283

he'd met at the Crime Club over the years and others he'd bumped into at publishers' parties and bookshop signings and readings.

Taken as a whole, the crime-writing set was a pretty democratic bunch, with aristocratic writers rubbing shoulders with those of working-class background like himself. That was one thing he liked about the quarterly Crime Club dinners – their inclusivity; the idea that everyone was in the same trade irrespective of class or background. That and, of course, the fact that the Albemarle had a fine cellar and served excellent food.

Mallory said, 'Do you think Agatha C herself will attend tonight?'

'Not for the spring dinner. She comes to the do every year just before Christmas.' He looked at the bulky detective. 'I didn't have you down as a fan.'

Mallory smiled. 'Taken as fantasies divorced from the real world, I think they're fine. You?'

'Not my usual fare, but I reviewed a reprint of her *Cards on the Table* last year and it was rather good.' He laughed. 'She's a big pal of Dame Amelia, who named her dog after Poirot.'

'You move in elevated circles, Don.'

Langham blew a billow of smoke through the window. 'I'd hardly say that.' He pointed across the road at the Albemarle with the stem of his pipe. 'This is about as posh as it gets for me.'

'My apologies for not allowing you to attend.'

'Apologies accepted.'

They sat in silence for a few minutes. Langham scanned the street to the left and right of the

284

club's porticoed entrance. It was a mild, clear night and pedestrians were out in force – couples heading into the city for a night on the town and workers making their way homewards in the other direction. There was no sign of a small, portly ginger-haired man amongst their number.

He looked at his watch. Seven thirty ... the chairman would be banging his gavel any second now and calling the meeting to order. First would be the announcements, which included everything from the introduction of new members to the listing of awards won by members, then a fifteen-minute speech by the specially invited guest, followed by the dinner itself.

'Perhaps he's thought twice about showing himself,' Langham said, 'after announcing his intentions to Maria.'

'Or he was too drunk to make it,' Mallory said. 'I had a man check the pubs around here and where he lives, on the off chance that he'd nipped in for a shot of Dutch courage. Nothing.'

'He might well have sobered up since two o'clock,' Langham said. 'I don't know what might be better – Martin showing up sozzled or sober.'

'In my experience it's easy dealing with a drunk,' Mallory said. 'They resort to fisticuffs at the drop of a hat, giving you the excuse to put the boot in ... in a manner of speaking, of course.'

'Of course, Jeff,' Langham said.

Mallory looked at his watch. 'I'll give it a few minutes, then go over and rouse the troops. I don't want them slacking because Martin hasn't shown up yet.'

'Mind if I pop across with you?'

Mallory looked at him. 'Very well, but stick close to me, OK?'

'Understood.'

Langham looked up and down the street, expecting to see Martin's bullfrog form – as Maria had described it – approach at any second. The flow of pedestrians had slowed to a trickle now, in theory making the sighting of their subject that much easier. Two big plainclothes policemen stood sentry at the top of the Albemarle's steps, watching every passer-by as they approached the club and hurried onwards.

'Right,' Mallory declared, pushing open the driver's door. 'Time to stretch our legs.'

Langham climbed from the car, knocked out his pipe and followed Mallory across the street.

He felt at once an anticipation that Martin might still show himself, and yet a growing sense of anticlimax as he realized that the chances were that Gideon Martin had fought shy of making an appearance after so rashly announcing his intentions to Maria. At least now, he thought, the police had an identity with which to work. It could only be a matter of time before Gideon Martin was apprehended.

Mallory chatted quietly to the men at the door – selected obviously for their strapping physiques – then led the way inside. The foyer of the Albemarle was a visually tasteful medley of plush red carpet, palms in brass pots and beeswaxed oak panelling. A liveried receptionist stood to attention behind a counter, watching

286

them with an eagle eye.

Mallory spoke to two further plain-clothes officers stationed beside the lift, then led Langham into the elevator.

As they rose to the second floor, Mallory said, 'The members have just gone into dinner. They're using the dining room adjacent to the rearranged venue. We'll just pop in and I'll reassure the chairman.'

'I've no doubt the members will be loving this,' Langham said. 'Real-life crime after years of writing about it.'

Mallory snorted. 'They'll be racing to be the first to get this into their next work.'

'Let's hope they'll all be here to do that, come the end of the night.'

Mallory glanced at him. 'Pessimistic, aren't we? You don't think Martin'd get past the security I've set up?'

Langham smiled. 'He'd have to be super-human to do that.'

The lift bobbed, the doors sighed open and they stepped out into a green-carpeted corridor. Mallory led the way to the end of the passage and turned right. Two plainclothes officers stood before a polished double door, and they snapped to attention as Mallory approached.

'No sign of Martin,' Mallory said. 'But it's early days yet. Just popping in to give the chairman the gen.'

He tapped on the door, eased it open and slipped through, Langham entering after him.

The hubbub of conversation and tintinnabulation of cutlery modulated suddenly at their en-

287

trance. Two-dozen guests sat around a long table laden with silverware and loaded plates. Heads turned, and one or two people who Langham knew registered their surprise at his presence alongside the detective inspector. He'd be able to dine off this one for months.

Mallory gestured to the chairman, Edward Hume, a portly, silver-haired writer of Golden Age puzzle novels. Hume rose from his place and hurried around the table. 'Detective Inspector Mallory, Donald,' he greeted them. 'Well, we're all alive thus far,' he commented with gallows humour.

'No sign of the subject,' Mallory said. 'But I'd appreciate it if you were to remain in here until after the meal. I'm arranging for one of the bars on this floor to be opened at nine thirty, so you can retire there any time after that. I'll pop back and give you the go ahead. And just to reassure you once again, Mr Hume, that I have my men surrounding the place.'

'I have every confidence in you, Detective Inspector.' Hume nudged Langham. 'This'll feature in the next Sam Brooke, no doubt?'

'If you don't get there first, Edward.'

They slipped from the dining room and Mallory led the way along the corridor to a bar room. One of Mallory's men was supervising a bartender who was setting out tables and chairs. 'Nearly ready, sir.'

'Good man. I'll let them out at nine thirty. Have Bryce and MacKinnon shepherd them along here, will you, and then guard the door. If you'd station yourself in here with the members...'

'Very good, sir.'

'What now?' Langham asked as they left the bar.

'I'm going to have a poke around on the top floor.'

'I might go back to the car, if you don't mind.'

Mallory handed over the car keys. 'The reality of police work, Don. Ninety per cent of the time it's bloody monotonous.'

Langham stepped into the lift and pressed the stud for the ground floor.

On the way down he had an idea, and when the lift reached the ground floor and the doors opened, he pressed for the first floor and waited patiently for the doors to trundle shut.

The lift carried him up to the first floor and seconds later he stepped out, turned left and hurried over the thick pile carpet to the dining room where the meeting of the Crime Club had been originally scheduled to take place. He paused before the door, expecting it to be locked, and was therefore surprised when he turned the brass handle and the door clicked open.

The light was on, and the fact set his pulse racing. He looked around the room, not really expecting to find Gideon Martin concealed somewhere within it, but fearing the possibility.

Chairs were set out in rows, and at the far end of the room was the raised table at which the committee would have sat. Behind the table, long red curtains were drawn across the windows overlooking Pall Mall.

Langham stood on the threshold, considering

289

his options. He eased the door shut behind him and stood very still, the only sound the pulse of his heartbeat in his ears.

The wall to his left was one long expanse of oak panelling. To the right, the panelling was interrupted by a door. He moved around the chairs to the door and eased it open. The room beyond was in darkness. He reached around the jamb, fumbled for the light switch and found it.

He stepped into the adjacent room – a dining room occupied by a long table and a dozen chairs.

He was about to retrace his steps when he heard a sound from the room he'd just left.

He whirled and approached the door. The long red curtains to his right were falling back into place, and directly before him a chair lay on its back. He stepped into the room in time to glimpse a figure flash through the far door and disappear into the corridor.

He gave chase, pulled open the door and raced out. He looked right and left and saw someone disappear up the staircase at the far end of the corridor. He set off, reached the staircase seconds later and took the steps three at a time.

He looked up at the curve of the balustrade on the floor above and made out a plump hand clutching it as the interloper ascended. He cried out, 'Third floor!' to whichever of Mallory's men might be nearby.

He reached the third floor and turned to climb to the fourth when he saw Bryce and MacKinnon racing along the corridor towards him. 'He's up here!' he cried, and set off in pursuit.

He came to the fourth floor and almost collided with Mallory. 'I saw him,' Mallory said, and set off up the staircase before Langham could reply.

He followed, his pace slowing with the unaccustomed effort of the ascent, and seconds later Bryce and MacKinnon raced past him. He experienced a quick sensation of relief that he was no longer in the lead, and the novelist in him noted the emotion for future use. Cowardice, he wondered, or common sense?

'This way,' he heard someone call above him. When he came to the fifth floor he made out a narrow, uncarpeted flight of stairs leading upwards, and caught sight of one of the plainclothes officers near the top. He followed, panting.

He came to the top of the mean steps and felt a gust of cool wind in his face. A narrow door flapped open before him and he crashed through it on to the flat roof of the Albemarle.

A laminated sunset stretched across the horizon of west London, and an indigo twilight was beginning to fall. He made out three figures moving between the chimney stacks and, ahead of them, a stocky form racing away. The man looked over his shoulder and dodged to his left, momentarily lost behind the curved shape of a ventilation outlet.

Mallory called out, 'Stop!'

Langham caught up with them and rounded the outlet.

Gideon Martin came to a sudden halt thirty feet away and turned to face his pursuers. Langham made out his full-jawed face in the twilight, his skin slick with sweat and his piggy eyes desperate. In his right hand he clutched a swordstick, hoisted before him as if to beat off would-be assailants.

He took a step backwards, approaching the raised edge of the building.

Mallory stepped forward and held out a hand. 'Careful,' he cautioned.

Langham stopped in his tracks, breathlessly watching what was happening with a sense of terrible presentiment. Beside him, Bryce and Mackinnon were frozen like statues, staring.

Mallory took another step forward. 'Think about it, man...'

Martin turned away from Mallory and in so doing lost his footing. Whether he was still drunk, or merely dizzy from the chase, Langham could not tell – but his feet caught and, with an oddly graceful motion, he toppled over the edge of the building.

He made not a single sound as he fell, and it was the eerie silence that Langham found so sickening.

As if released from stasis, he and the others approached the edge and peered over.

The body lay on the pavement far below, unmoving, and Langham could tell, from the awkward angle of the head in relation to the torso, and the dark pool of blood spreading across the flagstones, that Gideon Martin was dead.

Donald walked up the steps to Maria's flat and pressed the buzzer.

He heard her footsteps on the stairs, running, and she pulled open the door and gasped when she saw him. 'Donald!'

She was a vision – backed by the roseate light in the hallway – wearing a thick, belted dressing gown and pom-pom slippers on her bare feet. 'Oh, I've been worrying so much!'

He hugged her. 'I'm fine.'

'Come in. Can I get you a drink? Whisky?'

'I could kill a beer.'

She took his hand and almost tugged him up the stairs to her apartment. 'I only have some French beer my father gave me.'

'Wonderful.'

He sat on the settee while she poured it. 'Now, what happened?' she asked as she sat down beside him.

'Well ... Gideon Martin is dead.'

She thrust her head towards him and opened her eyes wide. 'Dead?' She looked disbelieving.

He took a long swallow of the beer and told her about discovering Martin in the dining room. 'He fled, but we chased him up the stairs and on to the roof. He ... he was either still drunk or exhausted. I don't think he deliberately...' He shrugged. 'He lost his footing or tripped. Anyway, he fell from the roof. Jeff said he must have died instantly.'

Maria heard him out in silence, then said in a small voice, 'Martin was an evil man, Donald, but even so...'

He pulled her to him, inhaling her perfume; she had just had a bath and smelled divine. 'I know, I know. I'm sorry.'

293

She looked up at him. 'But I thought you said that Jeff was going to surround the place with his men?' She shrugged. 'So how did Martin get into the building?'

He stroked her hair. 'We think he went straight there from seeing you. Apparently there was a period between two and three when no one was at reception. He'd attended a Crime Club dinner a while back as a guest, so he knew where we usually dined. He concealed himself in the room. It was only by chance ... a hunch ... that I decided to check.'

'It's horrible, horrible!' She lodged her head against his chest. 'I think he was a little crazy, yes? To kill all those people...'

They sat side by side for a long time, held each other and quietly talked.

TWENTY-TWO

The following morning Maria rang the hospital from her flat, and Langham watched her clutching the phone to her ear. 'Maria Dupré here. I was wondering...'

She listened to what the sister said, and Langham noted the whitening of her knuckles on the receiver. He sat up, suddenly tense.

'Ah, *oui* ... Yes, yes. Oh. Oh, I see.'

The torture was unbearable. He tried to attract her attention with a quizzical expression, but she waved him away as she concentrated.

At last she replaced the receiver and turned to him. 'Charles passed a bad night. There was some internal bleeding, which has now stopped. Sister said that he is stable again, but not able to see visitors.'

He crossed the room and held her. 'We had been going to visit last night, before all the brouhaha at the Albemarle.'

'Well, we could not have gone anyway, Donald. Oh, I so want to see the old man.'

Langham smiled. 'His nibs,' he said fondly.

She looked into his eyes. 'I have just a little work to do at the agency this morning. Perhaps you could come over with me, I could get the work out of the way, and then we could go for a tea, no?'

'That sounds like a capital idea.'

Fifteen minutes later they were in Charles's office. Langham lodged himself in a leather armchair and watched Maria make the first of several phone calls.

At one point she swivelled her seat away from the desk and pointed at him. 'By the way,' she said playfully, 'I've told my father all about you.'

'That sounds ominous.'

'And he would like to meet you.'

'The official vetting, hm?'

She smiled. 'He's pleased that I have found someone "solid and dependable", as he said. He even wants to read one of your books.'

He scowled. 'Well, that might put the mockers

295

on things.'

She looked at him. '"The mockers"? What is "the mockers"?'

He was about to begin an explanation when the phone rang. Maria turned back to the desk and picked up the receiver.

'Ah, *oui* ... I mean, yes. Yes, we do represent him. His phone number? But as a matter of fact he is here in the office as we speak.'

Langham sat up, wondering who the caller might be.

Maria listened, frowning, and twirled a strand of hair around her forefinger. At last she said, 'Very well, I will tell him...' and replaced the receiver.

'For me?' he asked.

'A policeman called Brady, from the Highgate station. They want to question you.'

'Question me? Did they say what about?'

She shook her head. 'No. He just said, "Please tell Mr Langham that we'll be around in ten minutes".'

Highgate ... Was it a coincidence that he had been in Highgate to see Justin Fellowes on Tuesday evening?

'I wonder what on earth they want?' He kept his fears to himself and sipped his coffee. 'I suspect it's Jeff Mallory, wanting to follow up something connected to last night.'

Maria changed the subject, telling him about her father's preferred reading – which ran to Sartre and Camus – and he tried to make the appropriate responses while wondering why the Highgate constabulary wanted to question him.

Five minutes later a loud knocking sounded at the front door, and Maria hurried to answer it. Langham followed her.

She escorted a small, pale-faced man in his fifties into the outer office, accompanied by a uniformed constable. 'Mr Langham? I'm Inspector Brady from Highgate station. I'd like to question you about your movements on Tuesday evening.'

Langham smiled, despite a sense of growing unease, and gestured to the inner office. 'Very well, perhaps...'

'I'd like you to accompany me to the station, sir, if it's all the same.'

'Is that absolutely necessary, Inspector?'

'I'd prefer it if you would accompany me of your own accord, sir.'

He glanced across at Maria, who was standing with her fingers to her throat and looking worried. 'I'd better go,' he said.

'Donald...'

He smiled at her and followed Brady from the office. A black unmarked police car, engine running, was waiting in the street. Langham sat in the back next to the uniformed constable while Brady took the passenger seat beside the driver.

'Do you mind telling me what this is about?' he asked as they set off.

'When we arrive at the station, sir,' Brady said non-committally.

Langham sat back and closed his eyes. He recalled Maria's expression of concern as he left and smiled to himself.

In due course the car drove around the back of Highgate police station and Langham was escorted down a blue-painted corridor to a tiny interrogation room. He was left sitting on a hard chair for five minutes before Inspector Brady slipped into the room, accompanied by a uniformed constable and a stenographer who sat on a chair in the corner, notebook poised on her lap.

'I would like you to account for your movements between seven o'clock on Tuesday evening and midnight of the same,' Brady began.

His worst fears were confirmed. 'Very well ... On Tuesday evening I was on my way back from Berkshire with friends, who dropped me off at Highgate a little before seven. I immediately called at the house of the writer Justin Fellowes.'

'And how long did you spend in his company?' Brady asked. He leaned forward, clasping his hands on the tabletop.

Langham thought about it. 'Perhaps ten, fifteen minutes. Certainly no more.'

'And what did you discuss while you were there?'

He took a breath. 'I went there to warn him to be careful about ... Look, if you liaise with Detective Inspector Mallory of Scotland Yard, he'll gladly bring you up to date with the details of—'

Brady said, 'We are in contact with Scotland Yard, sir, and we would like your full cooperation in this matter.'

Langham gave his best smile. 'And I assure you that you have it, Inspector. If you would tell me why I'm being questioned ... Is Justin—?'

'If you would allow me to ask the questions, sir. Now ... You said you warned Justin Fellowes "to be careful". And what was his reaction to your warning?'

'He took it seriously. He said he had a little work to finish, and then he'd spend some time with a relative down in Dorset.'

'And how was Mr Fellowes when you left him?'

'Ah ... sombre, I suppose. Reflective.' He gestured. 'Look here, can you tell me what's happened?'

Brady ignored the plea. 'Am I correct in thinking, sir, that you knew and had contact recently with Charles Elder and Nigel Lassiter?'

Langham gestured. 'Of course. Charles is my agent and Lassiter was a friend and colleague. If you're in contact with Scotland Yard, then you'll know I discovered Nigel Lassiter's body—'

Brady stared at him, his gaze intimidating. 'Would you say that that's something of a coincidence?'

Langham replied, 'What, Inspector, is a coincidence?'

'Your discovering Nigel Lassiter's body,' Brady said, 'and the events of Tuesday night.'

He knew, then, what had happened in Highgate. Numbed, he said, 'What "events"? Look, I think that if you liaise with Detective Inspector Jeff Mallory of Scotland Yard, all this can be cleared up in a jiffy. Last night I was with—'

He was interrupted by the sudden sound of voices outside the interrogation room. The voices rose in volume, too muffled for him to make out individual words. Brady cursed under his breath and was moving to the door when it opened and a flustered constable appeared. He muttered something to the inspector, who slipped from the room.

Langham heard the altercation resume, this time in lowered tones. He looked at the constable, who was standing to attention and staring at the wall, expressionless.

'Does this happen often?' Langham quipped. The constable elected not to reply. He noticed the stenographer correct her quick smile and consult her notes.

The door opened and Inspector Brady returned. He nodded tersely to Langham. 'That will be all now, sir.'

'I can go?'

Brady indicated the door with an ironic gesture.

Langham stood, nodded sarcastically to the inspector and stepped from the room.

Jeff Mallory was striding up and down the corridor, his bulk filling the confined space. 'I came over as soon as I heard you'd been taken in.'

He planted a firm hand in the middle of Langham's back and escorted him along the corridor.

'What the hell's going on?' Langham asked.

Mallory hesitated, then said, 'Donald, Justin Fellowes was stabbed in the heart with a silver stiletto – the award he won a few years ago. Forensics thinks he was killed on Tuesday evening between seven, when you left him, and midnight. His housekeeper had Wednesday off, and only found the body first thing this morning.'

'My word.' Langham stepped out into the sunlight, light-headed. 'I told him. I told him to get away.'

In his mind's eye, Langham saw Justin Fellowes gesture to his typewriter. 'He said he had just one more chapter to finish, then he'd leave London.' He stopped and looked at the detective. 'But why did Brady haul me in, after what happened last night...?' He gestured back at the station.

Mallory shook his head. 'Brady has some half-cocked theory that there was more than one killer. He thought it suspicious that you were at the scene of a couple of the incidents.'

Langham stared at Mallory, aghast. *'You* don't think...?'

Mallory laughed and clapped Langham on the back. 'Christ, no. I've known you ... how long, Donald? Twenty years? Come on, I'll drive you home.'

'The agency in Pimlico, if you don't mind, Jeff. I think I'll take Maria out to dinner tonight to celebrate my release.'

TWENTY-THREE

Langham awoke early the following morning and lay on the settee, blinking up at the ornate moulding on the ceiling of the sitting room. He thought back over the dinner last night and, later, the long kiss they had shared before Maria had pulled away and slipped into her room. It occurred to him that he was perhaps the luckiest man on the planet.

The telephone shrilled insistently from across the room, and before Langham could get up and answer it, Maria hurried into the room and picked up the receiver. She listened for a moment, then turned to him and said, 'Donald, for you. It is Jeff Mallory.'

He swore, wondering what Jeff wanted. He swung himself from the settee, pulled on his trousers and shirt, hurried across the room and kissed Maria on the lips.

He picked up the receiver. 'Donald here.'

'Don. We nabbed Kenny Wilson late last night, and first thing this morning I had him identify Gideon Martin's corpse...' Mallory paused.

'Go on.'

'Well, Wilson swears the body isn't the same person who set him up with Charles Elder and photographed the pair. Also, according to Amelia Hampstead, when her dog attacked her assailant the other day it bit his hand and drew blood. But Gideon Martin's hands are uninjured.'

Langham's stomach flipped. 'I see...'

'So it pretty well looks as though Gideon Martin wasn't the killer,' Mallory said. 'I have Kenny Wilson with an artist as I speak, giving him a description of the blackmailer. It's a long shot, but if it is anyone in the scribbling trade ... Look, would you mind coming along to the Yard and taking a quick shufty?'

'Not at all. When will the impression be ready?'

'Any minute now.'

'Right, I'll grab some breakfast and be right over.'

He put the phone down and turned to Maria. She was perched on the edge of the settee, biting her lip. 'Donald?'

Dazed, he relayed what Jeff had told him. Maria seemed to deflate. 'But ... but I thought it was all over, Donald. All the killing, finished with!'

He took her in his arms and kissed her brow. 'I'll get a quick cup of tea and some toast, then I'd better be off.'

It was just after nine o'clock when he pulled up on the Embankment and parked outside the ornate Victorian pile of Scotland Yard. He hurried into the building and told a desk sergeant that he had an appointment with Detective Inspector Mallory. Two minutes later Mallory emerged from a lift across the foyer, looking

303

tired and dishevelled.

'You look all in, Jeff.'

'I've been up most of the night.' They entered the lift and ascended to the second floor, then stepped out and turned right along a narrow corridor bustling with plain-clothes officers and secretaries.

'And I thought we'd nabbed the bastard and closed the case, all bar the paperwork,' Mallory said.

'You sure Kenny Wilson isn't mistaken about Martin?' Langham asked.

'Wilson is one hundred per cent sure – and he was intimate with the blackmailer, after all.'

Mallory's office was a broom cupboard next to a briefing room, with only room for a chair on either side of a desk piled with folders. A bookcase stood beneath a dusty window, the shelves crammed with legal and procedural tomes as thick as Bibles.

Mallory indicated a chair. 'Take a pew and I'll get the artist's impression. Tea?'

'Black, no sugar.'

Mallory returned two minutes later with a chipped mug and a battered folder. He passed Langham the mug and sat behind his desk, withdrawing a single sheet of paper from the folder.

He sipped the stewed tea and grimaced. Mallory passed him the artist's impression. 'Ring any bells?'

Langham took the portrait. The sketch showed a face in black and white, mawkish and overweight. He felt suddenly light-headed. He looked up at the detective, aware that his mouth was hanging open.

'Donald?'

He murmured, 'That's impossible...'

Mallory leaned forward. 'What is?'

Langham closed his eyes and opened them, but the face refused to change. An older, fatter version of the man he had last met almost ten years ago stared out at him: the same small, mistrustful eyes, the same ugly upturned nose and tiny mouth...

'It's Frank Pearson,' he said.

Mallory stared at him. 'Just a minute...' He referred to papers in the folder and said, 'Don, Pearson's body was discovered in Kent fifteen days ago.' He shook his head. 'That's *before* the blackmail demands were made and the money collected. Are you absolutely sure it's Pearson?'

Langham stared at the face. 'Absolutely. It's Pearson.'

'OK, 'Mallory said, 'how about this. There were two of them, working together to blackmail Charles Elder: Frankie Pearson and an accomplice. Pearson blackmailed Elder, then...' he pointed a finger at Langham, 'then the accomplice threw Frankie under a train to make it look like suicide and he collected the money, keeping all of it.'

'And the other deaths? Why kill Nigel Lassiter, not to mention Cartwright, Sidley, Southern and Fellowes? And why attempt to kill Charles and Dame Amelia?' He stopped and stared across at Mallory, realization hitting him like something physical. 'Hell...' he said.

'Donald?'

'I've got it – the connection between the victims.'

'Go on.'

'They all at one time, metaphorically, stabbed Pearson in the back, or that's how he saw it. Nigel Lassiter stopped collaborating with Pearson; Charles Elder dropped him from his stable in the thirties; Sidley rejected a Pearson novel and bought no more from him, and Cartwright ... Well, at some point he wrote vitriolic reviews of everyone in the business, and I doubt Pearson escaped his poison pen.' He stopped. 'Even me ... I once gave Pearson a stinking review.'

'And Fellowes, Southern and Amelia Hampstead?'

'I don't know – but the chances are that they slighted Pearson somewhere along the line.'

Mallory interrupted. 'You're forgetting one thing, Donald. Frank Pearson died, flattened by a train, *before* the killings.'

Langham recalled what Charles Elder had told him about Frank Pearson in his younger days and was suddenly overcome with a familiar sensation. He experienced it occasionally when the plot twist of a novel came to him, a gift of his subconscious. The feeling was one of euphoria, as the mental cogs turned and a solution offered itself.

He leaned forward. 'Jeff, has Pearson been buried yet?'

Mallory referred to his papers. 'He's still on ice. Various items identifying him as Frank Pearson were found on the corpse, but all dental records and any chance of identifying him from his fingerprints were destroyed by the train.'

'So he hasn't been *positively* identified?'

'No. He had no relatives, and even his agent couldn't make a positive identification. There wasn't much left to go on.'

'Did you see the body?'

'I was spared that.'

'Does the report say anything about distinguishing features?'

Mallory pulled a typewritten sheet from the folder. 'No, nothing.'

Langham sat back, releasing a long breath. 'According to Charles Elder, Pearson had a massive scar from a knife wound just below his ribcage. He was stabbed in a tiff with a lover in his twenties, and he wasn't averse to showing off the wound when he was pissed.'

Mallory scanned the report. 'Right. The body's in the morgue down at Hounslow. We can be there in ten minutes.'

They hurried from the building and a minute later were motoring south in Mallory's Humber.

Langham followed Mallory up the steps to the morgue, anticipation constricting his chest like an incipient coronary.

A surly mortuary attendant showed them into a tiled room, the entire right-hand wall of which consisted of square, enamelled white doors with big silver handles like so many domestic refrigerators stacked three high.

'Pearson, nine hundred and thirty-seven?'

Mallory nodded and the attendant pulled open a door at waist-height and hauled out a sliding tray. The temperature in the room, already cold, dropped appreciably as the tray trundled out with an exhalation of freezing mist.

A pair of blue feet with misshapen big toes protruded from under a white shroud. The attendant drew the shroud from the bottom up, revealing a pair of fat white calves, a shrivelled scrotum and a huge gut.

The first thing Langham noticed was that the right arm terminated just below the wrist and the left hand across the knuckles, the blood scabbed and blackened. Further up, the way the shroud was folded neatly over the shoulders was ample evidence that the London train had achieved a clean decapitation.

He stared at the protuberant belly, searching it for the tell-tale knife scar.

There was no sign of a scar anywhere on the pallid, pudding-like fat.

Mallory nodded and the attendant pushed the tray back into the wall.

They left the building in silence, returned to the Humber and sat for a few seconds before Mallory said, 'OK, Donald. Put your writing cap on. What happened?'

Langham had already thought through the likely scenario. 'This is a vendetta, Jeff. Pearson has it in for people he sees as having slighted him throughout his career. He was an unsuccessful hack who had to churn out potboilers to make a living. There was a time when Frankie had a good publisher in Douglas and Dearing, and Nigel Lassiter put the kibosh on that. Then Charles Elder dropped him. And others put the boot

308

in down the years, not that they would have seen it quite like that.'

'So Pearson decides to take revenge?'

'And dead men can't kill, can they?' Langham said. 'So ... he finds someone bearing a resemblance to himself, gets them drunk or kills them, puts his own papers or whatever about their person, then lays them on the track before the London train's due...' He shrugged. 'After that, he can start his killing spree with impunity.'

'Dead men can't kill...' Mallory repeated.

Langham said, 'It's like the title of a bad thriller.'

'And he's still out there...' Mallory paused and glanced at Langham. 'Have you any idea who else he might target?'

A rapid heat passed through Langham as he thought of the paperbacks. 'Just myself and Dame Amelia, of the writers,' he said. 'If, that is, the authors of the books he left at Streatham were the only ones on his hit list. But then there are the editors and critics he took against.' He stopped. 'Bloody hell...'

'Don?'

'It's just occurred to me...' He stared at Mallory, his pulse racing. 'No wonder the crossbow killing in the garden seemed so familiar. Christ! And the killing of Gervaise Cartwright – the executioner's hood. I thought I'd read something similar somewhere.'

'Don't tell me...' Mallory began.

'I reviewed one of his books, way back. It was terrible, and I went to town on it. The thing is, I'm damned sure it featured a crossbow killing in a country garden. And I read another one by Frankie ... and there was something in that one about a killer who stabbed his victims in the back and placed a hood on their heads.'

'So he's killing his victims in ways he wrote about in his books?'

'Without a doubt.' And what had Nigel Lassiter told him during their meeting at Tolly's – that Max Sidley had committed suicide in a manner described in one of his collaborations with Frankie Pearson?

'In his own books and his collaborations with Lassiter,' Langham went on, and told Mallory about the manner of Sidley's 'suicide'.

The detective was silent for a time. 'How many books did Pearson write?'

'Over a hundred, according to his agent. But the majority of those were under pen names. He wrote about six or so thrillers under his own name, and three collaborations with Nigel Lassiter.'

'And he's using methods described in his own books, and his co-written ones, to bump off his victims,' Mallory said. 'Right, I'll make a report for my super and call a briefing.' He looked across at Langham. 'If I were you, Don, I'd think about getting out of town, lying low.'

Langham considered his options. 'There's a hotel in Suffolk I'll book into with Maria. I'll leave you my contact details so you can keep me up to date.'

'Things have developed pretty fast on the Maria front, haven't they?'

Langham nodded. 'All in the last week. The

terrible thing is, if it hadn't been for all ... *this*, throwing us together...'

'Fate is a bloody strange arbiter, Don.' Mallory started the engine and eased the car into the road.

'Anyway,' he said, 'at least now we know who we're looking for. I'll get in touch with publishers. I still have contacts in the Crime Writers' Club. I'll put the word around that anyone who suspects that Frank Pearson might bear them a grudge should be extra vigilant. The thing is, I don't want the press to get hold of this. We have the advantage that Pearson doesn't know that we know he's still alive, and I want to keep it that way.'

Mallory drove back to Scotland Yard. Langham sat in silence for the duration of the journey.

Mallory glanced at him. 'Penny for them, Donald?'

Langham shrugged. 'I was just thinking about Gideon Martin. He was innocent...' He shook his head. 'We shouldn't have chased him on to the roof, Jeff.'

Mallory shrugged. 'He was up to no good at the Albemarle, Donald. And we weren't to know he wasn't the killer. Look, go easy on yourself, OK?'

Langham nodded absently, and five minutes later they pulled up outside Scotland Yard where they parted with an oddly formal handshake. Langham returned to his Austin and drove to Maria's apartment.

Over a cup of black Earl Grey, Langham told Maria about Frankie Pearson.

She sat in silence for seconds, then said, 'This changes things, Donald. You cannot go back to stay at your flat. It's too dangerous.'

'I'll just nip back to pick up a few books by Pearson.'

She looked at him quizzically. 'Aren't they the last things you'd want to be reading right now?'

'The odd thing is, each murder Pearson has committed is lifted from one of his own novels.' He shrugged. 'I don't know, but maybe I'll be able to second guess his next victim from the books.'

'But I thought he wrote hundreds?'

'He did, but only nine or so under his own name – and it's from these that he's copying the murders.'

Maria nodded. 'OK, you go, but be quick. I'll stay here today. The agency can go hang. When you get back I'll make you a nice cup of Earl Grey, yes?'

'I'll say. And I was thinking...' He took her hand. 'It'd be a good idea if we could get away for a while. Get out of London.'

She beamed. 'That would be wonderful.'

He told her about the letter he'd received last week from the hotelier on the Suffolk coast. If he took up the invitation, that would kill two birds with one stone: give them a welcome break and get them away from the capital while the police worked to track down Frankie Pearson.

'I'll ring later and book a room. Of course,' he went on, 'we might have to pretend to be married.'

She laughed. 'That might not be *so* difficult, Donald.'

He left Maria's apartment and motored over to Notting Hill.

He would spend no longer than was absolutely necessary at his flat, pack a few items of clothing and some books, then get away. He was struck at once by how absurd a notion it was that Frankie Pearson should still be alive and stalking those who had given him offence – and yet, despite the absurdity, he was gripped by a very real fear. Nigel Lassiter, too, would no doubt have laughed off any threat to his life if told that Frankie Pearson, a washed-up, alcoholic hack, was playing the part of an avenging angel.

He let himself into his flat and packed a case with clothing and toiletries. He moved to the study, slipped his portable typewriter into its case, and stood regarding the bookshelves against the far wall.

He was a creature of habit, and kept all of his books not only in alphabetical order but in chronological order of publication. Even his notional 'to read' pile, which now filled several shelves and consisted of a few hundred books, was thus regimented.

He found three hardback novels by Frank L. Pearson which he hadn't read – publisher's review copies he'd set aside with the intention of one day selling to the second-hand bookshop around the corner. He took them from the shelf, then caught sight of the complete run of the *Capital Crime* magazine.

He'd reviewed one of Pearson's novels for *Capital Crime* just after the war. He pulled down the six issues of the bimonthly magazine from 1947 and leafed through them one by one, looking for his column. He'd been mistaken – he must have reviewed the book *after* 'forty-seven, as the column that year was under the byline of Justin Fellowes. He was about to replace the issue when he caught sight of a title. *The Silver Stiletto* by Frank L. Pearson.

He sat at his desk and skimmed Justin Fellowes's hatchet job on the novel.

There occasionally comes within the remit of the reviewer's lot a book so bad that it must be finished, rather than flung across the room, so that the magnitude of its direness can be fully appreciated – and The Silver Stiletto *is one such volume. The plot involves the murder of a literary critic who is stabbed in a manner described with stomach-churning relish ... Pearson's prose is not only inept and well nigh unreadable, but purple and slapdash ... The dénouement is contrived and lacks the slightest understanding of the finer points of human motivation ... A word of advice to Frank L. Pearson, whoever he might be: seek alternative employment rather than inflict another dire penny dreadful upon the unwitting reading public.*

Justin Fellowes had attended Frankie Pearson's memorial service last week, and Langham wondered now if that was out of a sense of long-held guilt.

314

Poor, poor Justin, he thought.

He replaced the magazine on the shelf and found the run of issues from 1948. A minute later he was reading his own dismissal of Pearson's novel *Death on the Farm*.

Pearson will never win any prizes for euphonious prose, and his characterization is no better. The plot is ramshackle, and so patched together with authorial convenience as to be laughable. Even worse than the unlikely pay-off is the unlikelihood of such an inept detective working out the killer's crimes, never mind his motivations. Death on the Farm *is on every level a turkey.*

He reread the lines he had written seven years ago with a prickling sensation across his scalp.

He looked at his watch. He had been in the flat for less than fifteen minutes.

He found the letter he'd received from the hotelier last week and dialled the number. A minute later he was through to a man who appeared to be suffering from a bad case of flu, and introduced himself. 'And I was wondering if I might avail myself of your kind offer from tomorrow for two or three days...? If we stay any longer, then I'll gladly pay the difference.'

The hotel had a double room available this week, the proprietor informed him, and Langham made arrangements to stay for three days beginning tomorrow.

He picked up his case and typewriter and hurried from the flat, feeling relieved that he'd

315

organized the break and glad that he was finally off the premises. As he climbed into the Austin it occurred to him that, as he was on Pearson's hit list, then there was always the chance that he might be under surveillance. The thought sent a blade of ice slicing down his spine.

He drove at speed from Notting Hill and cut through the back streets to Kensington. He would spend the rest of the day with Maria and first thing in the morning they would escape to the Suffolk coast.

She was curled up on the settee, reading a book, when he returned.

She looked up. 'Did you get what you needed from the flat?'

'Everything, plus three books by Frankie Pearson.'

'Snap,' she said, holding up a tatty hardback and pointing to the coffee table where six books formed a neat tower. 'I popped out to the library,' she said. 'I didn't know which ones you might bring back so I withdrew everything they had.'

He picked up the book on the top of the pile. *'Murder is Easy* by Frank L. Pearson.' He looked at her. 'That's sickly prophetic.'

The other titles were the three collaborations with Nigel Lassiter and two solo efforts, one of which duplicated a novel he'd brought from his flat.

'I've already started this one, Donald. And in it...' She shook her head. 'He describes someone breaking into a country house and shooting the owner through the head, making the killing look like suicide. Just as he *tried* to do with Charles.'

'He's sick,' Langham began.

'And that was only the first killing,' she said. 'So many murders, and I'm only fifty pages into the story. He certainly likes to describe knife killings.'

And he likes to perform them, Langham thought to himself – among others.

He set the books aside. 'A little light holiday reading,' he said, and pulled Maria to him.

TWENTY-FOUR

Sunlight streamed into the sitting room through the bay window and Langham heard birdsong in the trees that lincd the quiet street. Half-awake, he propped himself up on one elbow and looked across the room. Maria was sitting on the window seat in her dressing gown, her bare feet lodged on a chair and the gown open to reveal her legs. She was absorbed in a book, head bowed, and the expression on her face intent. She looked across at him briefly, concerned.

'Good book?' he murmured, turning over. She didn't reply. He closed his eyes and sank back into semi-sleep, cheered by the thought that today they were going to the coast.

He came awake some time later and glanced at the wall clock. It was eight thirty. He turned over at a sound. Maria was striding up and down the room like a caged tiger, her right hand pressed to her mouth.

'Maria?'

She sat down quickly on the settee and stared at him with stricken eyes. He repeated her name, wondering at the change that had come over her.

'We can't go to Suffolk, Donald.'

He reached out and took her hand. 'What?'

'I woke up at six and I could not sleep. I began reading – one of Pearson's books. I couldn't put it down.'

'You're sounding like the back-cover blurb—'

'Be serious!' She stared at him. 'I had to keep reading. The book is about ... It's silly, but a character wants to kill his wife's lover, so he devises a way of luring him from London.' She hurried across the room, grabbed the book from the window seat and returned to the bed.

Langham took the book. *Death by the Sea.*

He looked up at Maria. 'I don't understand...'

'The husband writes a letter to his wife's lover, saying he is the proprietor of a hotel and inviting him on a free holiday as some kind of promotion. The lover takes up the offer, with the wife, and when they get there...' She gestured at the open book. 'Then the husband strangles them both ... It's horrible, horrible!'

Langham began to say that it was merely a coincidence, but Maria silenced him with a finger pressed to his lips.

'Don't you see? Pearson planned this. He wants to lure you to the coast, with me, and there he plans to...' She continued, 'It's just too much of a coincidence, Donald. He killed all those

318

writers in ways he wrote about in his books – and this is how he plans to murder you ... and me.'

He opened the book.

'It starts on page one hundred and seventy,' she said, 'when the lovers arrive at the hotel on the coast.'

Donald began reading feverishly, skimming the overwritten prose and stilted dialogue. The scene lasted for five pages, padded with unnecessary exposition as the husband tied up his wife and her lover and explained his motivations. It had never been his intention to kill just the lover – he intended to kill them both, as due punishment. He strangled the lover, and then did the same to his wife.

Langham stopped reading, sickened by the gratuity and relish with which Pearson described the killings. Had Pearson's books been a kind of sublimation of his need to commit murder – a subconscious desire he was now making real?

He laid the novel aside, considering this latest turn of events. 'So we know where he'll be...' he said.

Maria stared at him. 'What?'

'You're right – all this, the invitation – it's a set up. But we're ahead of him. We know where he'll be.'

She nodded. 'So we call Jeff Mallory and the police will go and arrest Pearson.'

He said, 'Or I go alone, confront him...'

She stared at him, aghast. 'I won't let you go, Donald!'

'I'll go armed,' he found himself saying. 'I can

319

pick up a revolver on the way.'

'No. This is madness. I won't let you!'

He reached out and squeezed her hand. He thought of Frankie Pearson and what he'd done to his friends, Charles and Nigel, and to Justin Fellowes and the others. He looked into himself and realized that what he really wanted was vengeance; he wanted to shoot Frankie Pearson dead.

'I'm sorry,' he murmured. 'I've been alone too long. I was thinking only of ... I want to punish Frankie Pearson so much for what he's done, for the hurt he's caused.'

'But killing him,' she whispered, 'won't lessen that hurt.'

He realized then that the choice was really no choice at all: what he felt for Maria was far stronger than the need for vengeance.

He said, 'I'll call Mallory, explain the situation. They can go and arrest him.'

She plastered his cheeks with tearful kisses of relief. 'Thank you, Donald.'

He dressed, splashed his face with cold water, then got through to Mallory and explained the situation. The detective heard him out, then observed grimly, 'Hoist, I think the saying goes, by his own petard. I'll be over in thirty minutes. I'll need to see the letter he sent – you have it with you?'

'It's in my case.'

'Good work, Donald. I'll be right over.'

Maria was standing beside the kitchen door, watching him. He crossed the room and held her. 'Don't worry,' he said. 'It's coming to an end.'

320

'It has been a nightmare.'

He had an idea. 'When they've arrested Pearson, let's celebrate.'

'Celebrate?'

'Let's find a quiet hotel on the coast and spend a long weekend away from London – a legitimate hotel, this time.'

'That would be wonderful,' Maria said. 'I'll make some coffee. I feel too sick to eat, but I think I need coffee.'

'Earl Grey for me.'

They sat at the dining table in the bay window and drank their beverages, saying little and staring out at the trees swaying in the spring breeze.

Mallory's Humber pulled up fifteen minutes later, followed by a second unmarked police car. Mallory crossed the pavement accompanied by two plain-clothes officers. While Maria let them in, Langham fetched the novel and found the letter in his suitcase.

'Donald,' Mallory said, his face set solid. This was a side of the detective Langham had not seen before, entirely focused on the endgame. His navy pinstriped suit looked even more dishevelled than usual, as if he'd spent the night in it. He introduced the plain-clothes officers as Howson and McNeil from the CID.

They sat at the breakfast table and Maria fetched a tray of tea and joined them. Mallory scanned the relevant pages of *Death by the Sea*, then passed the book to the CID men.

Mallory clenched a china cup in his big hands,

staring at Langham. 'We considered sending you in first,' he said, 'as per what Pearson is obviously expecting.'

Maria took Langham's hand and opened her mouth to say something, but Mallory went on: 'But we're dealing here with someone who's clearly mentally unhinged, not to say psychopathic. There's no saying that Pearson would stick to the script.'

Maria squeezed his hand.

'So we'll surround the place with undercover men and I'll send a team into the hotel. We're taking no risks here. Fortunately the hotel is secluded – a mile up a headland with only one road leading to and from.'

One of the CID men set the book down on the table. 'We know Pearson will be there, awaiting you. We hold all the aces.'

Mallory stood, his bulk looming in the bay window and occluding the light. 'I'll be in touch just as soon as we've wrapped it all up, Don.' He nodded to the CID men and they took their leave.

Langham stood before the window with Maria and watched them drive away.

He looked at her. 'How do you feel?'

'I don't know ... Edgy. Nervous. I can't believe that soon it will be all over. You?'

He smiled. 'I feel ... like you, oddly nervous. And I won't believe it's all over until I've heard from Jeff. What are you doing today?'

She worried her bottom lip. 'I really must go into the office.'

'How about lunch later? I could pick you up

at twelve.'

'That sounds nice. I might feel more like eating by then. What are you doing?'

He thought about how to fill the morning until lunch. 'I'll take my things back to the flat. I have a short story that needs finishing. I might look over that for an hour or so.'

It would be beneficial to get back to work, immerse himself in the machinations of imaginary characters and try to forget the events of the past few days.

He carried his case up the front steps, let himself into the flat and stood on the threshold of his study. It was as if he were seeing the room – his writing desk and serried books denoting a sequestered, almost monastic existence – for the first time. Nine years he had lived here, ever since being demobbed; he'd written a dozen books in this room, a hundred short stories ... and all he had to show for that industry were the volumes of his own work that filled the bookcase beside the desk. He could not help but contrast what he had back then with what he had now, namely Maria; and he knew that his old self would be shocked that she had relegated his writing, which had consumed his life and thoughts for so long, into second place.

His reverie was interrupted by a knock at the front door. He hurried down, expecting the postman with a parcel too bulky for the letterbox. He pulled open the door.

A small, balding man wrapped in a stained grey mackintosh smiled up at him. 'Ah, Mr

323

Langham.'

'Can I help you?'

'I think you most certainly can.'

Only then did Langham see that the man was holding something.

He looked again at the man's face – and saw that the artist's impression had got it right. The fat, the unhealthy pallor, the tiny eyes and the small, vindictive mouth.

Frankie Pearson aimed the pistol directly at Langham's chest.

He managed, 'What do you want?'

'Oh, come, Mr Langham. That's hardly an original line, is it? A trifle clichéd? Prompted more through fear, I suspect, than genuine enquiry. It sounds as stilted as a line from one of your books. What do you think I want?'

Later it came to him that he should have jumped Pearson there and then, on the threshold in full view of the street, where he might have been more circumspect about shooting. But at the time he was too frozen with shock to think of anything as elemental as survival.

Then the moment was over.

Pearson gestured with the pistol. 'Turn around and walk up the stairs.'

Langham turned slowly and dragged one foot after the other up the stairs. He heard Pearson enter the hallway and the sound of him kicking the door shut with his heel. He expected to hear the Yale lock click. When the sound failed to reach him, he stored the fact away for possible future use. The door had not shut fully, so if in the next few minutes he were able to overpower

Pearson and flee, then he would not have to waste valuable seconds unfastening the catch.

If only he could overpower Pearson, he thought.

He reached the top of the stairs. The only sound he could hear was the thud of his own heartbeat, and when Pearson spoke it seemed to come from a long way away.

'In there.'

Langham obeyed. He walked into the study and stared at his desk and his books which, just minutes ago, had seemed like the belongings of another person. Now their welcome familiarity seemed, to him, heartbreaking.

'Sit down at the desk and turn the chair to face me.'

Langham sat down, and when he turned the chair he saw that Pearson had perched himself on the armchair beside the window, holding the pistol in his lap. It would only take him a second to raise it, take aim...

Langham decided to bide his time and hope Pearson wanted to talk.

The little man seemed inordinately happy. 'You walked into it, Langham.'

The words wrong-footed him. 'Into what?'

Pearson laughed. He really was a most obnoxious little man. He seemed to have shrunk since the last time they had met, almost ten years ago, and he was also fatter and seedier. His face had the pasty pallor and the rheumy eyes of a seasoned alcoholic.

'I mean the hotel ruse,' Pearson said. 'I could not really lose, could I? Either you went to the hotel like a lamb to the slaughter, having not put two and two together and realized what I was doing, or you worked out my ruse and called in your police chums. All I had to do was keep watch on your little girlfriend's place this morning and, as soon as I saw Mallory arrive, I knew.' He smiled. 'I imagine they'll be on their way there as we speak. What a surprise they'll receive when they find a small hotel run by a retired colonel and his wife.'

'But I spoke—' Langham began.

'Of course you spoke to me, but the number you rang wasn't the hotel's. Not that you should castigate yourself for not checking. How were you to know of my little plan, after all?'

'And if we'd not suspected anything and gone to the hotel?'

'I had a room booked in your name, and I'd booked myself into the neighbouring room. I would have followed you, and...' He smiled. 'But now you will die in a different way.'

Langham stared levelly at Pearson. He would have thought that in the situation he would have felt fear. The odd thing was, despite knowing what Pearson intended, he felt calm: he felt not so much fear, he realized, as disbelief that the events would work themselves out in Pearson's favour.

He was determined to retain his dignity, and smiled at the thought. Maria would have laughed at his typically English, stiff-upper-lip attitude.

'What is it that you find so funny?' Pearson enquired. 'Humour, I assure you, is not at all the appropriate emotion to be feeling now.'

Langham said, as words now were his only weapon, 'I was thinking how utterly pathetic you are, you and your wasted life: the dreadful hackwork, and now the murder of people better and more talented than yourself.'

'Dreadful hackwork? I like that. That's truly rich coming from your lips, the man who made the formulaic detective story his forte. I could never work out your popularity, Langham. Your novels are no better than mine, but I suppose it's a case of not what you know, but who you know. You got in with that terrible queen Charles Elder, and isn't one of your editors an old army chum? How could you fail, with friends on the inside to pull the strings?'

Langham smiled, refusing to be drawn. 'That's what it's all about, isn't it? Jealousy. Is that why you're here, Pearson, because you're envious of my success?'

The small, plump hand holding the gun twitched, and a spasm of irritation crossed Pearson's face. 'Jealousy? Do you really think I'm motivated by an emotion as shallow as jealousy? It has nothing to do with jealousy, Langham, but with vengeance – a much more valid motivation, don't you think?'

Langham shrugged. 'That, Pearson, is a matter of opinion.'

'I worked hard at my craft. I worked on my first book for a year, and you can't even begin to imagine my delight when Elder took me on and found a publisher. And what happened then? Three books down the line, the bastard cut the lifeline, set me adrift...'

Langham said, 'The books were bad, Pearson. They didn't sell, and Charles was a businessman. There's no room for sentimentality in his line of work.'

'I could have allowed that to set me back, Langham, but I told myself I was better than that. I wouldn't stop what I loved doing just because some talentless agent didn't like my work. I sold a dozen books after he dropped me. I proved him wrong.'

How could he be so deluded, Langham wondered; the dozen books he'd sold in the thirties were pseudonymous westerns.

'And then I struck lucky. My persistence was rewarded. I met Nigel Lassiter. Young Nigel. I had quite a thing for him, at the time. Not that I let him see that – not Nigel, big, bluff, homophobic Nigel. We wrote three good thrillers together, and then he did the dirty, ditched me ... and immediately after that Max Sidley turned down my solo effort with a rejection letter so cruel I never forgot a word of it. I even quoted it while killing him.'

Pearson's eyes glazed over, and a smile came to his lips as if reliving the moment he murdered his ex-editor.

'But I soldiered on, as you do. I went back to the cowboy books and knocked out half a dozen a year for good old Hubert and Shale. When the war came I was exempted from military service on medical grounds, so I continued writing between periods of fire-watching. Boys' adventure stories, school stories for the girls' annuals – I churned it out, no keeping me down. Then I

328

made a lucky contact after the war, met an old school chum who worked as an editor for Pritchard. They were looking to start a line of detective stories, and I thought here I go, a second chance at respectability ... They took a couple, which sold reasonably well, and were about to commission another two when Gervaise Cartwright's vitriolic review of the second book came out and scuppered any chance of that deal.'

Langham couldn't help smiling. 'You're looking for excuses, Pearson, and people to blame. The bad review did nothing to queer the deal, if you'll excuse the phrase. Do you think Pritchard would have given a damn about what Cartwright wrote, however critical?'

Pearson stared at him. 'It certainly didn't help.'

Langham said, 'Your pride was hurt – admit it. No one likes bad reviews.'

Pearson looked around the study, at the ranked books, the watercolours, and his gaze alighted on the row of Langham's titles on the bookcase beside the desk. He said, 'So I went back to Hubert and Shale like a kicked dog.'

Langham stared at the little man and was surprised to see tears in his eyes.

'And do you know the one person who stood by me during all those years? Who believed in me and my novels? My agent, good old Dorothy. She was a stalwart, finding me work during the lean years, constantly reassuring me, fighting my corner. She *believed* in me.'

She pitied you, Langham thought, and she wanted her seven-and-a-half per cent.

329

'And then, in 'forty-seven, I had another break. A deal for Wilkins to produce three whodunits with the promise of more if they sold ... And what happened?'

'Let me guess. They didn't sell?'

'And why was that?'

Because they were truly terrible, Langham thought, but bit his tongue. 'You tell me.'

He saw it coming. Pearson pointed at him with his free hand. 'Because you, you self-serving, vindictive bastard, wrote a review of the second book so vile, so cutting, that the director of Wilkins hauled my editor over the coals and asked him how the novel came to be published by his company. And the upshot was that the third book was cancelled and I was out on my arse again.'

Langham leaned forward and said, 'And I stand by every word of that review. It was a bad review because it was a bad book.'

Without warning Pearson raised the gun and fired.

What was so shocking about the gesture was that Pearson pulled the trigger in sudden, splenetic fury, and the bullet could have gone anywhere.

Langham felt a dull blow in his lower leg, not so much a pain as a sudden, intense ache, and when he looked down he saw blood soaking into the carpet beside his shoe.

He looked up. Pearson was shaking, holding the gun in both hands, aiming directly at Langham's chest.

'The next one ... the next one will be in your

heart.'

Langham told himself that if he didn't move, if he kept very still, then the pain would remain at a tolerable level, a mere ache. He glanced down at his foot, surrounded now in a slick of dark blood, and he knew that if an artery had been hit in his lower leg he would die from blood loss in a matter of minutes.

'I soldiered on over the next few years, as you do. I lived from one measly contract to the next, picking up work where I could. When I look back, I wonder how I managed to keep body and soul together.' He shrugged. 'I put it down to dogged persistence, a belief in the worth of my work...'

Langham closed his eyes and tried not to laugh.

Pearson was saying, 'And then six months ago Hubert and Shale decided to drop their line of westerns, and suddenly I had no more commissions, nothing more to write, and ... and what would I do without my writing?'

Langham gritted his teeth against the mounting pain that pulsed up his leg. He stared across the room at Pearson. The man was crying now, weeping real tears as he lowered the gun to his lap.

The phone rang, startling him with the fact that there was an ordinary, sane world out there and that someone wished to speak to him. Instinctively he reached out and picked it up.

Pearson snapped, 'Drop it, Langham!'

He dropped it, and the receiver clattered into the cradle.

Pearson nodded, licked his lips and resumed. 'A few days after Hubert and Shale dropped me, I remembered your review. I dug it out and read it again, and that reminded me of all the others, and I unearthed Cartwright's hatchet job.' He smiled then, almost beatifically. 'And it came to me, just as the plot of a mystery novel comes to me – a series of murders that would rid the city of vile and disreputable scum.'

'You're mad,' Langham whispered to himself.

'And as I mulled the idea over, more ideas came, neat twists and turns, worthy of my very best efforts. Why not, I thought, kill my tormentors by methods used by the murderers in my own books? How novel, how fitting ... And I used another neat trick from one of my books. A dead man cannot commit murder, can he? So I found someone not dissimilar to myself, someone who would not be missed by family and friends, because he did not have family and friends – a homeless tramp I befriended and even gave my old clothes to. Then I got him blind drunk one night, drove down to Kent and arranged him on the London line with my papers in his pockets.'

He paused, smiling at Langham as if awaiting a round of applause.

Langham looked down at his foot. The pool of blood, he thought, appeared not to be getting any larger. Perhaps he'd been lucky and the bullet hadn't hit an artery.

'Max Sidley was easy,' Pearson went on. 'He hadn't heard about my "death", and he let me into his house when I called with the news, spurious of course, about the sudden illness of one of his co-editors at Douglas and Dearing. He was a weak old thing and he put up no resistance when I dealt with him.'

Langham stared at Pearson. 'With a drill...' he said.

Pearson smiled. 'A method derived from one of my very best novels, *Death in the Night*.'

'Sick,' Langham said.

Pearson waved this away and continued, 'Gervaise Cartwright was an especial pleasure, Langham. I'd never liked the man's cruel little columns, even before he penned that poison review of my novel. I posed as an avid reader wanting him to sign one of his books, and he was only too willing to oblige. I slipped the stiletto into his back while he sat at his desk – and the hood was a little touch I thought might amuse those in the know.

'I took great delight in planning the death of Charles Elder because he began it all, many years ago. He showed me hope, then withdrew it, and I always found him a conceited snob. You should have seen his face when I turned up at his country pile. He looked as if he'd seen a ghost – little Frankie Pearson, back from the dead. I must admit that he recovered from his shock and was the perfect host.'

'You intended to make it look like suicide?' Langham said.

'As per my novel *Murder in the Mansion*, yes. But then you and your little French floozy turned up and spoiled my fun.'

Langham said, gaining satisfaction from the

words, 'You didn't kill him, Pearson. Charles is going to pull through.'

The little man's cruel lips lifted in a smile. 'Then I shall have to make doubly sure that, next time, I succeed.'

'If there is a next time,' Langham muttered.

Pearson chose to ignore the remark.

Langham said, 'And Alexander Southern and Amelia Hampstead? What grudge did you bear them?'

Pearson smiled. 'Southern was a reader for Gollancz in the late thirties, and he advised them not to touch what I thought then was my best novel to date. So he had to die. I drove down to the village where he lived near Canterbury and watched him for a few days. He was a creature of habit, and liked to take a quiet afternoon stroll. In one of my novels an old major is killed by a hit-and-run driver, a method I employed to great effect with Southern.'

'And you killed Fellowes because he gave you a bad review?'

'With his own silver stiletto award,' Pearson said. 'A method taken from one of my more recent titles. The old boy put up quite a fight.'

He paused, then went on: 'And I would have successfully drowned Dame Amelia in her own moat – from my *Death at the Castle* – had it not been for her damned hound...' He held up his left hand, and for the first time Langham made out the bandage wrapped around his wrist.

'What on earth did you have against Amelia?'

'She blocked my election to the Professional Crime Writers' Association in the early forties, on account that she thought my work "sub-standard", as she later told a friend – a slight for which I never forgave her.'

Langham closed his eyes. His lower leg felt as if a red-hot poker was being stabbed into the muscle with agonizing regularity. He wondered if he would pass out, and fought against it: if he slipped into unconsciousness now, then who knew what sadistic pleasures Pearson might exact?

'But Nigel Lassiter was the best. I really enjoyed what I did to old Nigel,' Pearson said, almost reminiscently. 'The look on his face when I turned up at the cottage ... He had already discovered the grave, having found the front door locked and wandered around to the back garden. I approached him from behind and clear-ed my throat. Oh, how he jumped! And jumped again when he saw that it was I. And jumped a third time, backwards this time, when I shot him through the chest with a crossbow, a device I used in...'

Langham stopped him with a raised hand. 'Spare me the details, Pearson.'

'And now,' Pearson went on, 'now it comes to you. The element of surprise is no more, but there will be something about my killing of you that will give me more satisfaction than any of the others. Perhaps because I despise your work the most, perhaps because your review cut the deepest.'

He pulled something from the inside pocket of his mackintosh, and Langham saw that it was a copy of the *Capital Crime* magazine, the very

335

one which carried his review of *Death on the Farm*.

Pearson opened the magazine and smiled across at Langham. Then he began to read. '"The plot is ramshackle, and so patched together with authorial convenience as to be laughable..."' Pearson looked up. 'Rather like your own novels, no? How about this: "Even the lead character is so flat as to be one-dimensional." And then your parting shot – did you think yourself oh so clever when penning this, Langham: *"Death on the Farm* is on every level a turkey"?' Pearson smiled, almost sadly. 'Do you regret what you said, Langham?'

A retraction, at the eleventh hour, would do nothing to placate the madman. He said, 'I stand by every word, Pearson. More, I could have been crueller.'

'Really, Langham? Then perhaps you will regret never again being able to have the chance...' Pearson tore the pages from the magazine and wadded them into a tight ball.

'This will be my finest work, Mr Langham. The critic *eats* his words. You will open your mouth and eat these pages and then I will take great delight in shooting you.'

Langham made himself laugh.

'Oh, you find that amusing, Langham?'

'What I find amusing is that to kill me you'll have to deviate from your master plan. This scenario was never envisaged in any of your potboilers.'

Pearson smiled, revealing a collection of yellowed teeth. 'Ah, but that's where you are very

336

wrong, Mr Langham. Very wrong indeed. You see, I am working on a novel right now, and I rather fancy that the final scene will be a rendition of our little *tête-à-tête*, with the critic eating his words before his brains are blown out. I shall enjoy writing that scene ... I shall enjoy writing it very much.'

Langham recalled something. 'Which is why you didn't shoot me at the mill, when you had the chance...'

'Oh, I was tempted, Langham, sorely tempted. But that would have spoiled my fun.' He laughed. 'I will very much savour writing the final scene ... but even more enjoyable will be the day I submit it under an assumed name to the Charles Elder agency, and then sit back and think of your little French piece reading it.'

Hardly before he knew what he was doing, Langham pushed himself from the chair in rage and dived across the room. Startled, Pearson stood and fired. Langham felt something impact with his torso, a great blow that at once winded him and sent him sprawling on to his back.

He lay staring up at the ceiling, thinking about Maria and wishing that things could have been very, very different.

He was only dimly aware of Pearson as he strode across the room and stared down at him, smiling.

TWENTY-FIVE

Maria sat at the desk in Charles's office and stared at a patch of sunlight on the carpet. The French windows were open, admitting a warm breeze, and she could hear blackbirds piping away in the garden. She recalled her shock that morning on reading Pearson's dreadful book featuring the hotel murders, and her relief that Donald had seen sense and summoned Jeff Mallory. Soon all this ghastly business would be over; life would resume its usual rhythm and she could give Donald Langham all the love he deserved.

She had spent the morning reading the first few pages of a novel submission and answering a string of phone calls from editors and writers. Well-wishers were still calling for news of Charles, and she relayed the latest information she'd received from the hospital that morning: that Charles was making good progress and would soon be able to entertain visitors.

She finished speaking to the last caller and glanced across at the wall clock. It was after twelve; Donald would be arriving soon to take her out to lunch.

She pulled her compact from her handbag and powdered her face.

She wondered how soon Donald would hear from Mallory about the arrest of Frankie Pearson. She stopped what she was doing – lipstick poised – as it occurred to her that, because of her actions in reading the Pearson novel, the murderer would soon be arrested. She wondered if Pearson had been a fool in making his motives so obvious, or if on some subconscious level he had wanted to give the police a fighting chance of arresting him.

She finished her make-up, thinking that perhaps neither was the case. He was simply a madman who wanted vengeance, and the egomaniac in him thought it appropriate to mete out punishments first written about in his own novels.

She watered the aspidistra, and then glanced at her wristwatch. It was twelve thirty. Donald was late, which wasn't like him. She wondered if he'd become absorbed in the short story he'd mentioned.

She perched herself on the edge of the desk and rang his number.

It was answered almost immediately. A silence, followed by a man's faint voice, 'Drop it, Langham—'

The connection was cut.

She sat with the receiver pressed to her ear, frozen. She felt suddenly sick and light-headed, and stared through the window at a sycamore stirring in the breeze.

There was someone with Donald in his flat, someone who had not wanted him to answer the phone.

She found herself standing, moving towards

339

the door as if in a trance. Then she was out of the office, hurrying down the steps and climbing into her car. Her short-term memory seemed to be functioning imperfectly, for what seemed like seconds later she was turning into her street in Kensington without being able to recollect the intervening drive. It was so unfair, she repeated over and over, so unfair that she had thought the affair ended, and now...

She found herself running up the steps to her apartment, unlocking the door and running breathless up the stairs and unlocking the door at the top, only then realizing that she should have phoned the police from the office.

Without thinking, she crossed the room and unlocked her bureau. Then she was standing with the small, silver pistol in her hand, staring down at its impossible delicacy. How, she wondered, could something so lethal be so beautiful?

Gideon Martin had said that it was loaded with one bullet.

She picked up the phone and dialled 999. It seemed an age before someone answered. She had no idea what she was going to say until the words came out. 'This is urgent. There is ... someone is holding my friend hostage. He's probably armed...'

'Please, miss,' said a woman's patient voice. 'Now, slowly...'

Maria repeated herself, wanting to scream in frustration at the precious seconds ticking by, and finished by giving Donald's address.

She slammed down the phone. It seemed that her heart had expanded in her chest, was a massive organ beating out a rapid tempo that almost deafened her. She struggled to her feet and pushed herself towards the door. Seconds later she was back in the car and driving through the busy streets.

The other person in his flat could only have been Pearson, she told herself. Who else would not have wanted Donald to answer the phone? Ten minutes ago, she knew that Donald had been alive ... But what might have happened to him in the interim?

She found herself stuck behind a slow omnibus on the main road half a mile before the turning to Donald's street. She was crying now, repeating his name over and over and weeping uncontrollably, her throat raw and tears stinging her eyes.

She reached into her coat pocket. The pistol nestled there reassuringly.

She approached the side road and turned at speed. The building where Donald had his flat was a hundred yards down the street on the left. She brought the Sunbeam to a halt behind a line of parked cars twenty yards from the front door and jumped out, clutched suddenly by a cold terror.

She hurried along the pavement, wondering where the police were. They should have been here by now ... but what could they do, she asked herself – unarmed policemen against someone who would most certainly be armed with the weapon he intended to use to kill Donald?

She stopped at the foot of the steps, looking back and forth along the road for the first sign of a police car.

Then she looked up at the front door, and what she saw decided her. The door was ajar, open six inches. She found herself racing up the steps and pushing open the door. Before her, the interior stairs rose to Donald's flat. She climbed them, looking down to see that she had pulled the pistol from her pocket and was clutching it in her right hand.

The door at the top was shut, but was it locked?

She was reaching out for the handle when a sudden explosion made her jump. She had heard the sound of gunfire in films, but then it had never sounded so loud. Sobbing, she turned the handle and pushed ... and she was inside and striding towards the study where Donald had his phone.

She feared what she would find, but knew that her fear would do nothing to prepare her.

She pushed open the door and saw Donald lying on the carpet, and the blood, so much blood – a pool of dark liquid surrounding him – and a little man, an obnoxious, fat, balding man on his knees, reaching out towards Donald's body with something ... Maria thought it a hand-kerchief at the time ... reaching out towards Donald's open, gasping mouth.

Trembling, she raised the gun. One bullet. She had to get close to make sure. The ugly little man looked up suddenly. He appeared comically shocked to see her bearing down on him with the gun outstretched. He fumbled on the carpet for his own pistol which he had set aside, and there was something pathetic about the way he stared at her in shock and patted the carpet for his weapon as she stepped closer and closer to him.

One bullet.

Donald lying in a pool of his own blood...

Get close.

Aim and fire before he finds the gun.

Donald lying in a pool of blood...

She pulled the trigger, and the gun clicked impotently, and she pulled again.

And again...

Crying now, she pulled the trigger a fourth time, and the expected detonation did not happen. She squeezed again, for the fifth time, and the pistol still did not go off.

She knew she had one more chance.

She pulled the trigger for the sixth time. The same dull, empty click – and she had time to laugh hysterically through her tears at the thought of Gideon Martin's cowardice in threatening to shoot himself with an unloaded gun.

She let out a cry when Pearson's hand found his pistol and sudden hope lit his face.

Without thinking, she stamped her stiletto heel down hard on the back of his hand and heard his piercing scream. Then she found herself swinging the pistol, using it as a cosh, and smashing the weapon with all the force she could muster into the side of Frankie Pearson's ugly head.

He cried out and rolled away, and Maria dropped her pistol and reached out for Pearson's. She grasped it with a sob of relief and pushed herself to her feet and backed off. She came up against the wall, the impact startling her, and slid on to

343

her haunches. She crouched there, directing the weapon at Frankie Pearson.

'If you make one move,' she said, 'I promise you I will shoot!'

Frankie Pearson curled on the floor, staring at her with a strange mixture of malice and fear in his eyes.

She started as she heard a shout from the stairwell, then the pounding of feet as the police climbed the stairs.

'In here!' she cried, and as they burst into the room she let the pistol drop to the floor, held her head in her hands, and wept.

EPILOGUE

One week later Maria parked in the grounds of the Chelsea Royal Hospital and took the clanking lift to the second floor, then hurried along the corridor and paused outside the private room. She leaned against the polished oak door frame and peered in.

Donald sat up in bed, his torso strapped like an Egyptian mummy and his left leg swaddled in bandages. He was reading a novel and clutching his empty pipe between his teeth. She could hardly stop herself from laughing at the outlandish sight he presented.

He heard her, looked up and grinned. 'What's so funny?'

She ran to him, leaned over and kissed him on the lips, once he'd removed the pipe. 'You are, lying there with that silly empty pipe stuck in your face!'

He gestured with the implement. 'Well, of course it's empty. They won't let me smoke.'

She sat down on the side of the bed. 'How are you feeling today?'

'Far better than yesterday, I'll tell you that. I'm feeling a little better every day. Chipper, in fact.'

He reached out, wincing at the pain the gesture caused him, and stroked her cheek.

She whispered, 'Why is the world like this, Donald? Why do evil people like Pearson do what they do? And always at the expense of good people like you and Charles and Nigel Lassiter and...'

'I don't honestly know, Maria. I write crime novels about people who do terrible things to each other, and do you know something? I have no real idea how people can bring themselves to do what they do.' He stared at her for a while, then said, 'Perhaps you're right – perhaps I really should write something other than mysteries.'

She gripped his hand. 'I was being cruel. You do them so well.'

He changed the subject. 'Anyway, I've had two visitors already today.'

'Well, you are the popular one. Who were they?'

'The first was Caroline Lassiter.'

'How was she, or is that a silly question?'

Donald gestured with his pipe. 'Bearing up, as they say. She came to thank me for being such a close friend of Nigel's, and for finding his body.' He shook his head. 'There was little I could say by way of condolences. But I promised we'd visit her when I was out of here.'

'Of course we will.' Maria squeezed his hand. 'And the second visitor?'

'Jeff Mallory, with news of our friend Frankie Pearson.'

She pulled a sour face. 'Him!'

'The latest is that the wound in his hand has turned septic, and apparently he's still sporting

346

the shiner where you clocked him with the pistol. He was formally charged with the murders, and the attempted murder of myself and Charles, and he should come to trial in a few months.'

She considered how she felt about what would happen then. The odd thing was that, when she'd repeatedly pulled the trigger of the pistol, she had had every intention of killing Frankie Pearson. She had wanted nothing more than to see him dead, for the crimes he had committed and for what he'd done to Donald.

She shrugged and said, 'But I find the thought of him being hanged ... I don't know ... but it's repulsive.'

'I agree. The world will be a better place without Pearson – but that "better place" could be achieved just as well by locking him up for the rest of his life.'

'Oh, let's not talk any more about that horrible man!' She looked through the window and smiled. 'Look, the sun is coming out.'

He said, 'You look more than lovely against the light.'

She reached out and traced the line of bandages strapped around his chest. The bullet had missed his heart and lungs and passed through his upper chest, causing him severe blood loss but not threatening his life. The wound to his leg had been superficial, despite the copious quantities of blood.

'Has the doctor been around today?'

'He said I could get out of bed for a little while.'

'In that case,' she announced, 'I have a little surprise for you.'

She hurried from the room and returned with a wheelchair, and then assisted Donald out of bed.

'Don't tell me...?' he began.

'*Oui*,' she said. 'We are going visiting!'

Charles Elder sat up in bed and beamed when Maria pushed Donald through the door.

'Oh, my word!' he said, tears twinkling in his eyes. 'Donald, Donald! Oh, my boy, my boy! Look at you, just look! There is nothing as tragic as fallen youth!'

Donald laughed. 'Well, I wouldn't exactly call myself youthful...'

'To me, dear boy, you are both youthful and heroic! Maria brought me up to date with everything that has happened over the past two weeks. The timely intervention of both of you saved my life, though thankfully I have no recollection of the incident at all! And Maria – heroine *nonpareille*! Her exploits in bashing Frankie Pearson no doubt saved your bacon too, Donald.'

Donald reached out and gripped her hand. 'She's quite some girl, Charles.'

Maria found herself blushing and made to swipe the wheelchair-bound invalid.

Charles said, 'Oh, to see youth bound in *amor* with all of life ahead and the world their oyster; it brings joy to an ancient heart. But promise me,' he swept on, 'once we have recovered sufficiently to be released from this institution we shall all three resume the weekend at my place so cruelly curtailed by Mr Pearson.'

'That would be wonderful,' Maria said.

'There is but one cloud that slightly mars the horizon,' Charles said. 'That being, of course, my little appointment with her Majesty's judiciary. But on that score I have a scintilla of good news. Mr Winstanley dropped by yesterday and informed me that the gods look kindly upon me: to wit, that the judge at my trial has been appointed, and the bewigged officiator is known for his liberal tendencies. That, with the fact of my travails of late, according to Mr Winstanley, will show in my favour. The good man believes I will get no more than six months.'

Donald shook his head with disgust. 'That's still six months more than you deserve, Charles.'

'After the torture I have endured since the shooting, my dears, a spell at her Majesty's pleasure holds absolutely no fears!'

'Good for you!' Maria cried.

Charles dabbed at his lachrymose eyes with a lace kerchief and declaimed, 'But we are three friends, and survivors all. Look, the sun shines and we live to fight another day!'

He peered past them and said, 'And I do think this is the tea trolley on its way, if I am not mistaken. Now, would you care to join me in a pot of Typhoo's finest?'